Room Service
To Die For.

Whilst some places and businesses in this book do actually exist, all the events and characters in this story are entirely fictitious. Any resemblance to real events or people is entirely coincidental.

First Published : 2023.
© 2023 Errol Butcher.
All Rights Reserved.

Thanks to the many people who have influenced me in the process of writing this book, especially those who live in Belper and its surrounding villages for providing the backdrop to the story.

A special thanks also to my friend and fellow author, Alexandra Smith, for the many hours she put in reading and offering advice on the various drafts I sent her, without complaint.

Finally, thank you to those who read this novel and, hopefully, enjoy it.

Chapter 1.

'Don't Say Anything'.

"What kind of cretin are you?" the man's voice exploded into the bar, rising above the music and the noisy chatter of the customers. "I ordered a Cappuccino, not a bloody Americano."

David stood, just inside the entrance to the bar of one of his favourite hostelries, staring with a mixture of baffled amusement and disgust, at the man doing the shouting. The normally pleasant atmosphere was being disrupted by a very boorish man, shouting at Leah, one of the hotel's waitresses.
 "I'm sorry sir,....." the waitress began when the man finally paused for breath.
"Sorry, what do you mean, sorry?" the man interrupted, shouting down her apology. "I don't need you to be sorry, just go and get me a bloody Cappuccino; it can't be that difficult even for someone as brain dead as you."
'What an idiot', David thought, 'making all that fuss over a cup of coffee, there are far more important things to worry about in this world'.
He did, though, recognise the type of person immediately, small minded, self-important idiots who felt they had to bluster and bully to make people think they were important, but all they tended to achieve was to make themselves disliked, even hated. He had come across far too many such people in his wide and varied career to have any sympathy for them.

Turning away from the abusive man David edged his way further into the bar, joining about thirty other customers and staff who were watching what was going on, though there were some who were pretending they weren't interested.

"But I'm sure you did order an Americano," objected the waitress. "I wrote...

"How dare you try to tell me what I ordered?" the man baulked, his voice rising to even more querulous heights. "You must be deaf and stupid if you can't even get a simple coffee order right. I want to see the manager."

David sighed at the fact that he could still hear the moron and was seriously considering going over to tell him to stop shouting at the waitress.

As he was contemplating intervening; Leah, realising she had made a mistake in challenging the man's version of events, scurried away to get someone higher up the hierarchy, but, as it happened, the Deputy Hotel Manager was already on his way over to try and deal with the situation. He had been nearby and had heard the beginning of the altercation. Earlier in the day he had heard the man speaking to the receptionist when he had registered and recognized him then as a bully. However, being a consummate professional, he now put on his neutral face and quietly introduced himself.

"Good evening, sir, I am Tony Gordon, the Deputy Manager, what appears to be the problem?"

Taken aback by the man's calm demeanor, the complainant hesitated a moment, before answering,

"I ordered a Cappuccino and that half-brain idiot brought me an Americano, what sort of people do you employ at this hotel?"

"Leah is one of our best waitresses and doesn't usually make mistakes," the deputy manager informed him, still maintaining an even, neutral tone.

"Are you calling me a liar?" the man exploded once more.

"Not at all," the deputy manager explained, looking the man calmly in the eyes, though a slight smile tugged at his lips, "I was merely answering your question about the quality of our staff."

Clearly confused by this response, the complainant took a moment to respond, a perplexed frown crossing his face as he tried to gather his thoughts. He felt the deputy manager was

4

somehow putting him down; but couldn't work out how. Unable to think of any other response, he muttered lamely.

"I am a guest at this hotel,"

"Yes sir, I know, I was in reception when you arrived," Tony said, doing a very good job of keeping his dislike of the man off his face and out of his voice. Looking round the bar, the complainant informed everyone who could hear,

"Yes, well, my company spends a lot of money here."

Feeling that he hadn't quite fully made his point, he raised himself up to his full height of 5 ft 8 inches, adding,

"And I *demand* to be treated accordingly."

By now there was a great deal of whispering among the other customers, mostly regulars who knew that Leah was a very good waitress, whilst Tony was also very popular with the customers. Some of the whispers grew loud enough to hear.

"Git," one person muttered.

"Bastard," declared another, even more loudly.

Whilst it was clear the customers were on Leah's side, the Deputy Manager was in a tricky position, he didn't know whether or not a mistake had actually been made and though he suspected it hadn't, he obviously had no proof. Choosing his words carefully, he said,

"May I suggest that we replace the Americano with the Cappuccino you desire and the hotel will give you a discount on your evening meal? I hope that is satisfactory?"

"No it is not. That girl tried to say that I had ordered an Americano. She called me a liar. I want her sacked," he blustered.

"Don't you think that's a bit harsh?" Tony asked, looking the man firmly in the eyes as he said it.

"No, I don't," he stubbornly responded.

Tony continued to look the man in the face and starting to feel uncomfortable under the calm but firm gaze, he looked away from Tony and towards the other customers to see if he had any support there. However, by now, an increasing number of the customers were getting angry with the complainant and their comments about what he could do with himself were becoming increasingly hostile. The man's colleagues were also clearly getting embarrassed about the escalating situation and hoped he would accept the discount that Tony had offered him.

"Come on Phil, anyone can make a mistake," said the bravest of them.

Phil glanced contemptuously at him, but the not so quiet muttering of some of the other guests was starting to worry him. He decided it might be wiser if he did accept Tony's offer but, to try and save face, he did so with very bad grace.

"Very well," he said to the Deputy Manager, "but you'd better make sure the service improves."

Tony nodded briefly and left to place the order.

"What a crap hotel," the guest commented loudly, but only after Tony had left, whereupon he sat down and waited for his coffee. When it was brought, by a different waitress this time, he made a display of tasting it before he said to the waitress, with a smirk, "At least you seem to know one coffee from another."

The waitress stared at him with a blank face, keeping her contempt for him well hidden, before she left and the bar began to settle back down into its normal friendly atmosphere.

Now that the unscheduled entertainment had quieted, David was able to work his way to the bar and get Joe, the barman, to pour him a pint of Peroni. The evening continued without any further major interruptions, although every now and again, the complaining guest could be heard making disparaging comments about the hotel and its staff.

As the time approached 11pm, Mr. Hall was feeling very pleased with himself. He thought he had been very clever, as he had, in fact, ordered an Americano and not a Cappuccino, so the discount was actually for nothing. He didn't care in the slightest that he had verbally abused the waitress and called her a cretin;

6

she was only a waitress after all, a nobody, not the important businessman he thought himself to be.

As Mr. Hall made his way, somewhat unsteadily, out of the bar, the waitress he had verbally abused was walking towards him with Vicky, another member of staff from the Hotel. He gave them both a smirk as he passed them, before slowly climbing the stairs to his room.

"What a bastard, he definitely ordered an Americano," Leah confided to Vicky when they were out of earshot.

"Don't worry about it; that sort always gets their comeuppance sooner or later," Vicky replied.

"Well I hope he gets it sooner, rather than later," Leah said, with deep fervour.

Mr. Hall half staggered up the stairs, needing the support of the banister to stay upright and then weaved his way down the corridor towards his room. As he was searching his pockets for the key card to his room, the hairs on his scalp prickled and a vague sense of panic flooded through him. Suddenly sweating, a feeling of being watched overwhelmed him. He spun round quickly to see who was there. His half glazed eyes found no-one. The corridor was empty. Shaking his head to clear his thoughts, he made to enter his room, his trembling hands finding it difficult inserting the card into the lock.

"Bloody crap hotel," he said, his voice loud as he tried to fill the uneasy quiet. "Now the bloody key is bloody useless."

It took four attempts before his hands were steady enough to open the door to his room but, finally, he got the card to work and was able to enter his room. As he firmly closed his door, a shadow appeared to detach itself from an alcove in the corridor and make its way slowly passed Mr. Hall's room, before heading down the stairs.

Having finally managed to get into his room Mr. Hall switched on the light and went straight to the mini bar to get a drink to calm his shredded nerves. His hands still shook as he tried to open the whisky bottle, spilling a little of it on to the floor when the lid suddenly snapped opened. When, eventually, he was able to take a gulp of the whisky, he stood, breathing deeply for a few moments, trying to calm the pounding of his heart. Once the calming effect of the whisky had kicked in, he forced himself to go over to his laptop to check his emails in an attempt to restore some sense of normality.

As usual there were a lot of emails awaiting his response; he was the sales manager of his company, after all, he reminded himself, in yet another attempt to bolster his self importance, which he did even when he was on his own. He opened the first email, squinting as he tried to focus on the words, but with little success; clearly he was far more drunk than he had thought. For a moment, he considered making a cup of coffee to try and sober up, but decided just to finish his whisky and go to bed instead. He could check the emails in the morning. He did, though, send one email to his secretary, hoping to convince her that he was still working hard even though it was after 11pm, though the resulting email was certainly unlikely to impress her when she read it the following morning.
'Catrina, luve, I ned the figures for the monthyexpendtures.Can u sendd them by nooon tomorro w/ Make sore you send the blody rigth ones this tim. Any mor bloody mistakes an yu wil get saked. Phill Halll, Sales manger.'

Blinking like a befuddled owl, he stared at his laptop, trying to locate the off button. He discovered it eventually, hiding under his glass of whisky. Turning the computer off, he finished his whisky in two gulps, walked unsteadily over to his bed, pulled back the covers, before toppling unceremoniously into it. Pulling the covers over himself, he quickly started to snore, very loudly, the sound reverberating through the room like an asthmatic elephant. Even in his sleep he was still trying to impress people, it seemed. Eventually the snoring subsided as he reached a deeper level of sleep and it seemed the nearby world appeared to heave a sigh of relief at the ensuing quiet.

A couple of hours later, whilst Mr. Hall still slept soundly, the door to his room slowly opened and a figure slid silently into the room. Almost in response, Mr. Hall began to toss and turn; moaning in his sleep as if his dreams had become suddenly troubling. As he lay there in his bed, the figure stood over him for a few seconds, watching him with cold eyes. Then, almost gently, the figure leaned down and placed his hands around Mr. Hall's throat and began to squeeze. In the final moments of his dream, Mr. Hall felt those hands around his neck and, in a panic, surged awake, legs kicking and arms thrashing. Fear clutched at him as he found himself looking into a pair of coldly malevolent eyes, only a few inches above him. Realisation hit him, like a punch to the gut, these were real hands gripped around his neck, strong hands, and they were now squeezing tightly, very tightly.

Desperate, Mr. Hall struggled to fight off the attacker, but he was caught under the suffocating restraint of the bedclothes and his attacker's weight. Panic confused his thoughts, threatening to overwhelm him. The hands gripped tighter as his breathing became more and more laboured. His veins, turning dark, began to stand out. His pulse throbbed achingly in a head that felt on the verge of exploding. His strength was slowly, inexorably, ebbing away. He tried to plead for his life but he couldn't get any words out, the tightly gripping hands implacably constricting his larynx. Self pity flooded through him. He couldn't understand why someone was trying to kill him. 'What had he done to deserve this?' he thought, tears trickling across his face.

He knew he was dying. His strength now largely gone, he felt his life ebbing away as he looked up into the oddly blank face of his killer. All he could focus on now was that pair of eyes which seemed to stared coldly into his soul. Those eyes held him, and, unable to pull his gaze away, he stared into their unfeeling depths as his life continued to leach away. His last conscious act was to look at a face that was now smiling down at him, whilst an oddly wooden voice said,

"This is your fault, you brought in on yourself."

A vision of the waitress he had abused thrust itself unbidden, but with perfect clarity, into his mind. Then, Mr. Hall's body slumped and seemed to shrink into itself, twitching slightly a couple of times, before finally becoming still, though his still open eyes seemed fixated on the face of his killer.

If Mr. Hall still had eyes that could see, he would have noticed his killer move to the nearby table, pick something up and place it next to him, on the bedside table. It was an untouched Americano, still steaming and warm.

After staring at the body for a few moments longer, the killer slowly turned away from the bed, before walking to the outer door and opening it cautiously. Checking that there was no-one in the corridor, the killer left the room, closing the door with a click of finality, before walking away in grim satisfaction.

Chapter 2.

Life Goes On-For Some.

The following evening, David was making his way back into Belper after a hard and sweaty day's work gardening and was looking forward to a pizza and a nice cold Peroni. As he neared the hotel, he noticed there was a policeman standing, apparently on guard, outside the main entrance. He increased his pace, interested to find out what had happened.

As he got nearer to the hotel, he noticed there was another police officer standing at the side entrance, too. Drawing closer, he recognized the policeman standing there was his friend and neighbour.

Altering his approach towards the side door of the hotel, he strolled up to Mick and, affecting an attitude of indifference, he asked,
"Hi Mick, how goes it? What you doing here?"
"Hi, apart from being stuck out here for four hours without a break, I'm fine."
"Oh, what's happened then?"
Mick looked around to make sure that the no-one could hear, as he had been told, very forcefully, by his superior to keep the details of the incident secret for now.
"Murder," he said, with quiet bluntness.
"What?" David said, his head jerking up in surprise.
"Yeah. One of the guests. Found dead in his room this morning. Strangled apparently."
"Do they know who did it?" David said, looking speculatively through the hotel window as if he might somehow spot the murderer.

"I don't think so. Nobody's been arrested yet, as far as I know."
"Can I go in, I want a pint?"

Although David really did want a pint, he was, like most people, more interested in finding out more of the gruesome details from the members of staff he knew at the hotel. He had had a hard day building a rockery for a client in Hazelwood and felt he deserved a drink. He was to be disappointed though.
"Sorry no, the hotel is closed whilst forensic are inside. It certainly won't be open again today."
"Damn, I really needed a pint, too."
Sadly, David turned away and began his trudge home. He began thinking about what he was now going to eat for his evening meal when he remembered his manners. Turning back round, he said,
"See yer, Mick. If you feel like a pint later, let me know."
"No chance, I'm on 'til late. See yer," Mick replied.
"Maybe tomorrow," David called as an afterthought, but was unable to hear what Mick's reply was, and indeed David was now busy trying to digest the fact that there had been a murder in one of his favourite watering holes.

As he was genuinely hungry, he stopped off at 'George's Fish Bar' to get some fish and chips to eat as he walked home. Whilst he was waiting in the queue, he listened to the other customers and the staff. They were discussing the murder, so clearly it hadn't remained a secret very long. Apart from expressing feelings of shock, no-one knew any more than the little David had learnt from PC Sure, so, as he ate his small fish meal walking home, he worked out a simple plan to find out more. When he finished his meal and found a bin to put the rubbish in, he increased his pace in order to get home quicker. When he got home he got his phone and sent a text to Tony, the deputy manager, hoping he might be able to get a lot more information from him. However, much to his disappointment, he got no response to his text. He did recognise that, in the circumstances, Tony might well be busy with the police so, undaunted; he decided he would text Vicky, one of the front of house staff. Again, though, he received no response. He thought she was probably busy too.

Not one to be defeated easily, he then texted Nathan, one of the receptionists, but once again there was no reply. David realised that all of them were probably, either in the process of being interviewed by the police or had been told not to divulge any details until the police had finished their initial enquiries. Whatever the reason, it was clear that they were all unable, or unwilling, to respond to his texts. It was very frustrating, but David accepted that there was nothing he could do about it.

Having been unable to get any information from his contacts at the Hotel, David opened a bottle of wine, put on some music and spent the rest of the evening sporadically speculating about what might have happened at the hotel, working out various possible scenarios that he knew probably bore no resemblance to reality until finally, after consuming half the bottle, he decided it was time to go to bed.

Having spent a night sporadically dreaming about murder, he awoke next morning still intrigued about the murder at the hotel. He decided he would get the local paper before he went to work to see what had been reported there. They were bound to have written something up, even if they hadn't got too many details, as it would make a dramatic change from the usual stories you get in the local press. David was pretty sure that the murder would push the local livestock and farming show's largest vegetable off the front page, at least for that day.

Being a self employed gardener meant that, generally, he could start work when he wanted, so, on this occasion, he decided to have a leisurely breakfast whilst perusing the newspaper.

Obviously the murder was on the front page but, to his considerable disappointment, although there was a lot of speculation, there was very little concrete information available, other than the basic information about the victim. The report stated that the man, identified as a businessman, had apparently been strangled in his sleep sometime during the night. However, the police were unclear what the motive of the perpetrator or perpetrators might have been, as nothing appeared to have been stolen from the victim. The story also included a few interviews from staff and customers who had been at the hotel during the previous evening. From these sources, the altercation between the guest and the waitress was mentioned but this was reported as a minor argument and was not thought to have been the reason for the murder, particularly as this sort of behaviour from guests was a regular feature of hotel life and no-one had been murdered before. The paper did say though, as the initial investigation had been concluded, the hotel would be open for business as usual later that day. Having read what news there was, David realised that he would have to wait until that evening before he would be able to talk to his friends at the hotel and get some more concrete information as to what exactly had happened.

After reading the news, or lack of, he had to decide which garden he would work at for the rest of the day and settled on the one in Hazelwood where he had been working the previous day. He collected the tools he needed and set off for the garden. He worked steadily through the day, occasionally thinking about the murder, as he completed the planting up of the rockery he had finished building the day before. Finishing his work around half past four, he packed away his tools and returned home.

He returned to the hotel around 8pm that evening, and, unsurprisingly, found it was very busy for a Wednesday evening. 'It seems I am not the only one interested in finding out what happened?' he thought. He nodded to a few of the regulars as

14

he pushed his way to the bar to get his pint of Peroni and waited to get a chance to see Tony or Vicky to talk about the potentially grisly events. As he waited, he listened to the other customers discussing the crime and, forgetting his own lurid speculations of the previous night, wondered at the weird and wonderful explanations that some of the people came up with. One customer, who was admittedly already fairly drunk, explained that the guest must have seen the hotel ghost and, as a result, died of fright.

"But he was murdered, strangled," his friend reminded him.

"Yes, well, maybe the ghost strangled him."

"How could an ethereal being actually strangle him?" his incredulous friend demanded.

A puzzled look came over his friend's face as he asked,

"What's an ethereal being?"

"Er, it's like it's got no solid substance," his friend replied, a smile crossing his face, pleased with himself for remembering something he had read in a ghost story once.

"Oh, well maybe the ghost forced the guy to kill himself, then," the first man replied, determined not to give up on the idea of the ghost too quickly.

"Don't be daft, it's impossible to strangle yourself," his friend concluded with finality, giving his friend a superior glance as he claimed victory in their dispute.

A short time later, whilst he was at the bar replacing his empty pint glass with a full one, David heard another novel explanation.

"It was aliens," one man confidently announced.

"What do you mean, aliens?" asked one of his friends.

"There's loads of aliens about, the government don't let on, but they know they're here. The aliens probably tried to abduct him but he resisted so they killed him," he explained, looking carefully around to see if he could spot any aliens lurking in the bar.

"Why would they want to abduct him?" enquired another of the party.

"To experiment on him, of course, to find out about humans," the first man retorted.

"But if there are so many aliens about, don't they already know enough about humans," the second man objected, as he returned his attention to his pint.

David had got his refill by now and although amused by this sagacious discussion of aliens and fascinating as it was, he decided he had to leave that particular discussion behind. As he sat back down at his table, two women at the next table were discussing yet another version of what could have happened, though possibly with a greater chance of it being the truth than the aliens explanation.

"I bet his wife set it up, she found out he was having an affair and got a hit man to kill him," one of the women expounded.

"From what I heard he was a horrible git who no-one would have an affair with," her friend interjected.

"Oh, well maybe his wife organised it because she hated him then," the first women responded.

"That's more like it," agreed her friend, absently stroking her chin.

After what seemed an interminable wait, Tony was able to stop by David's table. David didn't bother with any preliminaries or niceties but simply asked, as Tony sat down,

"What happened, then?"

Tony, however, was a stickler for social pleasantries and asked, albeit with a sarcastic smile,

"Good evening David. How are you?"

"Sorry, I'm fine. What about you?"

"For some reason I'm a bit shocked, you know."

'Ok, now we've got the pleasantries over, what happened?" David asked, thoughtlessly tapping the table as he spoke.

"Well, it's like this," Tony began, and then, with a dramatic pause, he looked around the room before leaning closer to David, as if he didn't want the other customers to hear.

Subconsciously David leaned forward too, and, out of the corner of his eye, he saw several of the nearby customers leaning towards his table, trying to eavesdrop. Tony looked round for a bit longer, letting the tension build as he did so, before finally saying,

"Well, what happened was."

He paused once more, letting the tension built even higher, before adding, "One of the guests was murdered."

With that, he stood up and began to walk away from the table.

"Get back here, you git," David hissed, trying hard not to laugh at how easily Tony had sucked him in.

With a grin, Tony returned and said,

"I'm a bit busy at the moment; I've still got work to do. Wait until closing time; I'll be able to talk to you then."

As Tony walked off, David looked around at the customers close by, sharing a sheepish smile with them as they all went back to their drinks and conversations.

As David waited for closing time, he looked around the bar and thought about how the hotel had come back to life in the past few months. For many years it had been a dull, dingy place, where very few of the customers who actually entered the place, stayed for long. He had attended meetings there years ago and the meeting room had always been dirty, the beer cloudy and on one occasion the sandwiches had actually been so mouldy that he wouldn't have been surprised if they had begged for a decent burial. Now, though, it was a lot better, the new owner had put a lot of money into regenerating the place and had redecorated it in a modern style. It had paid off and although the crowd tonight was larger than normal, it wasn't that much larger. Lot's of people regularly met there, talking, chilling, shouting, laughing and watching the world go by. Bar staff scuttled from customer to customer, from tap to glass, from bottle to glass and back to the customer. Waiting-on staff moved deceptively quickly through the crowd, clearing tables, bringing food, mostly smiling or laughing and engaging with the customers in good natured banter. Behind the sound of the people music pulsed through the ether, rubbish as far as David was concerned but, he had to admit, it did seem to fit the atmosphere and was not too loud and intrusive. People often seemed to bounce up and down in their seats in time with the music as if to emphasise their conversation points.

As he finished his Peroni, he decided he was hungry and on his way to the bar he found Vicky, who oversaw the pizza section, passing through the bar and stopped to ask if there was a table free. He had known Vicky for several years now and had seen her develop from a shy and reticent 18 year old waitress into a very competent 25 year old woman. She had a very pleasant manner with people, putting them at ease instantly and making them feel particularly welcome. She dealt with problems with a serene disposition and easy confidence. On top of that, she was tall and lithe and had a smile that could have easily melted the ice caps. Being the front of house, she, like several of the other members of staff, was fitted with a two way radio system so that she could contact other areas of the hotel for information without having to waste time going from one part of the hotel to another. There was an earpiece and microphone on her head and a transmitter attached to her waist.

She spoke into her microphone then, conferring with Leah in the pizza bar, asking how long it would be before table one was free. On receiving her reply she turned to David,
"If you can wait a few minutes, I'll get you your favorite table where you can watch the rest of the room?" Vicky said.
"No problem, I'll wait," David replied.

Having known him for several years, Vicky knew he liked to watch and listen to the customers and staff as they interacted, providing him with insights which helped him to write his stories that someday he intended to try and get published. Vicky always tried to find him a table at the back of the room where he could

18

look out across all the other tables. Unknown to Vicky and the other members of the staff, however, it was his training in a previous occupation for the government that meant that he didn't like to have people or entrances behind him. It was second nature for him to constantly check who came in and who left the room.

As he waited for his table to become free, David stood, with his back to the pillar at the end of the bar, sipping his Peroni and doing what he usually did these days, watching the customers. There was the usual mix of humanity circling and re-circling through the bar. There were the couples who appeared to be early on in their relationships; nervous, excited, trying to impress and laughing a lot at very little. There were the couples who had been together for a long time and were comfortable in each other's company, often silent with only sporadic conversation, but still looking happy. There were groups of friends, talking, chatting, laughing at stories, jokes or reminiscences, maybe two or three of the group talking together for a while before moving on to others in the group. Then there were the business groups, disparate people thrown together by their company, trying to find things in common with each other and often ending up talking about sport or the business, or simply drinking quietly, alone, amongst many. Lastly there were the couples reaching the end of their time together, often barely speaking, looking around the room in boredom or distaste, snapping quietly at each other over nothing in particular, a physical and verbal distance growing between them.

All these people, together and apart, passed with a fluid motion through the bar, staying for a while before moving on, sometimes to other venues, sometimes home, sometimes returning later on to end their evening in the hotel.

A few minutes before his table was ready, a couple of older men came to stand near to David at the bar. They were discussing the hotel and how it had changed in the years since they had last been there. Whilst they agreed that the place was popular, they decided it wasn't really for them as it was too modern and lacked a great deal of its old charm and character, even if the grime had been removed. Also, like David, they really didn't like the music and they longed for old fashioned pubs which sold real ale and didn't serve food or have music playing. As they finished their pints and left, in a probably vain search for such a pub, David considered their views and found he shared them to a certain extent but he felt that the Lion fitted well into the modern world and had achieved a good balance, serving decent drinks and good food, with music that was loud enough to banish any unwanted silence but which didn't overwhelm people.

A few minutes later Vicky came over to show him to his table. As he sat down she asked,
"Do you need a menu or are you having your usual?"
He gave a brief smile and replied,
"The usual pizza, if you please."
"Ok," she said and went over to the pizza kitchen which, as is common these days, was located in the pizza dining area so the customers could watch the chef working on their food. That was supposed to somehow make the food more real and immediate, though David wasn't sure it was anything other than a smart marketing ploy. It was good food though.

Whilst he waited for his pizza, David looked again at the décor in response to what the two older men had been talking about at the bar. There were two main drinking and dining areas downstairs, as well as a main dining room, and all had been given a modern make-over, to entice a modern, relatively affluent middle class clientele. The tables were made of light wood and were a mixture of high and low tables. Some of the seats were leather sofas for groups to sit together. The walls were a mixture of varying shades of grey paint or modern wallpapers with the wallpaper on one wall made to look like old fashioned brick. The floors, like the tables, were made of light Ash wood which gave the rooms a light, airy feel. The general lighting was IKEA style lighting, lots of different lights bunched together with shades of different sizes and colours, whilst the lights above the main bar were set in top hats. The whole place had a modern, open feel and was very popular. It was a place to be seen in if you wanted to be part of 'the scene'.

When his pizza arrived David continued, in between bites, with his social voyeurism, catching a fragment of conversation between two fashionably well dressed middle-aged women at the next table.

"I don't believe it, you aren't?" he heard a shocked voice say.

"I bloody well am, my husband is away on business a lot and I was getting bored."

"How did it start?"

"You know Steve in the office, well, one day he asked a group of us if we wanted to go to the pub after work to celebrate his birthday. Well, Jack was away again so I went."

"And..."

At this point the two women leant close together and he could no longer hear but he filed the short conversation away for future use; such snatches of conversation were the sort of stuff he used to help flesh out his own stories and it would be easy to fashion an ending to the conversation.

When he had finished his pizza and coffee, David returned to the main bar to continue watching the interactions between the customers, as well as having occasional conversations with the members of staff who he knew. He also had a few passing conversations with some of the customers and occasionally fended off well meaning advances from semi-drunk business women staying at the hotel and hoping to take advantage of being away from their partners.

One conversation he had was with Leah, the waitress who had had the altercation with the now dead guest.

"I'm surprised to see you working tonight, after what's happened."

"Tony said I could have the night off but I thought I'd rather be amongst people at work than brooding alone at home. I feel partly responsible for what happened."

"You didn't kill him, did you?" David asked playfully.

"Of course I didn't," remorse in her voice and clearly upset.

David changed his approach and in a more serious tone asked,

"You don't think you were actually responsible, do you?"

"Well, I was talking to Vicky after the event and she said that people like him always get their comeuppance and I said I hoped it would be soon. I didn't mean for this to happen, though."

"Of course you didn't and you had nothing to do with what happened. I reckon it was just some nutter, probably high on drugs, as well. The police will get him, don't worry."

He gave her a quick smile of commiseration, receiving a wan smile in return before she returned to her waitressing duties.

"I still feel a bit guilty, though," she said as she left.

'Oh well', he thought, not intending to be patronising, 'she will soon get over it. She's young'.

Finally it was closing time and most of the customers, sated on alcohol and murder, were gone. There were just a few hotel guests left, alongside some of the staff, engaging in some end of evening chat. Rather than stand, David sat at a table with Tony so he could gently quiz him on what he knew of the previous day's events.

Tony was the Deputy Manager at the hotel and David had known him for several years. He had previously worked at a very good restaurant that David and his then partner had frequented every week. He had got to know Tony a lot better when Tony had asked him, as someone who wrote a lot, if he would read and edit a book he had written about the hotel trade. After that they had met often to discuss his book, as well as life in general, all whilst consuming copious amounts of alcohol. Working on Tony's book had also helped David deal with the break up of his long term relationship which occurred shortly after he started editing the book, providing something to focus his wandering thoughts on other than a failed relationship. That period of time had been a difficult one but, as always happened, was now slowly passing into history. David had just about come to terms with the fact his partner had left and wouldn't be coming back, but he didn't feel ready to move on with his life yet, at least in terms of another serious relationship. This was one of the reasons why David usually sat by himself and watched others interacting. It was also probably why he could be a bit difficult and prickly; well, very difficult and prickly, at times, his natural cynicism occasionally exacerbated by a dark mood fuelled by alcohol.

"So, what happened?" David wanted to know.
"I was in the office next to reception when Peter rushed in, white faced and shaking. It took him a few moments before he could speak and then he just blurted out that a guest was dead in his room."
"God, how is he?"
"Shocked, it was the first time he had seen a dead body, especially one that had been murdered. I've told him not to come back to work until he is ready."
"Why did he go to the room?"
"Mr. Hall hadn't answered his morning alarm call and his colleagues hadn't seen him at breakfast, which apparently, was unheard of, as he always made sure to get his money's worth. He didn't answer his door when his colleagues knocked, so they had gone to reception. Peter had taken the master key and let himself into the room. He saw the dead body and rushed back down to reception to call the police."
"What about his colleagues?"

"Luckily, they had gone back to their rooms, so I was able to go up to the room to check," Tony continued to explain, reaching for one of the pints he had brought. He took a long drink, set the glass back on the table then, voice shaking a little, he added,

"It was the first time I'd seen a dead body, as well. It was horrible; the man's face was all swollen and blotchy. I don't understand how anyone could do that."

David remained respectfully silent as Tony stared at the table, his mind obviously back in the man's room recalling what he had seen.

After a few moments staring blankly, Tony shuddered, before looking up at David with haunted eyes. Slowly recovering himself, he went on to explain that when he had got the story from Peter, he had called the police, who told him to make sure no one else went into the room. Tony had gone back upstairs to make sure the room was locked and to keep the staff and guests away from the room. The police arrived, sealed the hotel and interviewed everyone who was still there. Forensic teams combed the bedroom, as well as the corridor outside the room.

"Do they have any idea who did it?"

"I don't know," Tony replied, though they wanted to know if we knew the names of anyone who had been in the bar last night.

"Did you give them my name," David asked, taking a sip from his pint.

"Yes."

"I bet they'll want to interview me then."

"I should think so; they were very interested in the row with Leah."

"Have they interviewed her?"

"They've interviewed all the staff who were on duty, but Leah couldn't have done it as she had left the hotel and gone home by half eleven last night."

All the time he was talking, Tony's hands were absently tearing up one of the beer mats.

"Surely the Police don't suspect her."

24

"I don't think so, but I don't really know."

"Did anybody see anything?"

"Nobody has said anything."

"Did the police say how he died?"

"They said he was probably strangled but they were waiting for the results of the post mortem."

"What about the man's colleagues?"

"After they were interviewed by the police, they all left. They obviously didn't want to stay after the murder."

"I can't say as I blame them."

As there was very little more concrete news, talk of the murder petered out and David and Tony joined the other staff members who were still in the bar for a drink or two. David could see clearly that their faces still held a mixture of shock at what had happened and concern that there was a murderer at large. Comments on the murder kept returning sporadically, as people thought of some new aspect or question. Chris, the owner of the hotel, though, did say he hoped it was sorted quickly as he wanted the hotel to get back to normal as soon as possible. The murder of guests wasn't really all that good for the reputation of a hotel, he said.

A couple of days later David was interviewed by a detective who came round to his house. The detective asked if David had seen anything suspicious but as all he had seen was the altercation, he couldn't really add anything to the investigation. David asked if the police had any suspects but the detective refused to answer, merely saying inquiries were still ongoing.

It wasn't until the following weekend that David found out a bit more about the case from the police's point of view. David went for a drink with his neighbour, PC Sure, who was able to give him a few more pieces of information. After a few preliminaries, asked purely for the sake of politeness, David asked Mick about the murder.

"So, was he strangled?" David asked.

"He was, he died between 2-3am, so that excluded a lot of potential suspects."

"Any idea of motive?"

"None at all, nothing was taken, so it wasn't theft. Forensics could get nothing from the room other than from the victim and staff members who were supposed to go into the room. Actually, C.I.D. is at a bit of a loss over it, the only unusual thing they found was an untouched cup of coffee next to the table, an Americano."

Mick took a drink from his pint and then took some crisps from the packet on the table.

"The one that was at the centre of the disagreement with the waitress, that certainly is strange."

Mick didn't reply straight away as he finished eating his crisps. Finally he said,

"That it is, the only thing that was out of the ordinary was the row over the coffee, but all the people involved in that had alibis and anyway, who is going to murder someone over a cup of coffee?"

"It does seem a daft idea."

"The only thing they are pretty sure of is that the murderer must be male."

"How come?"

"They reckon it had to be someone pretty strong to hold down a full grown man, struggling for his life."

"I suppose so."

After they finished going over the murder, David and Mick had a few more drinks and crisps whilst discussing the madness of the world in general. After that they called it a night and walked together back to their respective homes which were only three doors apart on the same street.

Over the next few weeks the police appeared to make no progress on the murder, a fact confirmed by PC. Sure; certainly there were no arrests and, slowly, life at the hotel began to return to normal. People started to lose interest in the murder as it faded into the background and everyday life intruded itself back into their consciousness, after all, Strictly and X Factor were apparently much more important as people spent their time discussing the various acts on the shows and argued over whether they agreed with the judges. Who really cared about someone that nobody knew and who had been killed a few weeks earlier, at least now that the initial shock and intrigue had worn off?

Life goes on, it seems. Well, it does for most people anyway.

Chapter 3.

And So It Begins- Again.

Nathan stared disinterestedly at his computer, trying to avoid doing a stock take of the office equipment and stationary, a task he hated doing. It was late afternoon on a dismal Thursday. Rain lashed against the office window, but Nathan preferred to reflect on the more interesting events of two months earlier when a guest had been murdered. Too soon, though, his reverie was rudely interrupted by the sound of the bell at Reception clanging wildly. He heard the bell crash back down onto the counter and sighing, Nathan got up and went out to the front desk. It was obvious from the way the bell had been rung that whoever was out there was far from happy. He braced himself,

"Yes, madam, can I help you?" he said to the woman on the other side of the reception desk.

"I want to see the owner immediately," she demanded, banging her fist on the desk.

Nathan thought a little civility might have been nice, but merely said,

"May I ask what it's about?"

"Some of my jewelry has gone missing and I think one of your cleaning staff has stolen it," she replied, her voice climbing in volume and aggression as she spoke, whilst punctuating her words with thumps on the desk.

"Just one moment, madam," Nathan replied, "I will get the Deputy Manager to assist you."

"I don't want the Deputy Manager, I want the owner....... immediately," the woman yelled at him.

Remaining calm and unruffled, Nathan clarified the position,

"I am very sorry madam, but the owner is not here today, Mr. Gordon, the Deputy Manager, is in charge."

"Very well, I want him here right away."
"If madam would take a seat over there, I will send for him immediately."

Nathan pointed her towards a set of leather sofas located at the other end of the foyer. As the woman strode briskly towards the sofas, Nathan went back into the office, sat down at the desk and picked up the newspaper and began reading. Like most people, he had never liked being shouted at and was going to take his time before calling for the deputy manager.

However, much to his disappointment, the Deputy Manager walked into the reception area at that moment and joined Nathan in the office. He had been in the bar that adjoined the reception area and had heard the woman shouting, even over the music playing there, and so had come through to try and calm her down, before too many people heard her complaint. Accusations of theft by staff, a bit like murders, are not good for a hotel's reputation and Tony wanted to reduce her volume level if he could.

After a moment or two, Tony and Nathan came back out of the office. Nathan made himself comfortable at the reception desk, then nodded towards the woman pacing around at the other end of the foyer. Tony stood up straight, braced himself and walked over to the woman.
"Good afternoon, madam, I am Mr. Gordon, the Deputy Manager. What appears to be the problem?"
"Some of my jewelry has gone missing; your staff must have taken it. I want you to call the police."
"I see," Tony responded, his heart sinking at the volume level she was using so early in the conversation. "Before I call the police, can we just check that the jewelry has disappeared? Have you searched the room thoroughly?"
"Of course I've searched, it's gone. It was there last night, I have been out all day and when I went to put it on a few minutes ago,

it was nowhere to be found," she screeched back at him. As the volume of the woman's voice continued to rise, Tony winced at the possible damage it could do to his hearing and was seriously considering whether he should fetch some ear plugs.

"Calm down madam, there is no need to shout. We will get the whole thing sorted out," exhorted Tony, as he knew most of the bar could hear her, as well as the staff members and any guests who walked through the reception area.

"I will not calm down, my jewelry has been stolen and it has to have been the cleaner who does my room, she looks like a thief, with her dyed hair and tattoos," poking at him with her room key for emphasis.

"I beg your pardon," replied Tony, moving out of range, "all members of our staff are very carefully checked prior to being employed here. None of them are criminals. May I suggest that we go and search your room, just to check? If we still can't find the missing jewelry, then I will call the police."

"It's a waste of time, it's been stolen and you are giving the thief time to get rid of it."

"Nevertheless, I think we should check first," insisted Tony.

"Very well," the woman hissed at him.

Tony returned to the reception desk and asked Nathan to call Sandra, the Service Manager, on the radio and get her to meet him at the woman's room. He certainly wanted another person to be with him as a witness and to help with the search of the room.

"Do you know what room it is?" Nathan asked.

"12," Tony informed him, having seen the number on the key card she had been trying to poke him with.

"Find me her name, can you?" Tony whispered to Nathan.

Nathan quickly checked the computer,

"Ms Johnson."

Tony nodded his thanks and then returned to the guest.

"Ok then Ms Johnson, let's go and see if we can find your jewelry."

"It's a waste of time; it's not in my room. The cleaner took it; I told you."

Tony turned to Nathan, rolling his eyes; hating these types of situations but, taking a deep breath, he followed Ms Johnson up to her room.

When they arrived at the woman's room, Sandra was outside the room, waiting for them. The woman opened the door and they all went in.

"What exactly is it are we looking for," Tony enquired.

"A silver pendant with a ruby set in the centre," the woman replied.

"Where did you last have it," Sandra asked.

"I must have put it on the bedside table," the woman replied, suddenly a little uncertain. She did not want to admit to them that she had drunk quite a bit the previous evening and her memories towards the end of the evening were a little blurred, to say the least.

Tony and Sandra searched around the bedside table then spread out, moving everything in the bedroom, but no pendant emerged from the dark shadows.

"I told you it has been stolen," the woman asserted, with a strange tone of satisfaction, seeming to prefer to be vindicated rather than find her pendant.

"Now can we call the police, I want the cleaner arrested?" she demanded.

Just then Sandra asked,

"Did you remove your make-up last night when you got in?"

"Of course I did, what sort of person do you think I am?"

"I'll just go and check the bathroom," Sandra told Tony.

The woman scoffed and, chafing at the delay, paced up and down, before stopping in front of Tony to tell him,

"This is all a waste of time."

Tony opened his mouth to reply but was interrupted by an exclamation from the bathroom. A moment later Sandra emerged, holding a silver pendant.

"Is this it?"

"Yes, that's it, where did you find it?"

"I found it behind the waste bin. You must have taken it off to wash and it slipped off the surface and fall behind the bin without you noticing," Sandra concluded.

"Well done, Sandra," Tony said, his face neutral but silently exultant that the woman had been wrong, "It's a good job you checked."

Sandra handed the pendant back to the woman, who almost snatched it from her.

"Well, I'm pleased that's sorted, have a pleasant evening," Tony said as he and Sandra went to the door, sighing gratefully as they left.

As Tony and Sandra were walking down the corridor, Tony asked how she had thought about looking in the bathroom.

"Once she was unsure where she had put it, I thought she may have taken it off in the bathroom as she cleaned off her make-up. I often do that myself when I get in at night."

"Well done anyway, we don't need any more allegations ruining the hotel's good name."

Sandra was just about to answer when they heard a door crash open. They turned to see what was happening, when they saw that Ms Johnson was charging after them.

"Oh God, what now," muttered Sandra, but not loud enough for Ms Johnson to hear.

"The cleaner must have heard me telling you about the theft," Ms Johnson shouted at them. "She must have come back and put the pendant behind the bin."

"I don't think so, there was no time," Tony asserted, now walking briskly down the stairs back to reception, hoping Ms Johnson would stop following them but, to his great disappointment, the woman continued after them.

"She must have done. I want you to call the police. I want her sacked."

By this time all three of them had descended the stairs and reached the reception. Tony went over to Nathan and asked him to check what time the cleaners had left that day. Nathan checked the log out times and said that all of them had finished before midday.

"She must have come back and returned it," the woman insisted.

"And how would she have known to do that. No, I'm sorry madam," Tony explained to her, "There is nothing more I can do. You have your pendant back and it seems it simply fell behind the waste bin."

At this clear dismissal, the woman stormed off back to her room. Tony watched her leave and then breathed a sigh of relief and looked at Sandra, who simply raised her eyebrows and walked off.

Feeling herself completely humiliated by the hotel staff, Ms Johnson decided not to eat in the hotel that evening, but went to one of the nearby restaurants, a local Indian restaurant, the Elaichi and enjoyed a very good meal there. Somewhere around 10pm, she returned to the hotel and, rather than sitting alone, sulking in her room, she decided to go to the bar for a last drink. It did, though, take her quite a while to get served at the bar, which was, admittedly, quite crowded, but the bar staff, somehow, repeatedly seemed unable to see her standing there. Eventually, one of the customers politely said to the barman,

"This lady was before me," gesturing to Ms Johnson, who nodded her thanks.

"What can I get you?" and there was a short, but noticeable, delay before he added, "Madam."

"Large white wine," Ms Johnson requested, also delaying before she added, "Please."

"Of course, madam, any particular one?"

"Sauvignon Blanc."

"New Zealand or French?"

"New Zealand."

"Right away, madam."

Having heard about the accusation made by Ms Johnson, the barman carefully measured the wine out, making sure not to go over the line in the glass, before he then handed the glass over to Ms Johnson.

"That will be £6-40 please."

"Put it on my room, please, 12."

"Certainly, madam."

Ms Johnson sat down at the only vacant table in the bar and started drinking her wine, deciding to take it slowly, not wanting to repeat her level of drunkenness from the previous night. Glancing around the room, she noticed a man sitting at the next table and after a few moments, when no one came to join him, concluded he must be on his own. She decided it would be fun to chat him up. It was always awkward, as a woman, sitting alone in a bar, and whilst it would be nice to chat to someone else, he might also offer to get her some more wine, especially as he already appeared a little drunk. If it led to nothing else, it would save her some money, so putting on her most winsome smile she turned to the man, asking,

"Are you a guest here too?"

The man shook his head but then added,

"No, I live locally; I just come here for food and the odd drink."

Although his speech was just a little slurred, Ms Johnson thought the man had a nice voice and a pleasant smile. He also appeared to be willing to talk, so she began talking about how long she was staying at the hotel and some of the places she had visited locally. She was pleased when he appeared to be interested in her comments, nodding and smiling in encouragement. After a few minutes, she started to tell him the story of her pendant and its theft, moving on to explain how the hotel had covered it up by giving the cleaner the chance to put it back in her room. She also told the man that she thought that such things probably happened a lot at the hotel. The man, though, rather than sympathising with her as she had hoped and expected, had actually called her a 'daft cow', adding that the staff there wouldn't do that.

To his apparent surprise, Ms Johnson was offended at this response and had decided to take her wine up to her room, saying she would prefer to leave, rather than stay there and be verbally insulted and by a drunk, at that. The man watched her leave, though he had to screw his eyes up a bit as he was having difficulty locating her as she quickly left the bar.

As she passed the reception on the way to her room, wine glass in hand, she decided that, to make leaving in the morning a lot easier, she would pay her bill there and then, so she requested that the receptionist get her bill ready. The receptionist directed her to the sofas whilst she prepared her bill. As she waited, she slowly sipped her wine, thinking she would be glad to leave the hotel as her stay had been very humiliating. After a couple of minutes the receptionist called her over and gave her a copy of her bill to check. Having carefully checked it over, Ms Johnson presented her credit card so that payment could be made. Once the transaction was complete Ms Johnson asked the receptionist to make sure she received an alarm call at 6-30am in the morning.
"Of course, madam," replied the receptionist. Like all the other staff members on duty, she had heard the account of Ms Johnson's accusations against the cleaner, who was a friend of hers, so she deliberately wrote '5-30am alarm call, Rm 12' on the 'to do' list for the morning receptionist.

Having paid her bill and organized her morning call, Ms Johnson turned and walked through the foyer to the steps that led up to her room, whilst the receptionist smiled smugly at her departing back. Ms Johnson reached her room and was about to put her key card into the lock when the hairs on the back of her head tingled and she shuddered as a chill swept over her body. An oppressive feeling of panic swept through her. Feeling she was being watched, she spun round quickly, trying to see who was there, but there appeared to be no-one else on the corridor. She shook her head, trying to clear her thoughts and then opening the door to her room, rushed inside, closing the door quickly and firmly behind her. With the door closed behind her, she did not see the shadowy figure that seemed to slide slowly passed her room.

Still feeling disturbed, Ms Johnson definitely didn't want to go to sleep straight away and, as she still had wine to finish, she decided to pass some time sat in the armchair, reading her Kindle. Whilst she was reading, she heard a couple of people in the corridor outside her room and then heard them enter the room adjacent to hers. She continued reading for about an hour, before deciding that, as the following day would be a long one, it was probably a good idea to try to get some sleep. Although she could occasionally hear the murmur of voices coming from the room next door, they were not intrusive, so it wasn't long before she fell asleep.

Earlier that same evening, David had gone to the Lion for a drink, well several drinks in fact. His former partner had been to his house earlier to collect some mail and, for a while, the house had seemed welcoming again. When she had left, David, not wanting to spend the evening brooding and drinking alone, had decided to go the Lion for a bit of company and people to talk to, rather than talking to the appliances in the house.

Trying to show a bit of restraint he did, in fact, have something to eat whilst he was drinking, though, his skills of observation became increasingly blurred as the evening and the amount of alcohol he consumed, wore on. He vaguely recalled talking to a guest who was moaning about the hotel. She had claimed, quite loudly, that one of the cleaners had tried to steal some jewelry from her but the hotel had hushed it up and allowed the cleaner time to return the item. She had wondered how many people had had stuff stolen but thought they had just lost it. She had said she was going to post a very poor review on Trip Advisor, which, apparently, 'would show them'. David vaguely recalled thinking that she was a 'daft cow' but couldn't be entirely sure whether he had just thought it, or whether he had actually said it out loud. Probably the latter, he thought, as he did seem to recall the woman storming off at some point.

It was a short time after this that Tony intervened and decided that David was too drunk to stay in the bar and far too drunk to go home, so he gently escorted him to one of the hotel bedrooms which was vacant and sat talking with him until David finally went to sleep. With a final look of sadness at the state his friend was in, Tony let himself out of the room. He went down the corridor to the next room, where he had decided to spend the night. It was 1am, after all and he couldn't be bothered to go home. Admittedly, it wasn't that far to walk to where he lived but he, too, had drunk a fair bit whilst listening to David and so he felt he deserved just to crash at the hotel. He used his pass key to let himself into room 10, undressed quickly and slid under the sheets, passing into a kind of drunken oblivion very soon after.

Everything in the hotel had ground to a halt and a brooding quiet hung over the place. Nothing moved until, at around 2am, the door to Ms Johnson's room was slowly opened from the outside and someone, slid quietly, but purposely into her room. At the same time Ms Johnson stirred in her bed, maybe totally coincidentally or possibly subconsciously aware that something, or someone, had entered her room. A figure walked stealthily, if a little woodenly, over to the bed and stood looking at her. After a few moments, two hands reached down to grasp her by the throat and started to tighten, obviously determined to squeeze the life out of her. Ms Johnson's eyes burst open, confusion on her face, which quickly turned to horror as she saw the figure leaning over her. Now terrified, she realised it wasn't a nightmare. The hands around her throat were very real. Panic clouded her ability to reason clearly and she started to thrash around in the bed. She tried to grasp the hands at her throat, desperately needing to loosen their grip, but her hands were caught under the covers and in her confusion she couldn't find a way to get them free. Increasingly finding it hard to think, her actions began to appear pointless, as the hands implacably tightened, squeezing her life away.

Despite her confusion, she continued to struggle. Somehow, she managed to get one hand free from the covers and made a grab at one of the hands gripping her throat. Using the final remnants of her strength, she managed to pull the hand from her throat. As the pressure on her throat lessened, she took a deep, shuddering breath. The sudden rush of oxygen hit her lungs and, regaining a little strength, she threw herself to one side. Her desperate movement caught her attacker by surprise and she fought free. With nothing to restrain her she fell wildly out of the bed. As she did so, her head smacked hard against the edge of the bedside table. She slumped to the floor, barely conscious. Her blurred eyes looked up into the face of her attacker and, with a start, she thought she vaguely recognised who it was,
"You," she croaked; her voice barely audible. "What have I done to you?"
As she said this, the attacker leaned in closer, fingers grasping her throat once more. Barely able to move, as the blow to her head had left her weak and disorientated, Ms Johnson just stared, paralysed, into the face looming above her. Slowly, inexorably, the fingers tightened once more on her throat, this time with a grim sense of finality.

She felt her eyes drawn upwards to her killer. All she could focus on now was a pair of eyes which stared coldly at her. Those eyes held her and she stared into their depths, knowing with absolute certainty that she was going to die. She was terrified, but those eyes held her immobile, paralysing any movement, except for a few spasmodic twitches that shook her body.

Out of the blue, her attacker spoke,
"This is for the cleaner you accused."
The words echoed in her mind, calling up a vision of the cleaner. With that final image engraved in her mind, Ms Johnson slumped, her body becoming still and seemed to shrink in on itself. Disdainfully, the killer picked up the body from the floor and placed it back in the bed and, almost gently, placed the covers over her. The killer then found her bag of jewelry and arranged some of it neatly on the bedside table as a memento and also a warning.

The shadowy figure stood over her dead body and regarded the victim with grim satisfaction. After a few more seconds, the killer turned away from the bed, went over to the door, opened it carefully and looked out. When sure the corridor was empty, the killer stepped out, closing the door with a click of finality and walked away without a backwards glance.

Chapter 4.

'Old Friends'

David struggled to open his eyes, not that he really wanted to, because his eyelids felt they were stuck together with superglue and grit. He tried flexing his cheek muscles, scrunching up his face as he first tried to prize open his right eye and when that failed, his left eye. Having failed to successfully open either, he sank further into his pillow and decided it might be easier to restore his mouth to some sort of working order first. He ran his tongue around his mouth to introduce some moisture to it, but quickly gave up as he could not make any impression on the layer of silt that seemed to cover his tongue.

He was certain that he really didn't want to wake up, but a persistent knocking in his head had intruded on his sleep and woken him up, and now his mouth was begging, silently but fervently, for water. He certainly didn't feel great but, selectively forgetting the amount of alcohol he had drunk the night before, he told himself that it was simply because you don't sleep that well when you are in a strange bed.

Using his fingers, he finally forced his eyelids apart, reached out to put the bedside light on and, struggling out of bed, went to the bathroom to get the drink of water his mouth was begging him for. This was certainly a win/lose situation for him; the water felt like balm for his parched throat, but the light caused unpleasant eruptions in the pain sensors of his brain. Luckily, he didn't have a hangover, as such, he just felt very weary, but he did feel a bit dehydrated. He went back into the bedroom, fumbled for the kettle, filled it and switched it on. The other downside was that the knocking noise was still going on in his

40

head, only now, he could hear a voice as well. Slowly he realised it was coming from the corridor outside, and the voice belonged to Tony, who was calling out,

"Ms Johnson, are you awake. Reception has been trying to contact you with your alarm call."

More knocking followed, and David was very pleased to note that the noise did not seem to cause any repercussions in his head. He was forever grateful that he had a very robust constitution which, once the initial symptoms of distress had been dealt with, didn't seem to complain or try to get revenge if, occasionally, he abused it.

The most recent bout of knocking was, once again, followed by, "Ms Johnson, Ms Johnson, can you hear me?"
As David was still dressed, not having bothered to get undressed the night before, he opened his bedroom door and looked outside, to find Tony stood outside room 12, with his ear pressed to the door whilst knocking every few seconds.
"Morning Tony," David called quietly. "What's up?"
Tony swung round, looking slightly less dapper than usual, squinting at David with eyes that reflected a certain amount of torment.
"Morning, are you ok?"
"Fine," David replied, "You?"
"I've felt better," he replied, a wan smile crossing his face.
"What time is it?"
"About six forty-five."
"Good god, I can't remember the last time I got up at that hour. Someone not answering, then," David enquired, nodding towards room 12.
"No, I've been here for a good ten minutes with no answer; I think I'll use my master key. Can you vouch for me?"
"No problem."

Tony took his master key out of his pocket, knocked again before he opened the door to room 12. He stayed just outside the room and called again,

"Ms Johnson, are you awake? It's Mr. Gordon, the deputy manager."

There was still no reply and so he reached inside the door frame, found the light switch and depressed it, calling out again as he did so but, once more, there was only silence from the interior of the room.

Whether or not he was feeling over sensitive, due to the previous murder, or possibly his hangover, the whole situation was screaming to Tony that something was seriously wrong. He looked back down the corridor at David and said,

"Something's wrong, I feel it, I'm going in."

"Ok." David acknowledged.

Tony slowly entered the room and David could hear him continue calling to Ms Johnson. A few seconds later David heard a sharp intake of breath, followed by,

"Oh God."

He then heard rushing feet and Tony emerged from the room, a shocked look on his now pale white face.

"She's..., she's..... dead," he finally managed to blurt out.

"I thought that might be the case," David said, shocking Tony with the calmness of his response.

"Dead," Tony repeated, "I think she was murdered like the other one."

At this point, David decided that, with Tony in the grip of some sort of emotional paralysis, he would be better equipped to deal with a situation like this, so he took charge and just let Tony come to terms with the after effects of shock.

"I'll check," he told Tony.

Tony could do no more than nod.

David could almost physically feel Tony take hold of his courage and then, taking a deep breath, he led the way back into room 12. Feeling it was wise; David closed the door before joining Tony at the side of the bed. David glanced up and down the bed, searching for any details that immediately stood out. He then leant over the body, placed his fingers on Ms Johnson's neck, trying to find a pulse. Failing to find one, he did the same with her wrist. When he was sure that there was no sign of a pulse he turned to Tony, who had just stood there, hoping against hope that David could find some sign of life. He seemed to shrink a little when he heard David say,

"Yep, she's dead alright and by the marks on her neck, I would say that she has been strangled like the other victim."

Tony looked across at David, shocked almost as much by his calm manner and matter of fact approach, as he was by the actual death. As far as Tony could tell David did not seem in the least upset or panicked. He did not know exactly how he had expected David to respond, but this definitely wasn't it. The thought that flashed unbidden through Tony's mind was that David acted was almost as if death was a routine occurrence to him.

David's matter of fact approach did seem to have a calming effect on Tony, though, and he was able to start processing the reality of the situation.

"I had better call the police," Tony ventured, "but what this will do for the reputation of the hotel, I dread to think. Two murders in a couple of months will not exactly improve the hotel's image."

David felt a pang of sympathy for Tony and the owner, Chris. As he stood there looking at the body, several thoughts sped quickly through his mind about the effect the murders could have on their lives and the rest of the staff and so, for one of the few times in his life, he acted impulsively.

"Go and fetch Chris, but do it quietly and, for now at least, tell no one about what's happened. I have an idea that might help," David commanded Tony.

For a few seconds Tony stared blankly at David, unable to process what his words actually meant. As that meaning slowly came into focus, Tony looked carefully at David and noted the detached and thoughtful look on David's face.
"What do you mean?" he asked.
"Just go and fetch Chris and bring him here. I repeat, don't tell anyone about the murder. I want to talk to you both, and don't call the police."
"Ok, but I don't understand."
"You will, shortly."

Tony left quickly and returned a few minutes later with Chris. Whilst Tony had been gone, David had been looking around but without touching anything and had noted some interesting facts about the murder. Chris, like Tony, looked shell-shocked and sick when he saw the body, even though Tony had quietly told him what had happened on the way up to the room. He had waited until they were on the stairs near the room and no-one else was around to hear but hearing about a death is a lot different from actually seeing the body.
"Bloody hell, why does this keep happening; what have I done to deserve this?" Chris burst out, half to himself. It wasn't that he didn't care about Ms Johnson; it was just that he was overwhelmed with fear for the hotel.

Unable to contain himself any longer, Tony turned to David and asked why he had wanted them to keep the murder quiet.
"Surely we need to contact the police, or they may think we had something to do with it," he said to David, turning to Chris for confirmation. Chris, though, was still staring at the body, his eyes seemingly riveted. Tony lightly touched his shoulder in compassion, remembering the disorientation he had felt on first

44

seeing the body. Chris shook himself weakly and looked at Tony gratefully. He obviously had heard what Tony had asked, even if he hadn't responded immediately, because he nodded in agreement and he too, turned to look at David.

In order to allay some of their immediate worries, David said,
"What I have got to say will only take a few minutes. The police don't know exactly when we found her, so are not likely to be suspicious, if you do decide to call them when I have finished."
As he was saying this, a look of both determination and, strangely, resignation, crossed David's face. It was almost as if he had been fighting an internal battle with himself. He nodded, more to himself than to Chris and Tony, and then spoke.
"What I am about to say, you need to keep just between us three. Do I have your word?" David demanded.
Both Tony and Chris looked confused but uncertainly agreed. Tony wondered fleetingly if David had had something to do with the murder and was going to confess. He cast a slightly suspicious look at him.
"I need a better response than that," David told them.
Chris and Tony looked at each other and nodded, before turning to David once more and, this time, their agreement was much more certain.
"Ok then," said David.

David took another look around the room, his gaze lingering briefly on the dead body on the bed, before continuing,
"If this murder goes public, there are going to be police crawling all over the hotel and because they still haven't solved the previous murder, they will probably keep the hotel closed for quite a while, whilst they investigate. Also, if you look at the bedside table you will notice that the woman's jewelry has been neatly set out. What does that tell you?"
Obediently, Tony and Chris turned to stare at the bedside table, but when they turned back to face David it was clear that neither of them had seemed to grasp his words or be capable of giving

an answer. David's sigh in response to their blankness was gentle and understanding, so he continued,

"What it tells me is that this murder and the previous one are linked."

Tony managed to struggle out of his stupor and asked, his voice cracking,

"How do you reach that conclusion?"

"Well, first and most obviously, both victims were strangled in their beds at night. Secondly, both victims had been involved in altercations with, and been abusive to the staff. Lastly, in both cases, the murderer left clues as to why they were murdered, the untouched Americano for the first murder and the jewelry set out on the bedside table, this time."

"Oh?" said Chris, who was now beginning to shake off his immediate shock at the murder, whilst also taking note of the apparent change that had come over David as he made these observations.

"So," responded David, "that gives us a clue as to who is behind the murders and that won't be good for the hotel."

"It has to be one of the staff," stated Tony, in a shocked voice.

"Yes," agreed David, "one of the staff or someone close to them."

"My god," exclaimed Chris, "I can't believe one of the staff would do this."

"You'd better, because that is what the police and everyone else will think if this goes public. What will that do for your reputation? Who is going to stay at the hotel if they think there is a murderer on the staff?"

"My God, I'll be ruined," murmured Chris, looking completely broken as he leant against the wall for support.

"But what can we do about it; we can't just ignore or hide the murder. We have got to call the police, haven't we?" Tony asserted.

"There is possibly another way to deal with it," David told them, "but you will have to trust me."

Both Tony and Chris stared at David, identical looks of complete bewilderment on their faces, having no idea where David was leading.

"How?" they both said at the same time.

"Listen. I used to work for a 'government department', shall we say which had certain skills that we could utilise. Now, I still have contacts there who owe me a few favours. I could ask them to come and do a clean up job which will make it seem that nothing ever happened here."

"But what about the body?"

"They will get rid of it."

As their initial shock began to fade, both Chris and Tony began to see potential problem David's solution.

"But she must have family or friends who knew she was staying here. Surely they will report her missing to the police who will come here and investigate just the same."

"I said trust me, she will disappear in a way that casts no suspicion on the hotel.

Believe me, we used to do that all the time," David let slip.

By this time Tony and Chris were in an even deeper state of bewilderment, not only as a result of the second murder and from David's suggestion that they do not tell the police, but, equally, from the revelations of a past occupation they would never have suspected.

'No wonder he wasn't shocked by the body', Tony thought, 'obviously he has had experience dealing with dead bodies before'.

"However, if you want me to do this we need to get on with it, before anyone starts asking questions." David told them.

Chris looked at Tony and then David, obviously unsure what to do. Clearly, this whole situation was beyond his experience and he was seriously torn over what to do. On the one hand, as a fairly law abiding member of society, he felt he should report the murder. After all, that's what people were supposed to do, but and it was a big but, he really felt his livelihood was at stake, not to mention the thousands of pounds of his own money he had put into renovating the hotel. If there was a way he could protect all that, it would be good. It was a huge decision to make, but if he was being honest, self preservation was certainly moving him towards agreeing with David's suggestion, but then he was stopped by a chilling thought,

"What about the murderer, if you just lose the body, how will we find out who he is? We can't just let them go free and possibly kill another guest."

On asking this, he turned to David, fervently hoping he had an answer to that question. If David could not come up with an answer, Chris felt that he would feel compelled to say no, but it would be a reluctant 'no'.

"I was coming to that. Obviously we need to apprehend the killer; you can't have someone killing guests left, right and centre. It is possible to hide a couple of bodies but if it happened on a regular basis, someone would notice. If you have no other immediate objections, I have some ideas about how to catch the killer, quietly and without anyone knowing. Hopefully, I can catch them unawares and if I can get some help from my former colleagues, who would then be involved in the case, we would be able to say it was an 'official' investigation, carried out under the auspices of an official government department."

"Can you guarantee you will catch the killer and the hotel won't be dropped right in it?" asked Chris.

"Nothing is guaranteed, but I will obviously do my best and my former colleagues are experts in their field. If they are involved the chances of catching the killer are very high and you would be able to say you didn't call the police because there were security implications. After all, the police haven't caught anyone yet for the first murder so there is no guarantee they would do so this time." David said.

Chris looked across at Tony.

"What do you think," he asked.

"It's not really my decision, is it?"

"No, but I would like your opinion."

Tony took a few moments to consider the various aspects and assess the chances of success, compared with the effect that reporting the murder of another guest to the police would have on the hotel. He wasn't totally convinced that David could deliver, or even if he totally believed his claims, but he was able to tell himself that if there was a chance of successfully keeping the murder quiet and catching the killer, it was probably worth taking the chance.

"Well, if it works you won't lose everything you have invested in this place, and the rest of us will still have a job. Also David says he knows what he is talking about so, yes, I think I would take the risk." Tony said at last.

It appeared that Chris was in agreement with Tony and had only been waiting for Tony to say he thought it was the right option as, immediately Tony finished, he turned to David,

"Ok," he agreed, "do what you need to do."

Once the two of them had agreed to listen to him, David had been fairly certain that they would agree to his proposal. After all, self preservation is a very motivational factor and his option was the one most likely to keep them their livelihoods, so whilst they had been thinking his proposal through, he had been considering how best to deal with the situation. Surprisingly, old routines clicked into place very quickly.

"Right, first things first, we need to keep the staff out of this room and especially the cleaners. Tell them that it is out of bounds, there is a suspected electric fault in here that is potentially very dangerous and no-one must enter until it is sorted. An electrician is on the way. If anyone asks about the customer; what's her name, by the way?" he looked to Tony.

"Ms Johnson."

"Ms Johnson, so if anyone asks, just tell them she checked out early this morning. One of you will need to do the paperwork for that straight away, but keep it under wraps until I get the ok to proceed."

"Ok," Tony and Chris replied, in unison.

"Right, I'm going back to my room to make a phone call and get the ball rolling. Make sure you lock this door so no-one comes in and make sure you do Ms Johnson's paperwork as soon as you get downstairs."

Both Tony and Chris nodded in agreement and all three of them left the room, locking it and putting a 'Do Not Disturb' notice on the door handle.

As Chris and Tony set off downstairs, David went back to his room. On the stairs Tony said,

"I hope we made the right decision."

"Me too," replied Chris fervently, physically crossing his fingers and metaphorically crossing everything else.

When David was back in his room, he sat down for a minute to compose himself. When he had left 'the department' he had thought he would not be contacting them ever again, let alone after only a few years. He had left because he had started to think that some of the jobs they did were too extreme and could be done through other means, but now he would be going back to them, admittedly unofficially, to get them to circumvent a potential official police enquiry and get his friends out of a difficult situation. The irony was not lost on him and he expected to receive some caustic comments from his previous colleagues. After a few minutes vacillating over the issue, he took a deep breath, checked the time, which was 7.24am. Using the hotel phone so as not to leave any record of the call on his mobile, he took a few deep breaths and then dialed the special number that he doubted he would ever forget. There was someone on duty 24 hours a day so, even though it was relatively early, after the usual four rings the phone was answered,

"Yes, can I help you?" a voice enquired.

"Can I speak to Mark, please; my name is David, code name Firefly. It's been a while since I used it so you may need to check back."

Mark was second in command at the department and all routine calls were referred to him initially. He then decided if they needed to be referred upwards to Sir Peter Nichols, the person charge of the department, who was simply referred to as 'Sir' most of the time.

"Wait one moment please."

Fingers drumming the table, David tried to remain calm whilst he waited, knowing that the operator was both checking his code name and ensuring that his location was being traced in case his code name was either, not recognised, or proscribed. After a couple of minutes the operator came back on the line,

"I am putting you through now."

It was obvious that the operator had already talked to Mark because he answered almost before it had been transferred, clearly knowing who was on the line.

"Is this a ghost on the line?" he asked.

"No ghost, flesh and blood," David replied.

"Well, that's ok then," said Mark, "glad you remember the drill."

"Of course I remember it; the training will stick with me forever."

"Well, well, David, to what do we owe this pleasure?"

Mark was not the sort of person to forego the chance to be both sarcastic and condescending; though David knew he was an excellent operative.

"I need a favour. I need a clean up squad to get rid of a body from a hotel and make sure there is a trail leading away."

"You've not started killing people again, have you, David, you know you can't do that without our permission?" Mark asked, only half joking.

"No I haven't," responded David, "there has been a murder of a guest at my local hotel in Belper and I would like to keep it under wraps."

"Sounds intriguing, old boy, do tell me the details." Mark requested, his tone sounding disinterested, though David thought he had detected a quickening of interest and an intake of breath when he had said, 'murder at my local hotel'.

David then went on to explain all the details of the two murders and his hunch that the murderer was connected to the hotel in some way and the effect that bad publicity could have for his friends. Mark listened carefully, occasionally asking a question for clarification. When David had finished, Mark said,
"Leave it with me; I will get back to you when I have spoken to the boss. How do I contact you, at the hotel or on your mobile?"
"I presume you have the hotel number?"
"Oh yes, the receptionist checked that for us."
"Ok, I am in room 11."
"You didn't get drunk again, did you?" Mark bizarrely asked, before he severed the connection and David was left staring at the receiver.

When he had finished talking to David, Mark looked at the receiver for a few seconds, thinking about what David was asking for, before walking the short distance to the office of his boss. He knocked and entered to find his boss drinking a cup of coffee and casually watching the CCTV screens of the building and its surrounds, frowning at what he was seeing. He looked up from the screens as Mark entered and said,
"I think we need to keep the operatives a bit more active, they seem to spend a lot of time just sitting around, I'm not exactly certain that trying to throw cards into a hat is the best form of training."
Mark watched the screen for a few seconds before saying,
"He is very good at it though."
Sir Peter just grunted. Mark smiled to himself, than added,
"Well. There might be a chance of some action for them, as it happens."
"Oh yes, what's that?"

Mark recounted his conversation with David and the request he had made.

"Very interesting, this sounds very similar to the situations we are investigating. David's little problem might very well give us the entry point we need. We could solve our problem case and have a potential scapegoat should something go wrong."

"That's what I was thinking, it does seem very fortuitous."

"Yes, it does. Give me a few minutes to think about it and I will let you know."

"Ok," said Mark, leaving the office.

Sir Peter sat for a few moments thinking about David's request. Whilst it would certainly be unusual for the department to carry out such a favour for an ex colleague, it was not totally unheard of. The fact that there might be a tie in with a case they were currently investigating would be fortuitous. Also, some of his operatives around the country could do with some live action. Finally, and possibly most importantly, David had been a really good operative and Sir Peter acknowledged it would be very good if he could be persuaded to return to the department. Maybe helping him out could have that beneficial result, as well. All in all, it seemed like a win-win situation. Having reached his decision, Sir Peter left his office to tell Mark his decision.

"Ok, I think we can help David."

"Right. Do you want me to tell him about our operation?"

"I don't think so. Not yet anyway. We can always tell him later if we need to."

"Ok, I call him back and tell him the good news."

Back at the Lion Hotel, David waited for the response from the department. He made himself a cup of coffee, hoping the caffeine would give him some 'oomph' and start to rectify the effects of last night's drinking. He had nearly finished his second cup of strong black coffee when his room phone rang, which David thought was suspiciously quick unless, of course, it was going to be an emphatic 'no'.

"David, I've got the ok from 'Sir'. He is prepared to do this favour for you; some of the boys are already in your area and need a bit of practice. The boss thought a live event was much better than training. Do you have a cover story for the operation?"

David gave a quick smile of relief and explained that the cover story would be an electrical fault, so the operatives needed to pose as electricians. He gave the address and the names of Tony and Chris as the people to contact when the agents arrived at the hotel and that they could park round the back of the hotel.
"Ok, they will be with you within a couple of hours."
"Thanks."
"Oh, don't mention it, old boy," Mark nonchalantly responded, "We have to look after our own, don't we?"

After the call ended, David checked his mobile to get the time and calculated that the operatives would arrive between 9 and 10 am. David then went down to reception to tell Tony and Chris that everything was in place. There were a couple of other staff members at reception so he merely informed them that he had been in touch with his electrician friend and they would be there within a couple of hours.
"Let me know when they get here," David told Tony, who would be at reception, "they are old friends but I haven't seen them in a while, so it would be good to catch up."
This latter was for the benefit of the other staff members that were at reception, to explain why David was hanging around at the hotel rather than going home as he normally would.

David excused himself and went to the restaurant to get some breakfast. As he sat eating his full English, a couple of things Mark had said came to mind and cause his hand to pause, fork halfway to his mouth, whilst he considered them. 'We have to look after our own', Mark had said. Slowly, the fork continued its path to David's mouth as he considered that. I suppose he could have simply meant doing him a favour as an old member of the

54

department, David surmised and hoped. Still, he knew that the boss might want to get him back in the department and he might use this to try and entice him back. He had better be on his guard, he concluded. The other thing Mark had said was even more puzzling. Why had Mark asked if he had got drunk again and then rung off before David had a chance to respond? Also, why hadn't he asked why he was staying in the hotel when he only lived about two miles from the hotel? In fact, David thought, Mark had been surprisingly disinterested in asking him any details about his current life. With a sense of certainty, David realised that he definitely needed to be careful.

Whilst David was enjoying his breakfast, the phone rang in another office located about 5 miles from Sir Peter's department. The man seated behind the desk noted the number and, recognising it as his informant in Sir Peter's department, picked up the receiver,

"Yes," he said.

A voice answered,

"Hi, just to let you know, Sir Peter has just agreed to help out an ex-colleague deal with a murder at our Hotel, just low level help at the moment, but I thought you would want to be informed."

"That's very interesting, do you know the details."

"All I know at the minute is that a former operative asked for help in getting rid of a body and Sir Peter agreed. I will let you know if I find out more."

"Thanks," said the man behind the desk and put the phone down.

He stared thoughtfully at his phone for a few moments, then swore briefly before picking up the phone again and called his second in command.

"Joshua, I have just had our insider in Sir Peter's Special Ops department on the phone. It appears their department is going to get rid of our dead body at the Hotel."

"I see Sir, do you know why they are involved?"

"No details yet, but it seems one of his former operatives asked for help getting rid of a body and Sir Peter agreed. Hopefully nothing will come of it and they will just do this one favour."

"I see, but it might compromise our operation a bit, won't it?

"Not if it's just the one favour, it might become more problematic if they decide to fully investigate it. Hopefully it won't become a problem."

"Yes Sir. Do you want me to inform the operatives about this?"

"Not at the moment, we can use it as a test to see how robust the whole operation is."

"Very good, Sir."

David continued to eat a long slow breakfast and some time later, with the food part of his breakfast finished but with his third cup of tea in front of him, one of the hotel staff came to find him to tell him Tony wanted him at reception. He made his way quickly, but without appearing to rush, to reception. Two men were stood there, their backs to him, wearing work men's clothes but, even after the passage of years, David recognised one of them immediately.

"Hi Johnnie ," he called across the foyer, "it's been a long time, how are you?"

Johnnie looked round, "Good ta see ya, Davie, you're lookin' good."

David approached Johnnie and clasped him by the arm and shook his hand effusively. Johnnie turned to the other man with him and said,

"Bill, this is Davie, the bloke I told you about; Davie, this is Bill, he works with me."

Bill shook hands with David, both sizing the other up.

"Hi ya Davie, Johnnie's told me a lot about you, good ta meet ya," he said in a good-natured way.

"Well, if you work with Johnnie you must be good," David responded.

David turned to Tony and suggested,

"If it's ok, I'll take them up to the room, we have a lot of catching up to do?"

"No problem," smiled Tony, catching on at once, "Be my guest, here's the key."

"Ok, follow me," David said, as the two men picked up their equipment and followed him to the stairs and up to the room.

"So, how's the electrical trade doing?" asked David, loud enough for the benefit of any staff that happened to be within earshot.

"Busy," responded Johnnie, equally loudly and they continued making small talk as they climbed the stairs and went down the corridor to the room. When they got to room 12, David moved the 'Danger, Do Not Enter' sign that now covered the lock so that he could unlock the door and they entered quickly, after which David closed and locked the door again to make sure no-one else could get in by accident. With the door safely closed, Johnnie turned to David and asked,

"Ok, what's the position; Mark said you would explain the details to us and oversee the operation. What do you want us to do?"

"Just the usual, we need to lose the body on the bed and set up a false trail so that it appeared that the woman actually left the hotel and disappeared somewhere else."

"No problem. I thought you had left the department though?"

"I have," David confirmed.

Both Johnnie and Bill gave him a very skeptical and amused look at that bit of information, but said nothing else. They all went further into the room to size up the task.

"Is there an easy way to get the body out of the hotel? Bill asked.

"Not really, we need to work on that. We can keep the room locked all day, pretending you are working in here. The first thing is to set up the false trail. Have you got a local female agent who looks anything like her?"

Johnnie and Bill looked at the woman on the bed, looked at each other, and then said, at exactly the same moment,

"Chloe!"

"Call her, will you, Bill and see how long it will take her to get here."

"Ok."

Bill reached into his pocket to get his phone out as he went to the other end of the room and dialed Chloe's number. Chloe answered fairly quickly and Bill spent a few minutes talking to her.

"Apparently she has been on an operation in Nottingham and can be here in about forty minutes, one of the department's drivers will drop her off and I have arranged to meet her at the train station so she is not seen at the hotel." Bill informed them both.

"Good," said David, "It will still be early morning, so I think she should catch the train from Belper to Derby. She needs to use cash for that journey so it can't be traced and then no one will be able to find out what time she left Belper."

"I can give her the woman's coat when we meet and tell her to get the train to London from Derby. I will need her credit card so Chloe can use it to buy a train ticket from Derby? I'll get her pin number on the way from tech boys."

"Ok. Good. She can catch the train to London around 11 to 11-30 so it would look like she had been shopping in Derby before she caught the train," David added.

Bill got the coat, put some of the dead woman's clothes in her small luggage bag, put them both in his work bag, found the credit card in Ms Johnson's bag and then left to meet Chloe, having got directions to the station from David.

"I'll stop off at reception and tell the guy there you will talk to him as there is a serious problem and it will be a big job," he informed them as he left.

"He seems very efficient," David said approvingly to Johnnie.

"Oh yes, he's one our best. He arrived after you left but in the last couple of years he has shown himself to be very capable. So, what shall we do about the body, how do we get it out?" asked Johnnie.

"I'll go and have a close look at the hotel layout and find the best route. Lock the door after me. Do a bit of banging now and again to make it seem like you are working."

With that David left the room and walked casually down the corridor to the room he had stayed in overnight so he could give his face a quick rinse to freshen up and make himself another cup of coffee. As he was sitting at the table, sipping his coffee, he thought over what had happened since he had been woken up that morning and, for the first time wondered why he had broken his cover and decided to help Tony and Chris. With an abrupt shock, he realised that, although he was dealing with a brutal murder, he was actually enjoying himself and the experience of overseeing his former colleagues in a live operation had started to rekindle a sense of purpose and excitement in his life which had been missing, particularly since he and his partner had split up. Since that had happened, he knew he had been largely drifting and whilst he generally enjoyed his job as a gardener, the rest of his lifestyle was so mundane that the thrill of trying to solve the murders had brought some life back into his veins. He wondered if he was starting to need a sense of purpose and the thrill of that sense of adrenalin rush again. Also, it had to be said, he was also feeling a certain sense of satisfaction in that what he was doing was also helping his friends, particularly Tony who had done a lot to help him deal with his situation.

He finished his coffee and left his room, wandering slowly down the corridor, as if deep in thought, though, in reality, he was looking closely at the layout of the hotel, the distance from room 12 to the stairs and the staff elevator. He went down the stairs and turned to look carefully around the foyer, trying to see if the elevator came out at this level. It didn't appear to, so he continued his turning and when he faced the reception, he asked

59

the receptionist if Tony or Chris were in the office. He probably could have walked straight in, but he thought it would look better if he asked; after all he wasn't a member of staff. The receptionist opened the office door and called to Tony, who came out a few seconds later. The receptionist nodded towards David and Tony, obviously now over his slow start, asked,

"How's the electrician doing? I got the message that there is a problem, will it be sorted out today?"

"Apparently it's a pretty big problem. He needs to show you."

"Ok, let's go and see."

The two of them set off up the stairs to room 12, not speaking. When they got there, he knocked and when Johnnie came to the door, David announced himself. Johnnie let them in and then closed and locked the door behind them. When they went all the way into the room, Johnnie sat down and resumed drinking the coffee he had made himself and David began to explain the situation to Tony.

"We won't be able to get the body out yet, so we are going to have to say there is a major electrical problem, until we can move it, probably late tonight. We are setting a false trail for Ms Johnson so it appears she left this morning and then went to London, where she will apparently disappear. That's not a problem; did you sort out her bill?"

"We were lucky, I didn't have to. Apparently, she sorted her bill out last night and paid it before she came up to bed. Obviously, she had intended to leave early this morning anyway."

"Good, that makes life easier. Now, the only way I can see of getting the body out is to get it to the staff lift. Where does it come out?"

"In the basement; close to the rear door, which is very close to where your van is parked," he answered, looking at Johnnie.

"Ok, that's how we will do it then," said David to Johnnie, who nodded. Whilst this exchange between David and Johnnie was going on a look of surprise quickly passed over Tony's face. He had simply assumed that Johnnie would be the one in charge, but the way Johnnie deferred to David showed that wasn't the case. He was beginning to wonder even more about David's background. It seemed his friend had a lot of secrets in his past that he had managed to keep hidden, even when thoroughly drunk. He had certainly played his part well. Tony also realized that a small part of him was definitely angry at David. He had thought he had known all about David's life, but it was clear that he knew hardly anything, at least, anything that had happened before he moved to this area. These unwelcome thoughts though, were pushed aside when David said,

"So, what we need is a good excuse for keeping the room closed until tonight. What electrical reason can we give?"

"That's easy," Tony quickly exclaimed, "We can say that some of the older electric cables have frayed and need replacing and it will take until tomorrow to do the necessary repairs."

Both David and Johnnie looked at Tony with a certain amount of admiration for the speed with which he had come up with that explanation. Whilst obviously enjoying the admiration, Tony did not want to give a false impression about his talents, so he reluctantly explained,

"It happened at my parents' house a few months ago so it just seemed an obvious reason to use."

"Yeah, good, that will work. I can just stay in the room and bang about, sending Bill out every now and then, apparently to get some equipment from the van," concluded Johnnie.

"Ok, that's good. I will go home and return this evening for my normal drink and we'll move the body after midnight. Tony, you need to make sure that the room remains off limits until tomorrow, at least, and is not allocated or cleaned today."

"Ok, I will put a block on it on the computer and put a notice on the staff notice board that the room is being made safe. I will also make sure that either me or Chris is in the hotel all day. I can bring these two some lunch later on unless you want to eat in the bar. Also, what time will you be here 'til tonight?" Tony asked Johnnie.

"Better make it around 5-30 to 6 pm, we are supposed to be ordinary electricians, after all. We don't want to make your staff suspicious by working too long."

"Just make sure that the sign stays on the door so no-one on the staff forgets and tries to come into the room." David reminded Tony.

"That's ok, if Johnnie has the room key, I will make sure that only me or Chris has the master keys today, then no one will be able to get in."

"If the room is really secure, we will go and eat in the bar at lunch. We need to appear to be good, honest electricians who would definitely make the most of working in a place where there was a bar."

"Good, that's all sorted then," David concluded, "I just need to talk to Johnnie privately about the final arrangements and then I will shoot off until tonight."

Tony took his cue and left the room. He returned to the office to put all the arrangements in place. When he had gone, David discussed with Johnnie the final arrangements that needed to be put into place. Johnnie and Bill would return to the hotel at 1am and would park as near the back door as they could. David or Tony would let them in and they would collect the body. Whilst Johnnie and Bill would be the ones to physically move the body, David and Tony would be keeping watch to make sure that no one caught them in the act. Having agreed the details, David was about to leave when he remembered to ask,

"Will Bill be bringing a body bag back?" he asked.

"Don't worry, it's all organised. We have done this before, remember."

David gave a sheepish smile and apologised, acknowledging their expertise in such matters.

David then left the room, waited until he heard that Johnnie had locked the door behind him, before going downstairs to say goodbye to Tony. As there were a few members of staff around, David said fairly loudly,

"Those wires were pretty badly chewed but Johnnie is an excellent electrician, they'll get it sorted as quickly as possible. Anyway, I'll see you later."

Tony waved in response and said,

"See you."

David turned and walked out the door and made his way home. David had just let himself into his house and put the kettle on when, caught by a thought, he stopped,

"Shit" he swore aloud.

He had just realized that they hadn't thought about how they had supposedly found out about the electrical fault. He needed to think of something and tell Tony, just in case anyone asked. Admittedly, it was unlikely that anyone would ask but they needed to cover all bases and have an explanation just in case. David sat drinking his tea, trying to come up with a reasonable explanation, but nothing seemed to work. If Ms Johnson had left the hotel without speaking to anyone, which was the picture they had put in place, how had Tony known about the problem with the electrics. As Ms Johnson hadn't told him, Tony would have had no reason to go into room 12 in the normal course of events. How could Tony have known?

A sip of tea, one possible explanation explored, before being discarded. Another, sip of tea, another explanation assessed and discarded. This process went on through several minutes and several sips of tea. Eventually, as he was taking his last sip of tea, the answer came to him. As usual, the best answers are based on reality and, as Tony had actually gone to Ms Johnson's room when she did not answer her alarm call, they could say that she had, unknown to Tony, supposedly, left early without seeing anyone. When Tony went in the room he can say that the lights went off and when he checked the kettle and the TV, neither of those worked either. He also thought he could hear the electrics hissing, so he put the room out of bounds. That would work, David thought. All he had to do now was get that information to Tony.

He didn't want to use the phone so he decided to pretend that he had left something in his room at the hotel so he could have a quick word with Tony. He drove the few minutes back to the hotel, went to reception to get the key to the room he had stayed in. Nathan was on reception, which made life easier as he wouldn't ask daft questions.

"Hi Nathan, can I have the key to room 11, I think I left my work diary there last night."

"Hi David, sure, no problem," Nathan replied, turning to get the key for him, before saying, "The cleaner must have it; she is doing those rooms at the minute, so she might have found it."

"Thanks, I'll check."

David walked to the stairs and climbed them to get to room 11. As Nathan had said, the cleaner was in the room so David asked if she had seen his diary. Obviously, she said she hadn't, but David pretended to look for it anyway. When he had finished looking, he said,

"You're right, it's not here. Obviously, I must have left it somewhere else. Thanks anyway. See you."

With that he gave a wave and started to walk off. The cleaner, like most staff at the hotel knew him and called,

"See you David. Hope you find the diary."

David gave a last wave and left the room, almost walking directly into Tony.

"I heard you talking to Nathan, so I assumed you must have come back for a reason," Tony said.

David checked that the cleaner couldn't hear before saying quietly,

"Yes, I suddenly realised when I was home that we didn't have a legitimate reason for knowing about the so called electrical fault in room 12."

Tony looked quizzical, as he had thought that just saying he went to the room when Ms Johnson hadn't responded to the alarm call would be enough but, as David explained his reasoning and his solution, Tony's face registered his understanding.

"I suppose that could have been a problem, though I doubt anyone would have bothered to ask. Still, you are right, it's better to be prepared."

With that David returned to the reception, gave the key back to Nathan, explained he hadn't found the diary and then left the hotel to go home, once more. When he got home, he dropped heavily into his most comfortable chair and just sat there for a while, eyes closed, not even bothering to put the kettle on for a cup of tea!

Chapter 5.

The Night Shift.

After all the excitement of the morning, David decided not to do any gardening that day, preferring to spend the day resting, as well as re-hydrating his body after the previous night's drinking. So it was around 8-30 that evening that he walked the half hour to the hotel and, as he entered the bar, he bumped into Leah, "You're late tonight," she said.

It seemed a lot of the staff knew his routine.
"I don't want to be too predictable," he responded lightly.
"It's too late for food," she told him.
"That's alright, I've eaten at home. I just fancied a pint."

With that, he slipped past Leah and headed for the bar and ordered his usual pint of Peroni. He took a large mouthful whilst still stood at the bar, making it easier to walk across the bar without spilling it, to sit at one of the vacant tables. As he had expected, almost immediately Tony came and joined him, but before Tony had the chance to even open his mouth to say 'Hi', David said conversationally,
"Do you know, it's amazing how many secrets are discussed in public places like bars, when really they shouldn't be. I've heard lots of things people wouldn't want me to know simply by sitting near them. It's great for my writing. As a barman at times, I've bet you have heard a lot of things people wouldn't want you to know."
David had to give Tony his due, because he picked up on David's real meaning immediately.
"Oh yes, but a lot of the time people open up to the bar staff as if we were counselors, they seem to think that, somehow, we

can help them. Oh, by the way, your friend has done a good job so far on the electrics. He said he will be finished tomorrow. That will be good. We will need the room for the weekend."

"I told you he was good."

"So what are your plans for this evening?"

"I intend to get slowly rat-arsed, so I think we should drink until the early hours. I don't want to get home too early, if at all."

"Sounds good to me, I'll join you at closing time," Tony concluded, before wandering off to do whatever hotel related tasks he still had to do.

David decided to move over to a vacant table near the big TV screen to watch the sport, so that he could drink more slowly. It also made a pleasant change as he didn't have TV at home, well, he had a TV but as he didn't have either a license or an aerial, he mainly only used it to watch old DVDs.

As the evening meandered towards its close, people started to drift away and go home, or, in a few cases, possibly onto somewhere more interesting. Most of the staff who had finished their shifts only stayed for a short while to have a post work drink and to unwind a bit before going home. Around midnight there was only Tony, David and Vicky left, plus the night porter who stayed at reception in case any of the guests needed assistance, or rather, after midnight he slept in the office at the back of the reception. The few hotel guests had already gone to bed and the hotel bars and surroundings were quiet. The immediate problem for David and Tony was that Vicky would quite often stay late into the night drinking with them but, obviously, tonight they needed her to leave. They tried talking about writing and their books in order to bore her into leaving but, for once, in true sod's law fashion, she actually seemed quite interested, so they turned to football, which, admittedly, neither of them knew very much, and which, as it turned out, Vicky had far more knowledge than either of them. It was getting close to 1 am and Vicky was still there and they were beginning to get a little desperate. David wasn't drunk and so there was no need for him to use one of the hotel rooms, so he couldn't excuse himself and go upstairs. About 10 to 1 Vicky went to the toilet and David said quickly to Tony,

"I'm going to say I'm leaving. I will go and let the boys in and take them upstairs. You make sure to keep her in here until I have had time to take them up. Tell Vicky you are going to finish some paper work and then go home. Hopefully Vicky will then go. When you are sure she has gone, come and tell us."

"Ok."

So when Vicky had returned David finished his drink and said he was going home.

"What, so early?" queried Vicky.

"Yeah, I'm knackered and I really do have to do some work tomorrow, otherwise I won't be able to afford your excellent company," replied David.

"Wuss," Vicky told him.

David smiled and got up to leave,

"I know," he admitted, "I'm getting old. See you later in the week."

"See ya," they both said as David left the bar.

He went quickly to the back door and opened it. Bill and Johnnie were standing in the shadows. As soon as they saw David, they sauntered casually but quickly over and entered the hotel. David put his finger to his lips to make sure they were quiet and led them upstairs. When they got to room 12, Johnnie unlocked the door and they went in. David quickly told them about Vicky and they settled down to wait.

About fifteen minutes later, there was a knock on the door; David went over, made sure it was Tony and let him in.

"She's gone," he told them quietly so as not to disturb the guests who were in some of the other rooms.

"Ok, let's go," said David.

He sent Tony to the stairs to watch and make sure the coast was clear. Bill and Johnnie picked up the body bag and carried it to the door. David looked out, making sure there were no guests around and out of their beds, before beckoning them forward. They set off down the corridor, heading for the staff lift. David put out the lights in room 12, closed the door quietly and then followed them down the corridor.

When he caught up to them Bill and Johnnie were stuffing the body bag into the lift, which was actually a large dumb waiter that was mostly used for linen. When the body was in the lift, they shut the door and were about to press the down button, when they heard Vicky's voice from the bottom of the stairs,
"Hey Tony, I was just getting my coat from my car when I saw the room light from room 12 go out. I thought no-one was in there?"
David, Bill and Johnnie, stopped dead. There was nowhere they could go unless they went back to room 12 but that didn't seem like a good idea if Vicky came up the stairs to investigate. It was all down to Tony.
"That was me," he said quickly, "I just went up to check on the progress of the electricians before I finished so I could leave a report for Chris for the morning."
"Oh, okay. I just thought it funny that's all," Vicky explained.
"Glad to see you're on the ball," congratulated Tony.
"Ok, I'll be off then; goodnight."
"Goodnight."

They heard the sound of the door opening and closing and then Tony poked his head round the corner of the stairs and raised his thumb. Almost in unison, the three men upstairs wiped their respective brows and grinned.
"That was good, especially for an amateur," said Bill.
"Yeah, maybe we should offer him a job with us?" added Johnnie.
"Ok, let's get the job finished," David said to them, as if he was still their boss.
"Almost like old times," muttered Johnnie.

He pressed the down button and the lift set off slowly on its journey to the basement. The three of them joined a nervous looking Tony at the bottom of the stairs.

"Well done mate, quick thinking," praised Johnnie, as both Bill and David patted him on the back. "Are you sure she's gone?"

"Well, she went out the side door, so I presume she's gone home."

They made their way down to the basement and whilst David went to the rear entrance to make sure the coast was clear, Bill and Johnnie took the body from out of the lift.

"Give me the van keys, I'll open the back door," David said.

Johnnie put down his end of the body, fumbled in his coat pocket, found the keys, gave them to David and showed him which button to press, before picking up his end of the body again.

"All clear," Tony mouthed to them.

The two men carried the body across the room and into the staff car park, whilst David went ahead to open the van doors. They quickly put the body in the back and threw a blanket over it. They closed the doors, locked them and then all four of them relaxed.

"Right, we're off to get rid of this," Johnnie informed them, jerking his head towards the back doors of the van.

"What time will you be here tomorrow?" David enquired.

"Why do they need to come back?" asked a bewildered Tony.

"We have to pretend to finish the electrics," Bill reminded him.

"Oh yes, I forgot about that," admitted Tony.

"Good job we didn't", said Johnnie, "We'll get here around eight-thirty and finish around eleven. We'll leave a part of the wall newly plastered as evidence. Can I have the keys back, ready for tomorrow?"

"Here," said David, as he returned the keys, "Well, thanks for everything Johnnie, hopefully I won't ever need you again."

Johnnie just gave him a knowing look and replied,

"You never know."

"I doubt it," responded David, but he had a strange feeling that Johnnie might be letting him know something. Whether he was or not, a feeling of both excitement and anxiety went through him at the thought.

At that Johnnie and Bill got in the van and drove quietly and sedately away. Tony and David looked at each other and Tony raised his hand in the universal gesture of asking if David wanted a drink. David responded with a 'thumbs up' and they went back in to the bar. Tony poured a drink for both of them and they wearily sat down.
"Right," exclaimed Tony, "You have a bit of explaining to do."
"About what," David asked disingenuously.
"You know very well. You obviously have a past that you have managed to keep very secret. In view of the past couple of days, I think it's time you spilled the beans."
"Ok, but I can't tell you much, as I have signed the Official Secrets Act but, as is obvious, I used to work for the government in that line of work. I did it for several years before I began to feel that we were over-stepping our remit and asked to leave. They allowed me to resign, provided I always told them where I was and I never went abroad without telling, or rather, asking them, first."
"Wow, and we all thought you were just a retired office worker, with a good pension, who worked as a gardener to keep yourself occupied."
"In a sense, that's nearly true," David concluded vaguely.

Tony went to the bar to pour another couple of drinks and said,
"I think I might have a few of these tonight, I think I need it, what about you?
"I'll have a couple, but don't have too much; this has to be kept secret. If any word gets out we will be in serious trouble, understand?"
Tony gave a sardonic laugh and then replied,
"Yeah, I do realise that, I'm not stupid. Cheers."

"I know, but it's very easy to say too much when you are drunk and lose focus."

"You don't. How many times have we got drunk and you never let slip a single word?"

"Aah well, I've been trained haven't I?"

"Very well, it seems."

They clinked glasses and, as he took a drink, David realised that he no longer wanted to drink himself into oblivion. In one way, that worried him as much as the idea of wanting to drink so much, as he could feel the pull of his old life insinuating itself in the back of his mind.

"One more thing, at some time in the next few weeks the police will probably come and ask questions about Ms Johnson. Someone is bound to report her missing. Everything has been sorted, just show them the paid bill and leave it at that. Don't get creative or pretend to remember too much. Remember how many customers pass through the hotel and how many of them can you remember? Ok. The police could well get suspicious if you remember too much?" David told Tony.

"Ok," Tony accepted.

A short while later, David decided he had better get home. Even though he could work pretty much when he pleased, he acknowledged, at least to himself, that it might be a good idea to return to a more regular working pattern.

The next day, Johnnie and Bill arrived as expected, stayed until around eleven thirty, banged around a bit and then reported to Tony, in the foyer, before they left.

"Right, everything is sorted," Johnnie explained, talking just loud enough so that people could hear, "the electrics are working fine but if there is a problem get back to us, David has our number. There is a bit of painting that will need doing when the new plaster has dried. We will send you the bill in a few weeks."

"Thanks for your prompt and efficient service. It's been really good," Tony told them.

With that, the two of them left and Tony turned to the receptionist, saying,

"If you need me, I'm just going up to room 12 to check it over to see if it is ok for guests to use."

The receptionist nodded and Tony went up to the room to make sure what state it was in and, if truth be told, to satisfy himself that nothing of Ms Johnson's had been left behind, not that he didn't trust Johnnie and Bill, but accidents did happen. Also, some part of his subconscious wanted to get some sort of closure on the whole affair.

His inspection of the room elicited nothing untoward and, as he stood in the empty room, Tony was very satisfied with the choice he and Chris had made to try and safeguard the reputation of the hotel. He did a very good job of ignoring the questions that fluttered at intervals through his mind about whether Ms Johnson had a partner, or children, or a family, telling himself that the decisions they had taken would not change how other people were affected, she was dead and nothing could change that. In the depths of his mind though, he knew he was being slightly disingenuous with this line of argument, but he decided he would rather not think about it, if possible.

Tony noted that the room needed a good clean, but the plaster that needed repainting was out of the way and Tony was able to move the table and place the armchair where it would cover the new plaster from view until it was dry enough to paint. He left the room and as he closed the door, he breathed a sigh of relief that it was over. He was walking back to the stairs when he stopped in his tracks, as a harsh thought intruded into his relief, 'it's not over, we still don't know who the murderer is; he may strike again'. With that disquieting thought in mind, he decided he needed talk to David again, soon, to see what plan he had come up with to try and catch the killer before he struck again, which in all probability he would, after all some people were always rude to the staff.

Chapter 6.

The Quiet Before The Storm.

Over the next few days, Tony's life slowly began to return to some sort of relative normality as the everyday problems of the hotel crowded in on him, however, constantly lurking in the back of his mind was the fact that one of the people he worked with could well be a brutal murderer. He now looked at his colleagues in a completely different, somewhat suspicious way, but never actually getting any resolution. Tony was starting to get very stressed, as was Chris, when Tony told him how he was feeling. So it was that later that week that Tony went round to David's house to discuss the next step in finding the killer.

"The pattern seems quite clear. Guests who abuse the staff badly are getting killed," conjectured David.
"So it would seem," agreed Tony, "But who's doing it?"
"That's not so easy. It wasn't the same member of staff being abused, nor were they on the premises when the murders took place, so from that point of view, both had alibis."
"So, if it's not them, who is doing it and why?"
"That's the tricky bit. It could be one of the customers, but it would be very difficult to discover if any customer had witnessed both acts of abuse. We can't actually ask anyone, as officially only one murder has taken place. Logic says it has to be one of the staff, but I can't imagine any of them being murderers, but I think the facts suggest that it has to be one of them. I can't think how it could be anyone else."
"So what are we going to do?" Tony asked. "How are we going to stop them from doing it again?"
"The easiest thing would be if I was to stay in the hotel all the time, but that would be very suspicious. The killer obviously

knows about the second murder, but they must be really confused about what happened to the body and why the police weren't called. I don't want to draw attention to myself by being there all the time. The killer is obviously being very careful not to draw attention to himself. All we have to do is wait until another guest abuses one of the staff and we'll know who the victim is likely to be. If I'm not in the hotel, you will need to let me know as soon as possible, so I can get to the hotel, pretend to get drunk and you can let me stay in a room near to the guest. That won't be suspicious as it has happened on numerous occasions. I will then be able to listen for the sounds of a struggle and then catch whoever is doing it."

"Isn't it a bit risky, what if you fall asleep, or you don't hear anything and also, I can't guarantee that we will have a room close to the victim," Tony pointed out.

"Good point. Also, thinking about it, there is the problem of dealing with the potential victim, as well. They may well be a bit suspicious of the whole situation, if I suddenly turn up to stop them being murdered."

After a short while thinking the problem through, David sighed and swore under his breath.

"Mark will laugh his head off, but I need to contact the department again and borrow some equipment, if they will let me have it, so I can monitor the corridor outside the potential victim's door. I don't suppose you'll let me put a camera in the victim's room, would you?"

"What's wrong with that, if you save their life?" asked Tony.

David gave a short laugh and said,

"Think about it."

Tony did think and for a while he couldn't understand what David was on about but then, it hit him. What would happen if the suspected victim found the camera before anything happened? He could just imagine their outrage as they stormed down to reception and accused the hotel of taking illicit movies of their guests. So much for the hotel's reputation if that was

75

broadcast by a guest. Tony grimaced and metaphorically mopped his forehead at the prospect of what could have happened.

"Yeah, I get it, so what equipment could you use?"

"Once we know who the suspected victim is I can set up a camera in the corridor to watch their door. When I see someone behaving suspiciously in the corridor outside the room I will go and catch them. Hopefully I can subdue them without disturbing the guest."

"What are we going to do when we catch them?" asked Tony confidently, "Call the police or what?"

"That's the only real sticking point, I would need time to remove the camera; and depending on where my room is in relation to the victim's, I would need to be able to explain how I knew what was happening."

As he sat, thinking the situation through, David realised that there was another issue and added,

"One more thing, you will need to make sure that either you or Chris is in the hotel at all times to make sure that you know if an incident has occurred so you can contact me."

"I don't know about that, there are always occasions or emergencies that crop up that sometimes mean we are both away."

"Ok, you need to sort out something. At least make sure that one of you is always there in the evening. You also need to make sure you know if any incidents happen if you are both away from the hotel."

"Ok, I'll see what I can come up with," Tony said, pursing his lips and absently stroking his chin.

Silence fell again, as Tony and David were thinking through their respective problems. Out of the blue, Tony said,

"Got it, I just need to put in place a reporting system so that any type of abusive situation is reported immediately. I'm sure I'll be able to think of a good health and safety reason for it."

"Good."

David had decided that the issue of whether to call the police or not could be put aside for now. After that they spent a few more minutes discussing the issue of the killer's identity, but, as always, the discussion simply went round in circles. It had to be one of the staff but they could not think of any member of staff who could be a murderer, so maybe it was a customer, but a customer couldn't just come and go in the hotel late at night, so it had to be a member of staff, but....and so on, ad infinitum.

After everything had been discussed that they could either anticipate or plan for, they had another couple of drinks and then Tony went home.   Once again, David had noticed that neither he nor Tony seemed quite so in need of drinking excessively, although David wasn't certain that trying to catch actual murderers would be recommended by the medical profession as a good way to cure incipient alcoholism.

The next day, David rang the department's number again and, after the usual preliminaries he was put through to Mark, ready to suffer verbal abuse from his former colleague when he asked if he could borrow some specialist surveillance equipment.
"Hello, old boy," Mark greeted him, "nice to hear from you again, so soon. If you are applying for your old job, I can put you through to sir."
David decided to ignore that comment and simply asked, "I need to ask another favour."
"Ask away, old boy, we just love helping out old comrades."
He explained that he needed some surveillance equipment to help him catch whoever was murdering the guests.
"We did wonder how you planned to catch the killer. You do sound as if you are enjoying yourself, old boy, has this stopped your excessive drinking?"
"How did you know about that," David asked suspiciously.
"Oh, we like to keep tabs on old friends," Mark blandly replied.
"I see."
"I'm sure you do."

"What about the toys?"

"I will ask the boss and get back to you, ok."

"Ok."

Again, it didn't take too long before Mark rang David back to tell him the boss had agreed.

"He seemed strangely happy to give you some help, he must like you," Mark blandly informed him.

"I hope you didn't give him any reason to be happy," David retorted.

"Of course not, old boy, now I'll put you through to the technical department and you can discuss with them what you need."

"Thanks, for this," David said.

"Don't mention it, old boy. We have to stick together, don't we?"

After he had informed the technical department what the problems he faced were and discussed the latest gadgets and how they worked, he sat down and thought deeply about how helpful his former colleagues were being. There was definitely something going on, some ulterior motive; the department, or the boss at least, wanted something, but, at the moment, David had no real idea what it was. He felt he was somehow being used, but he had no clue as to how or why; after all, he had gone to them for help. Nevertheless, it was odd, they were being strangely accommodating. He thought there was a good chance the Boss was simply trying to get him to return to the department, after all, there had seemed to be several hints along those lines and he had been good at his job, but something, some instinct, was telling him there was more to it than that.

That evening, he went to the Lion around 8pm, ostensibly for his usual pint or two of Peroni, but mainly because he wanted to tell Chris and Tony that the department had agreed to let him borrow the necessary equipment and it would be there in a day or two. He also wanted to have a quick *recce* of the corridors where the hotel bedrooms were situated to make sure he would be able to use the equipment he had ordered. When he got there, Tony was sitting in on reception and as it was a public space, and there were a couple of people milling about, David had to be a bit circumspect in what he said to Tony.

"Hi, how are you tonight, my good man?" Tony asked

"Fine, my friend, you ok?"

"Jolly good, I too, am fine, old chap."

As usual, when Tony greeted him, David had the image of Tony as an old WW2 RAF pilot; he should have a mustache and a flying jacket and goggles with him. He had definitely been born sixty years too late.

Controlling his flight of fancy, David forced his mind to return to the present and continued,

 "You know I told you I was getting a super-duper new camera, well it should arrive in the next couple of days."

Tony looked confused for a second, but then the meaning of David's words registered.

"Great, you should be able to get some really good pictures then; you'll have to let me use it sometime."

"Yeah, no problem, I just hope it's easy to set up. I might need your help; you're more technically minded than me."

"I think the term is 'tech savvy' but it's no problem, just let me know."

As they were talking the foyer cleared and David said quickly,

"I'm just nipping upstairs to check on the best places to site the camera and work out how quickly I will be able to put them in position."

With that he went quickly up the stairs to the first floor. There were eight bedrooms in all, three on either side of the first part of the corridor and then the corridor made a right turn and there were two more bedrooms on that section, ending in a dead end. Thankfully, the smoke detector was in the perfect place on the corner so if he needed to replace that one, the surveillance camera could be trained on any of the rooms on the corridor. When he got to the second floor, he found it was a mirror image of the lower floor, which would make planning a lot easier.

He returned to the foyer and gave a thumb's up to Tony to let him know that all was well and then walked into the bar to get a well-earned pint. At least he told himself it was well earned, all this thinking and planning, as well as walking up and down the stairs, made a person very thirsty.

As he entered the bar, he saw that it was quite busy with both diners and people just out for a drink. He got himself a pint and found a good table from where he could engage in his hobby of people watching. One or two of the clientele he found particularly interesting to observe. There was one old couple, who obviously didn't go out to eat very often and were completely unsure of what they were supposed to do. After they had ordered their food from the waitress who came to the table, they would go up to the bar to ask about their food. Although I imagine the barman kept telling them the food was freshly cooked and would take a short while, they still kept returning to ask. They were all smiles though, when the food did arrive, and they appeared to enjoy it immensely. Whilst they were eating their food, the man drank his pint of bitter and the woman had a sherry. It was all very old fashioned and traditional, almost a relic from a bygone age and David silently raised a glass to the two of them.

Another couple, these much younger, were clearly very much in lust and spent most of the time kissing each other and fondling the parts other beers obviously couldn't reach. They appeared totally oblivious to their surroundings and how most people were trying to avoid looking in their direction through sheer embarrassment, or, possibly, jealousy, or both.

At yet another table, a group of businessmen, who obviously worked at one of the local companies, were entertaining a visiting dignity from their parent company who was probably staying at the hotel, as it was the best hotel in the area. They were having a very good time, drinking copious amounts of alcohol as they ate their meal, though being careful to keep complimenting the big boss, laugh at his jokes and not get too drunk and make fools of themselves.

Part way through the evening, David had an idea for a short story and took out his notepad and started to plot the story and the characters. Then, in his break, Tony brought over a couple of pints for the two of them and joined David for a short while.
"So, when does your new camera arrive then?" Tony enquired.
"Sometime tomorrow afternoon, I believe, by special courier."
"Oh, good; you'll be ready to take that classic shot whenever it crops up, then."
"Sure will."
With that they both raised their glasses muttering,
"Cheers."

Just then a loud burst of laughter came from the businessmen's table and both David and Tony glanced over, just in time to see a waiter, carrying desserts, step onto the dais where the table was, just as the big boss thrust his chair backwards. The two of them crashed together and the desserts, which the waiter was carrying, went everywhere, including over the boss' jacket, leaving a nice white, creamy mess as an impressive souvenir.

After a moment's stunned silence, during which everyone on the table looked at the mess in shock, the big boss man exploded,
"What the bloody hell do you think you're doing? My jacket is ruined, you clumsy oaf."
"I'm terribly sorry sir, it was an accident. You stood up just as I arrived. I couldn't get out of the way."

"Don't make excuses, you just over balanced and dropped them, all over me, you idiot."

Tony got up, muttering to David, 'I never get a moment's peace' as he walked over to the businessmen's table.

"Good evening, I'm the Deputy Manager, can I be of assistance?"

"Yes, you can, you can get this clumsy idiot out of my sight and tell me what you are going to do about my Jacket."

"As it happened, I saw the incident from just over there," Tony indicated to the table where he and David had been sitting, "and whilst it was very unfortunate, it clearly was just an accident, however, the Hotel will be more than willing to get your jacket dry cleaned for you."

"What do you mean, just an accident, it was clearly this clumsy idiot trying to carry too much.

Over the years he had been in the hospitality trade, Tony had come across a lot of self-important bosses whose concept of good management was bullying. Whilst never insulting such people, Tony always made sure he didn't let them bully him or his staff, so with a polite iciness, he replied,

"I'm sorry sir, but I happened to be watching just as the unfortunate event occurred and, to my view, it was clearly an accident. You happened to push your chair back and stand up at the very same moment the waiter was about to put the first plate on the table next to you."

"Rubbish, you are clearly trying to cover up for the Hotel's poor quality staff, if he worked for me he would have been sacked by now."

"Well, however that may be, in this hotel we do not tend to sack people for accidents."

All this while, the poor waiter was stood to one side, listening to this tirade against the hotel and him, feeling very miserable but also angry at how the guest was distorting the facts. He was also angry at the fact that the businessman's colleagues hadn't said a word in his defense, as they too, must have seen it had been a total accident. Obviously, like many employees, they didn't want to challenge the boss.

"I am not satisfied with your attitude; I would like to see the owner of the hotel."

"I'm afraid he is not here at present; he won't be here until around ten-thirty tonight."

"Well, make sure he is available to see me as soon as he gets here then. Now get us some more desserts and get this idiot to clean the mess up he made."

"I will see to the desserts immediately, sir." Tony said.

Tony took the man's jacket to get it cleaned and signaled to Martin, the waiter to go and sort out some more desserts and get one of the cleaning staff to clear up the mess. This drew an angry snort from the big boss, as he had clearly wanted to humiliate the waiter some more, whilst he was cleaning up the mess. Tony took the jacket to reception and told the receptionist to get it cleaned and then he walked back to continue the interrupted drinking of his pint, but he stopped short as he approached, David was staring at him, a very worried look on his face.

"What's up?" he asked.

"We haven't got the surveillance camera yet."

"What?" then he, too, realized the import of what had just happened, and he turned to look at the businessman. "Oh shit, what are we going to do?"

Chapter 7.

The Best Laid Plans.

Tony sagged heavily back down onto his chair, looking worriedly at David who had gone into analysis mode and was busy working out how to protect the company boss from a likely murder attempt, which, based on previous events, was a virtual certainty? As the pieces started to fit together in his mind, he issued instructions to Tony,

"Go and find out what rooms are free near the businessman, but be unobtrusive," he told Tony.

Tony sidled off to Reception, ostensibly to check when the jacket would be ready, but, in reality, checking on the current availability of the rooms.

"He's in room 8, the best room on that floor. Room 5 is free; it's down the corridor and on the opposite side, probably about 20 feet away," he told David a few minutes later.

"Ok" said David. "I will pretend to get drunk again and you can do your usual thing and make me stay in room 5 overnight. No-one should be suspicious. I'll just have to keep alert and listen for any sounds. I should be able to get to the killer before they get to the door to 8."

"Right."

Around 10-50 pm Chris, the owner returned and was told by Tony that not only did the businessman want to see him immediately, but also that he had verbally assaulted the waiter, so there was a good chance that the murderer might strike again, if he had seen the incident. Chris swore loudly, several times and then added,

"Please tell me that David is in tonight.

"Oh yes, and he has a plan on how to protect the businessman."
"Thank God," said Chris fervently.
"I should thank David if I were you," Tony replied, somewhat caustically.

When Tony had told Chris the details of what had happened with the businessman and the waiter, Chris asked Tony to bring him to the office so he could talk with him. Whilst the businessman was meeting with Chris, David decided that it was nearly time for him to go to the room. He signaled Tony.
"When I finish this pint in about five minutes, come across and tell me I've had enough drink."
"OK."

A few minutes later as David reached the end of his pint, he got up from his table, picked up his glass as if he was going to get another drink. As he did so, he deliberately staggered against the table, making a very passable impersonation of a drunk, unable to control his balance. Tony took the cue and came over to David,
"No more drinks for you tonight, David, come on; I'll get the keys for a free room for you. Sleep it off there tonight."

David pushed himself unsteadily up from the table to which he had been clinging and cautiously walked out of the bar, seemingly having trouble focusing his vision and in getting his feet to work properly. None of the other customers in the bar seemed to notice much, however, as they were too busy with their own drinking. A drunken customer was certainly not a rare occurrence and as David was not playing a noisy drunk, no one paid much attention to him.

When he got to the first floor corridor and saw it was empty, he went and had a quick look at room 8, before taking the key card off Tony and walked quickly to his room. He opened the door and went inside, with Tony following him.

"Right Tony, you need to get back downstairs and check what's happening, I'll get myself some coffee and get ready to listen for noises from room 8. Keep me posted. Oh, and make sure you and Chris stick to your normal routines."

"Ok."

Tony set off back downstairs and reached the office he shared with the owner, just in time to hear Chris say,

"I'm sorry Mr. Maitland, I will not sack the waiter for what my Deputy Manager assured me was a complete accident."

"That is simply not good enough, I will not be treated like this," Mr. Maitland replied and stormed out of the office, nearly knocking Tony over as he passed.

"Not a happy man," said Tony, when Mr. Maitland was out of earshot.

"Prat," said Chris and left it at that.

"David's in place and will intervene if anything happens tonight and he stressed that we have to behave as normal."

"Easier said than done."

"Yep."

For the next hour both Chris and Tony tried to behave normally, talking to people in the bar, or sorting out any problems that occurred, though they both seemed to look at their watches more often than normal. Near midnight, Chris decided to go home, as usual, and Tony was left to close up when the last of the guests had finished drinking and gone to bed. That night, the last person to leave the bar was Mr. Maitland, who finally went to his room at around twelve thirty. Tony quickly texted David to tell him he was on his way and then he went to the reception. He talked to the night porter, who acted as receptionist during the night and then said,

"God, I'm knackered, I think I'll stay in the hotel tonight, I can't be bothered to go home."

"Good idea," replied the receptionist.

Tony decided to take the key to room 16 which was located directly over the room Mr. Maitland was staying in. That way, he hoped, he should be able to hear if anything happened and go down and either help or, he admitted to himself, more likely, interfere, with David and the killer. On his way up to the room he stopped off to make sure David was ok. He knocked on the door and, after a moment, David let him in.

"Anything happened yet?" asked Tony.

"Yes, the murderer has been in, killed the guy and then left. I just waited here and let him do it," was David's sarcastic response.

"Yeah, sorry, stupid question. I'm just a bit uptight."

"Don't worry about it, do you want a coffee?"

"Yeah, I might as well before I go to my room, unless you want me to stay here and help?"

"No thanks, you would probably only get in my way. Let me deal with the murderer on my own."

'Well, that's put me in my place', Tony thought, though with a certain amount of relief, as the prospect of taking on a murderer was not high on his bucket list.

David made the coffee and they made small talk until around 1:30am, when Tony went up to his room. When he got to his room, he lay down on his bed, fully clothed and lay there listening for any sound. Before he knew it, and despite his best intentions, sleep crept stealthily upon him and he began snoring quietly, not that he knew that, obviously.

Down below, David now sat near the slightly open door to the corridor, in the dark, listening for any untoward and suspicious noises. As the time passed, he too, began to drift towards sleep, though his head falling forward onto his chest kept jerking him back awake. He looked at his watch and saw it was nearly 2-30 am so he cautiously looked out at the corridor and, seeing there was no-one about, he decided he had time to go to the toilet and wash his face to try and wake himself up. Feeling a lot more alert after dousing his face with cold water, David returned to his chair by the bedroom door. As he was about to sit down, he heard a muffled thud from somewhere down the corridor.

Instantly suspicious, he quickly but cautiously went out of his room and crept stealthily down the corridor to room 8.

He listened at the door and thought he could hear movement inside. He quickly tested the door handle and found that the door opened easily. Taking a deep breath, he quietly went inside and crept towards the bedroom. As he passed the bathroom, old instincts kicked in; intuitively he felt someone was in there but before he had chance to spin round, something solid hit him on the back of his head and he fell to the floor, temporarily stunned.

As he lay on the floor of the room, eyes closed, David, bizarrely, began to feel slightly euphoric and became transfixed by the light show that was going on behind his eyelids. A whole range of colours swirled and eddied, changing through red, yellow, green and deep blues in a steady flow that cascaded and coruscated in his mind, whilst shapes would briefly emerge, change and then reverse themselves continuously. Oddly fascinated by this light show, he became only aware that the bathroom light must have been switched on. Forcing himself to try and concentrate, he managed to force his eyelids open, only to find that all he could see was the carpet from very close range. He vaguely knew he needed to get off the floor, but before he could move someone knelt on his back and pinned his face even closer to the carpet. Focusing his scattered wits, he was about to try and struggle free when a strangely wooden sounding voice said,
"You are not the man who abused the waiter. Where is he?"
"I don't know," David weakly replied.
"What are you doing here?" the wooden voice continued, "you are not the one I was sent to kill."
"I heard a suspicious noise and came to check."
David began to struggle weakly but the person was able to hold him down easily. He was thinking about what to do next when another blow on the back of his head made his world dark again. The figure released him slowly, wary in case David was only

pretending, then stood over him for a few seconds before turning to leave the room. Whilst he wasn't unconscious, David was certainly dazed enough that it took him a few seconds to realise that the attacker had gone. As the import of that hit him, he forced himself to his feet, then staggered to the door to the corridor. As he looked out, he just managed to grab a quick glimpse of a leg and an arm before they disappeared round the corner of the stairs. He followed, slowly and somewhat groggily, going down the stairs to the reception area. When he got there, though, the area was completely deserted, with no sign of where his assailant might have gone. He took a quick look round but found no-one, except the night porter who he saw was asleep in the back office. Making sure not to disturb him, David went slowly back upstairs to room 8 to see if he could find any evidence of who the assailant may have been or where the businessman was.

Back in room 8, he splashed water on his face in the bathroom. Now feeling a bit more alert, despite the pain in his head, he carried out a thorough search of the room. However, there was very little to see, in fact the only thing of note in the room at all was an untouched Crème Brule on the bedside table. David picked up the dessert and, needing a burst of energy, quickly ate it as he went to search the bathroom. A quick search of the bathroom revealed nothing of interest, so David went back into the main bedroom to look for any clues which might suggest what happened to the businessman.

Of the businessman, however, there was no sign, his bed hadn't been slept in and there was no sign of any of his clothes or possessions anywhere. It seemed that the businessman had been a very lucky man and, for some reason, had left the room before the attack came. Obviously, they would have to wait until the morning to find out where the businessman had gone. They couldn't risk waking up the night porter who would certainly be suspicious if he found them carrying out their checks. At least he knew the man wasn't dead, as the killer had obviously expected him to be in the room and didn't know he had gone.

As he could find no clues or anything incriminating in the room, David decided to go back to his room and get some rest before the morning. He remembered to take the dessert bowl with him so there was nothing strange in the room to be found by the cleaning staff. On getting back to his room, he put the plate on the bedside table and then quickly undressed and got into bed. He lay there as sleep crept up on him, revisiting in his mind what he could remember of the attack on him. He remembered that the person appeared to be quite strong and held him down quite easily, though he had to admit that he had been groggy from the blow to the head but, other than that, there was very little else that appeared useful. Just as he was finally drifting off to sleep though, a thought intruded on his consciousness and he was dragged back towards a state of semi-alertness. Struggling against sleep, he realized that the leg and arm he had seen disappearing round the corner to the stairs looked as if they belonged to a woman. Although it was a startling thought, he was too tired at that point to consider it any further. He hoped he would still remember it in the morning, but for now, he simply couldn't force himself to stay awake any longer. As he drifted off into sleep he repeated to himself several times, 'they belonged to a woman, they belonged to a woman, they belonged to a woman'.

Chapter 8.

If Only It Had Arrived Yesterday.

David awoke early the following morning, though, technically speaking, it was the same morning, as it had been past 3am when he had got to sleep, with a thought tugging at his subconscious. Surprisingly, he had remembered that final thought when he had woken. Recalling it, he was certain that the leg and arm he had seen disappearing round the corner of the corridor had belonged to a woman. He was doubtful, though, 'A woman shouldn't have been able to hold me down that easily', he thought, though he did accept it was possible. Another possibility that struck him was that there might have been two attackers and it was only the woman's leg and arm he had seen when they ran off. That made a bit more sense, he told himself; though he wasn't totally convinced that was right either. Also, something else that was troubling him from the encounter the night before, but he couldn't quite grasp what it was. It was buried somewhere in his subconscious. 'Hopefully it will surface sooner rather than later', he thought.

He got out of bed and decided to have a shower. The shower was hot and physically refreshing but as he was toweling himself dry a burst of pain made him wince. He put his hand up to the back of his head and winced again when his fingers found a very sore spot. He looked at his fingers but didn't see any blood, which was good. He then thought he had better check his pillow which, again, was also free of blood, so at least there would be no awkward questions from the cleaning staff. He sat down quickly and closed his eyes. He'd had a lucky escape and he was honest enough to admit it.

He dressed and was just about to go down for breakfast when there was an urgent knock on the door. As he opened the door, a very agitated Tony pushed passed David, almost running inside. As soon as the outer door was shut, he virtually exploded, "Well, what happened, did you catch the murderer, why didn't you call or text me?"

David castigated himself for not thinking to contact Tony earlier and said,

"No, I didn't, I heard something in the night and I went into the room but someone clobbered me and virtually knocked me out."

"Oh my God, have they killed Mr. Maitland? Why didn't you text me? What are we going to do? We need to call the police."

"Calm down, the guy wasn't in the room. For some reason he had left, taken his clothes and gone."

"What, gone where?"

"I don't know where he went, but it appears that he had left before the killer arrived. When I turned up the assailant hit me from behind and then ran off and I lost him."

"Oh great, I thought you were supposed to overpower him."

"Well, if he had been attacking the man, as he was supposed to be, I would have done, I did not expect him to come out of the bathroom and hit me from behind."

"What are we going to do now? Why didn't you text me last night, when all that happened?"

"I haven't decided what to do yet, but the first thing we need to do is find out what happened to Mr. Maitland and why he wasn't there. After that I need to review all the facts. As to why I didn't text you, what could you have done, except maybe disturb the rest of the guests? It was the middle of the night, what would you have told the night porter you were up to?"

"You could have told me," a distraught Tony exclaimed, falling into a chair and putting his head in his hands. A few seconds later he wearily raised his head and muttered,

"You know, I'm not sure my heart can take all this stress."

"Come on, let's go down to breakfast and, for God's sake, don't look so worried, it's supposed to be just a normal day remember."

The two of them set off down to the restaurant to get some breakfast and for David to think about what to do next. As it was still quite early, there were no other guests in the dining room, so they were able to talk quite freely, particularly as breakfast was a self-service process and the staff only popped in occasionally to check that everything was ok and all the food containers were full.

David explained in full detail all that had happened the previous night, except for the bit about thinking the leg and arm he saw belonged to a female, deciding to keep that to himself for now. He knew he needed to think the whole thing through some more and to try to resolve what it was that was niggling at him, before he mentioned that there might be a woman involved. He didn't want Tony to go blundering about and start trying to investigate the women who worked at the hotel.

Part way through breakfast Tony could restrain himself no longer and went off to reception to see if he could find out what had happened to Mr. Maitland and why he hadn't been in his room. When he got to reception, the night porter was just handing over to the day receptionist. Tony said 'Good morning' to them both and then asked the night porter if everything had gone smoothly overnight. He always asked that if he was in early, so he didn't think the question would cause any suspicions, though Tony was starting to think he was definitely getting paranoid about trying to appear normal.

Most mornings the night porter would say that everything was fine, but this morning was different.
"Well," he began, "it was a bit strange. You know that fella' in 8, the one that shouted at Peter, the waiter, last night. Well, about

one in the morning, he rang me on reception and tells me to order him a cab 'cos he's goin' to another hotel. We didn't treat him right here, he said. He said to get his bill ready and he'd pay as he left. So I did, I got his bill ready and, sure enough, a few minutes later, down he comes with his luggage, pays his bill and waits for the cab. Then off he went."

After listening to the night porter's explanation, Tony returned to David and explained what had happened.

"A lucky choice," said David.

"Indeed."

When they had finished breakfast, David told Tony that he was going to go home and then go to work, so that everything appeared normal. He would spend the day whilst he was working going over everything that had happened and work out a new plan to catch the murderer. He also said that,

"The surveillance camera and equipment should come today, so that will make life easier the next time this happens."

"Part of me would rather it didn't happen again but, then again, I don't think I want this hanging over me, not knowing when it might happen again or whether we could deal with it when it did."

"I know what you mean."

With that, David went off to reception to pay his room bill for staying the night, though, in the circumstances he knew that Chris would quietly refund him. Having paid his bill, he said goodbye to Nathan, who was on reception that day and went home.

A few minutes after David had left, Tony went into reception and Nathan asked,

"Did David have another bad night last night? I hope he gets over his separation soon, this drinking is not good for him."

Tony looked momentarily blank before recovering enough to say,

"Yeah, but I think he is getting better, he wasn't anywhere near as bad as he has been; it was a little bit more of a happy drunk."

"Well, that's something, I suppose."

Despite the recent revelations about David's past, Tony saw himself as a good friend and he didn't want Nathan to think badly of him or think he was still in a bad way, when in fact the 'so-called drunkenness' had been an act. He had also noticed that David was much more focused and 'happy' in a strange sort of way, since he had taken on the role of catching the killer. He hoped it was a good sign for David's future. He also hoped that David was able to catch the killer soon, as although David may have been relishing the battle, Tony was definitely feeling the strain and was looking forward to a well deserved holiday when it was all over. In fact, he thought it might be a good way to distract himself if he were to spend some time on the computer this morning looking at various holiday destinations he might go to. Even if he didn't end up going anywhere, it should help keep his mind off the current problems at the hotel.

He went to his office, put the computer on and was just about to begin searching when Chris burst into the office, almost forcing the door off its hinges in his haste to enter.

"Well," he blurted out, only just managing to close the door in time, "What happened, did David catch the killer?"

Tony sighed and thought, 'well that bit of peace and quiet was short lived'. He clicked out of the holiday destinations on the computer and then concentrated on describing what had happened over night. When he had finished, Chris wiped his forehead and looked as if he was carrying the cares of the world on his shoulders.

"Is David ok?" he asked, "He wasn't hurt too much from the attack, was he?"

"I think his pride was hurt more than anything. He thought he could take the killer on quite easily, I think. He didn't expect to come off worse," Tony replied.

"What's he going to do now?"

"He said he was going to spend the day planning out his next move but at least the surveillance equipment is coming today so that will make it easier. If we'd had it last night, at least we would have seen that Mr. Maitland had left and David would have been far more prepared for the attacker."

"Ah, well at least he is ok."

Just then Vicky came into the office and Tony and Chris were forced to talk about hotel issues, which, in view of all that had gone wrong, was probably better for their blood pressure anyway.

"Can I have today's waitress rota for the restaurant?" she asked.

Tony passed the rota to her, but she dropped it as she tried to take it, wincing and grabbing her left wrist.

"What have you done to your wrist?" asked Chris.

"Oh, I don't really know, I must have hurt it without realizing it."

"Did you put it in the accident book?" Tony asked.

"I don't think I did it here, it must have happened at home, I noticed it when I got up this morning," she replied.

"Oh, that's ok, then"

"Don't worry; I might not sue the hotel."

"Uh!" was the best that Tony could respond.

"God, what's up with you, it was a joke."

"Yeah, sorry, I'm a bit tired this morning."

"Too much drinking with David. Is he ok this morning?"

"Oh yeah, drink hardly seems to bother him, he got up and merrily went off to work."

"Lucky sod."

"Anyway," Tony drawled, "will you be able to work today?"

"Yeah, as long as I don't try and pick up too many plates, I'll be fine."

"I think it's probably best if you just supervise the two eating areas today," said Chris.

"I was hoping you'd say that," said Vicky, grinning as she left.

After Vicky left, Tony decided it was time for him to go home as he was working again that evening. Chris also left the office to do the rounds of the hotel, checking that everything was ok and sorting out what needed to get done.

David meanwhile had returned home and changed into his work gear before going off to work. He decided to go to one of the gardens he looked after in Hazelwood where he knew that no one would be in. It wasn't that he didn't like his clients, but if they were at work it would give him the chance to think and plan without being interrupted. It also allowed him to take it a bit easy as his head still throbbed despite the pain killers he had taken when he got home. Luckily, the main gardening job he had to do was cutting the grass on his client's two large lawns. He went to the garage he rented, loaded his trailer, attached it to his car and drove to Duffield, before turning onto Avenue Road and then Hazelwood Road to his client's house. Once there he unloaded his lawnmower from the trailer, topped up the petrol and began walking up and down, putting nice lines in the lawns.

As it didn't require a great deal of thought to simply walk up and down the lawns, he was able to concentrate on the situation at the hotel. He went over the events of the previous night and re-examined all that had happened from the moment he had entered Mr. Maitland's room. It was certainly true that he had expected the killer or killers to be by the bed and if Mr. Maitland had still been there then that's where the killer would have been. Still, David accepted to himself, he clearly was a bit rusty. He should have quickly checked the bathroom first, just to be sure. Whilst it wasn't what he wanted to admit to Tony and Chris, he concluded that he needed to ask if he could go back to the department for a bit of training, to make sure the same thing didn't happen again.

As he was thinking about a refresher course in unarmed combat, David was startled to realise that he would actually enjoy such a workout. The whole situation at the hotel, despite its danger, had certainly restored a sense of purpose to his life. He hadn't really considered it in detail before and certainly hadn't made a definitive decision, but the idea of going back to the department wasn't anywhere near as disturbing to him as it might have been just a few months, or even weeks ago. In view of his previous reservations, and his reasons for leaving the department, he knew he would need to give these feelings some serious thought. It was one thing to enjoy this one-off situation; but did he really want to do this full time again. He decided that he was in no position to make any decision yet; he needed to sort out the situation at the hotel and then see how he felt when it was all over. Those decisions were far too large and complicated to be decided on a whim, so he decided to just concentrate on his current problem at the hotel for the time being.

With that decision made, or at least delayed, he went back to thinking about what his next move at the hotel should be. The obvious thing to do and which would cause the least suspicion was to simply wait for another situation to occur which would lead the killer to act again. Simple actions are usually the best, he concluded.

He was getting near to finishing cutting his client's grass on when he received a call on his mobile. His normal response was to ignore all calls when he was working, as he didn't think he should be talking on the phone whilst charging his clients for his time. On this occasion, however, he knew there was a good chance it might be the department contacting him about delivery of the surveillance equipment so, for once, he decided to answer, just in case it was them.
"Hi, David speaking."
"Hi David, this is Johnnie. Can you please confirm your codename?"
"Firefly."

"Ok, your delivery will be with you in about an hour's time. Can you make sure you are at home when it gets there, as the operative has been instructed to give the goods only to you in person?"

"No problem, I will be there."

With that Johnnie rang off. David quickly finished his work, took his tools back to his trailer and drove back to the garage he rented, before driving the short distance home in order to wait for the delivery.

'At least it won't be like a normal delivery where you wait around all day and still, somehow you miss the delivery driver, he thought.

Almost exactly an hour after the phone call, there was a knock on his door. David didn't recognize the operative who was delivering his equipment and supposed he must have arrived in the department after he had left. The operative checked that there was no-one in earshot before asking,

"Are you David?"

"Yes."

"What's your codename?"

"Firefly."

"Good."

With that, the man passed him a couple of boxes.

"Can you sign for them," he asked, pushing a notepad towards him.

"That's new, we never used to sign for equipment?" David queried.

"We still don't normally, but apparently you don't work for us anymore, so we need you to sign for our records. Mark said you were to use your real name."

"I don't have a real name," David reminded him. "What name should I use?"

"I'll just check."

He went back down the steps to his van and returned a few minutes later.

"Mark said to use the name you used when you worked for us."

David duly signed for the equipment with his old name and the delivery man left. As David closed the door, his mind thought back to the name he had signed. When he had changed his identity on leaving the department, he had kept the name 'David', as he had got used to responding to that name and had merely taken on a new surname and identity. He had thought he was going to be permanently rid of the old identity when he had left the department, but, obviously, life wasn't as straightforward as that. With a shrug, he put those thoughts aside and started to unpack the boxes to see what he had got and how he used them. When he had got everything out of the boxes, he was amazed at how much surveillance equipment had progressed since he had left the department. Everything was so much smaller and more compact now. The technicians had sent him detailed notes on how to set the system up and he spent the rest of the afternoon and early evening practicing to make sure he could get the system up and running in less than fifteen minutes. Satisfied that he had mastered the new technology he sat back, closed his eyes and tried to rest his weary brain.

Peace and quiet was a scarce commodity, however, for just as he closed his eyes and leaned back in his chair, his phone rang again. Sighing deeply, he opened his weary eyes and saw it was Tony's number, so he answered, praying fervently that Tony wasn't ringing to say another member of staff had been verbally abused. He certainly didn't need that level of hassle today.

"Hi Tony, what's up?"

"Just thought I'd see if you had decided where we are going next."

"I'm coming in tonight so we can talk about your book then, ok. I don't want to go into the details over the phone."

Tony understood immediately and replied, "OK, the book is getting a bit complicated now, so that's probably a good idea. What time are you coming in?"

"I'll be in around nine or so."

"Ok, see you then."

"See yer."

When he had finished talking to David, Tony turned to Chris, who had got him to make the call and told him that David would be in later to discuss the next moves. Chris dropped his head, looked down at his desk and gave a heavy sigh, clearly wanting more information, his patience having reached its limit. Understandably, they were both struggling to deal calmly with all that was happening.

Chapter 9.

When Someone Else Knows More Than You Do.

David sat at his kitchen table, taking a quiet moment to just sit still, mind blank, thinking of nothing. His eyes, however, seemed determined to close of their own accord, without bothering to ask his permission. Also, his head was beginning to throb painfully behind his eyes. Basically, he was shattered and so, despite what his doctor had told him about not sleeping in the day, he decided to have a short nap before going to talk to Tony and Chris, otherwise he probably wouldn't make it to the hotel that night. He could just imagine how Chris and Tony would deal with that. He had noticed the edge of stress in Tony's voice earlier when they had spoken on the phone and didn't want to make it worse by not giving them a plan tonight.

David lay on his bed, set his phone alarm for seven thirty and began reading a book to relax. The book was science fantasy, definitely not a crime novel. After reading just a few sentences, the book slipped gently out of his hand onto the duvet as he drifted off into sleep. David slept deeply for a while, but then his breathing changed, becoming quicker and shallower, whilst his body began to thrash spasmodically from side to side in the bed. He was in those final few seconds of a dream; that in-between stage between sleeping and waking. Although still technically asleep, he was subconsciously aware of what was happening in the dream. He was reliving the last few minutes of his entrance into the hotel bedroom the night before. He felt again the pain in his head as he was hit from behind. He winced in his sleep and jerked to the side of the bed. He again felt someone kneel on his back and the monotone voice talking in his head. As the person

102

released him and left the room, he tried to get up to follow. With a thud, he fell out of his bed onto the floor. He lay there for a moment, his pulse racing, his eyes frantically searching for his attacker. It was a few moments before he realised that it had only been a dream and he was actually lying on the floor of his own bedroom.

Gingerly raising himself into a sitting position, he tried to pull his scattered thoughts together, hoping his heart would stop pounding. As he sat there, he grasped with startling clarity what it was that his subconscious had recognized but he hadn't. The wooden sounding voice he had heard in the room the night before *had* belonged to a woman, which meant that the person kneeling on his back could well have been a woman, as the voice had seemed to be very close to the back of his head.

If that was the case, then David knew it was time for a major rethink. He went downstairs, made himself a cup of tea and returned to his bedroom. Sipping his tea in bed, he began to go through all the facts related to the two murders and the attempted murder. Several things now seemed to point to one of the attackers being a woman, but David still found it hard to believe that it was a woman who had pinned him to the floor so easily. One option was that there might be a man and a woman involved, but the man had kept deliberately quiet. If that was the case, then it must mean that the man could well be easily recognizable to David. That would be why it was the woman who spoke, though she too had tried to disguise her voice with the wooden monotone. The fact that she could continue to maintain the deception when the situation had gone so wrong, as it did that night, meant she was obviously very good and well disciplined; someone who needed to be taken very seriously. The situation now seemed to make more sense, but David was still left with a vague disquiet. He was fairly certain that he hadn't sensed two attackers in the room when he had been jumped. This was unsettling, but David was certain that the

103

woman whose arm and leg he had seen was small in build and so could not have pinned him down so easily. He decided that the blow to his head must have confused his senses. Then, a disturbing thought hit him. What if she was a trained operative?

David sat unmoving as the ramifications of this thought percolated through his consciousness. If she was a trained operative, it made the whole situation much more dangerous. 'But', he thought, 'what was a trained operative doing killing abusive guests in a Belper hotel. It just didn't make sense.' Again, his instinct told him that it hadn't been a trained operative, but he felt he couldn't ignore the possibility.

With that thought in mind, David then moved on to a consideration as to how he should deal with the new situation. Two possible attackers, or a trained operative, complicated the plot and made it less easy for him to tackle them on his own and keep it all quiet. Much as he was loath to do so, he decided that, if there were two attackers, his only safe option was to call on his former colleagues again and see if they would help him set up a trap to draw the attackers out. That way he could have one or two operatives in the bedroom ready to deal with any intruders. It would also allow him to be hidden in another room with the surveillance camera which would then enable him to come at the attacker or attackers from behind and so cut off any escape.

Having reached a new, but clearly serviceable plan, David settled back into his bed to rest until his alarm went off as, so far, his rest had not been that restful. With his new plan decided David was actually able to drop off to sleep more quickly than he expected and when his alarm went off at seven thirty, he felt more refreshed than he had expected to.

David had a quick shower and bite to eat before setting out for the hotel. On arriving at the hotel, he entered via the reception, waved to Tony at reception and then went to sit in the bar. As he expected, it wasn't long before the two of them came to join him. As it was a Monday evening, there were not too many other customers in the bar, so it was easy for the three of them to find a quiet corner of the bar, away from prying ears. Once they had got drinks, David explained his suspicions to them and outlined the plan he had come up with. Both Chris and Tony quickly agreed with David that getting help from the department would be the best way to deal with the situation. Although they hadn't said anything, that probably had something to do with the fact that he had been overpowered on the previous occasion. The two of them had seemed far too enthusiastic about having some other professionals there to help David deal with the attackers. David had the distinct feeling that their confidence in him had declined somewhat since the previous evening. Mind you, David couldn't really say their assessment of the situation was wrong, as he, also, was less confident of his current level of readiness as well, but he certainly wasn't going to admit that to them.

After finishing their drinks, Chris and Tony left to resume their duties, whilst David stayed to drink a couple more pints of Peroni, deciding that it might be suspicious if he left too quickly. After that, David went home to get a good night's sleep, having informed the two of them that he would contact his former colleagues the next day to see if they would agree to set the trap.

It was still early the following day when David rang his former colleagues, steeling himself for any comments that might come his way. He went through the identification processes with the receptionist before being put through to Mark. With a certain amount of embarrassment, he explained what had happened to him and was surprised when Mark didn't make any sarcastic remarks but just let it pass. When he had finished explaining how he had been overcome and explained that he believed there were two attackers Mark asked, somewhat abruptly,

"Obviously you didn't ring just to explain your failure, amusing as that was. I assume you need something else from us, apart from maybe a refresher course in unarmed combat."

David swallowed hard before replying,

"Well, I thought it would be a good idea to set up a trap, have someone insult one of the staff and then have one of your operatives in the room to help me catch them."

David wasn't exactly sure how he had expected Mark to respond, but he was certainly surprised when Mark, after a brief moment's hesitation, simply said,

"Actually that is a good plan. Obviously, I will have to ask the boss if he wants to commit the department that deeply, though. I will get back to you later after I have talked to him."

"Ok. Thanks."

When Mark put down the receiver, he stared thoughtfully at if for a few minutes thinking about what David had told him. There were certain details about the wider picture that Mark had not told David as he was no longer in the Department, but now, he thought it might be time to let him have the extra information. After another moment or two debating with himself, he reached his decision, picked up the phone and dialed the extension of his boss. He gave his boss a summary of everything that David had told him, as well the outline of the plan he had put forward.

"It is a good plan," his boss admitted, "I think we might go along with it, it might help us with our problem, after all."

"That's what I thought too, but do you think we should tell him all that we know? It would be easier working together if he knew the whole picture, particularly if there is a chance he wants to come back to the department. It wouldn't be good if he were to find out later that we kept information from him, especially when the details might have helped in creating the trap."

"I was wondering that, too; call him back and tell him I would like to see him."

"Should I tell him why?"

"No, hold fire on that; just tell him I need to talk to him before I can decide whether to give the ok. Oh, and sweeten it by offering him some practice time."

"When do you want to see him?"

"I am busy for the next couple of days, so see if he can be here on Friday, say, late morning, that way he can catch a morning train. You'd better send him a ticket too, to sweeten it a little more.

"Ok, when do you want me to ring him?"

"Better wait 'til this afternoon. We don't want him to think we are too eager to help. Let him stew a bit first."

"Ok."

As Mark put down the phone, a broad grin crossed his face at the thought of making David wait. However, there was definitely one fly in the ointment as far as Mark was concerned. His conversation with his boss had confirmed his suspicion that his boss really would like to get David to rejoin the department. Whilst Mark genuinely liked David, and had found him very good to work with, he wasn't sure he wanted him back. His main problem was that David really was very good at the job and the boss had always thought very highly, not only of his obvious talents, but also of his organizational and leadership qualities, which was why he had originally made David his second in command. It was entirely conceivable that the boss would replace Mark and make David his second in command again and Mark enjoyed being second in command and didn't want to lose the position.

David kept himself busy for the rest of the day, working on the gardens of two of his clients in Milford, enjoying gardening in the warm sunshine, but also nervously waiting for the call back from Mark. He kept wondering what was taking so long and whether that meant that they had decided that they had already done enough for him and so would not help him this time. He knew there was nothing he could do to force them to help, if that was the case. He knew, or at least he believed, that he could do it on his own if necessary, but he also knew it would be a lot easier and a lot more certain if he had their specialist help. However, as the time continued to pass and he was still waiting for Mark to ring back, the more certain he became that the delay in replying was being done on purpose to put him on the back foot. It fitted known patterns about the way the boss worked; if his answer had been a straightforward 'No', they would have simply told him so by now, as there was no reason not to. They wouldn't have to justify their decision, they would just tell him that he was on his own, they had done him a favour for old time's sake, but that was that. No, it was becoming increasingly probable that his former boss was playing his usual games, trying to keep him off balance. That meant, he believed, that they were virtually certain to help, but he was also convinced that they must have a particular reason for helping which they hadn't told him about yet. He thought that was why they were trying to keep him off-balance. It would be interesting to find out what that reason was. Were they simply trying to get him to return to the Department or was there something more to it than that? Time, and his former boss, would tell. If he was right, he predicted that Mark would return his call somewhere between 4 and 5 o'clock that afternoon.

At 4-20pm Mark did ring back. David had finished the job he was on and was waiting for the call. He had thought Mark would call around that time as he would wait long enough to hassle David, but not too long to make it too obvious. David answered the phone and after a brief interchange of pleasantries, Mark laid out the boss' response.
"Sir wants to see you. He hasn't made up his mind whether to help you or not, yet."
Deciding to test his hypothesis, David asked,
"What's going on Mark, he wouldn't normally want to see me, there's more to this situation, isn't there?"

Mark swore under his breath, noting once more, how perceptive David was, but he followed his boss' instructions and tried to sound vaguely indifferent,

"Don't know, old boy, I'm just telling you what he said. He wants you to come and see him; he also said you could get some practice in whilst you were here. Maybe he wants to see how you cope with that first. You might not be up to this sort of job anymore, you know."

David didn't know whether or not to believe him. Mark may be telling the truth, but David was certain that there was something else at play here. However, it didn't really matter, David had no choice other than to agree to the request, as it was the only way he saw of getting the help he wanted and they all knew it.

"Ok, when does he want me there?"

Mark metaphorically wiped his brow in relief and said,

"Can you make Friday, late morning?"

"Yes, it means I will be able to get the train; it's a straightforward journey, only takes about an hour and a half."

"Good, we will send you a train ticket."

"That's very decent of you."

"It's the least we can do for an old colleague."

With that Mark rang off and went to make his report to his boss.

"How did he take the news?"

"He knew there was more to this than you just wanting to see him."

"Good, it means he hasn't lost all his abilities, he always was astute."

"Too astute, sometimes," said Mark, inserting a gentle criticism.

"Mmm, possibly."

Whilst that conversation between Mark and Sir Peter was going on, David was also considering the phone call and the request to meet the boss. It certainly was unusual, but David had to admit that it was plausible that he simply did want to see David's physical shape and assess his mental abilities before he committed himself and his operatives. However, David was certain that there was more to it than that. For one thing, the boss had a department to run and had better things to do than check up on David's physical condition as an ex-member of that department. After all, Mark, and the senior physical trainer, would be the ones to actually assess his capabilities. Also, Mark had sounded far too smug, and his response had contained too much of an air of studied indifference for David's liking. Still, he only had to wait until Friday to find out if his suspicions were true.

He decided not to go to the Hotel that evening to let Chris and Tony know what was happening. He did not usually go there two nights running, so it might be a bit suspicious if he turned up again. He also didn't want to phone or send a text or email as they could be intercepted, if only by accident, so the two of them would have to wait to find out what the situation was.

Whilst he came to that conclusion, he also decided that it would be simpler if he didn't tell them about his planned visit to his former boss or that the plan hadn't actually been agreed by them yet. There was no need to worry the two of them unnecessarily as he was certain his former boss would agree, so they could wait a few days to find out.

The next day an electronic train ticket was sent to David's email. This confirmed to David that his former colleagues were indeed, monitoring him, as he had not given Mark his email address. Still, such things were only to be expected, electronic surveillance was standard procedure in such departments, it was one of the main reasons he always made sure the location tracker on his mobile phone was switched off, not that it made much difference these days but, at least, it made David feel he was making a privacy statement. At least it might slow Big Brother down a bit.

On the Thursday evening, he sent a text to Tony saying he wouldn't be able to meet him to discuss the next stage in the editing of his book as he had to make a sudden trip to London. Tony replied saying it was no problem and hoped it was nothing serious, as they could just as easily meet when he got back. David decided not to reply as he couldn't work out how best to phrase a reply.

The next morning David caught the 08-01 from Derby and after an uneventful train ride, arrived in London's Kings Cross station only 5 minutes late, at around five to ten. He quickly caught a tube to Bayswater and when he arrived there, took the stairs to street level and walked towards the once familiar building that housed the department he had worked out of for nine years, but which he hadn't entered for the previous eight years. He had to admit that he was feeling a certain amount of nervousness as he approached the faded old door which barred his way. He approached the doorway, stood on the step and faced the door, knowing that the hidden camera would be scanning his face and comparing it with their records to check his identity. A few seconds later the door clicked, David inhaled sharply, before pushing the door open and slipping inside. Once inside, he found himself standing in a sort of large cubicle, which was a new feature. He stood there for about 30 seconds before the inner door clicked open. He then passed through into the main reception area. Once there, he looked round with a certain amount of nostalgic curiosity. This part of the entrance room was virtually as he remembered; a modern looking foyer with a reception at the far end, where a woman sat behind the counter, though he noticed with a touch of surprise that the bullet proof glass that used to be in front of her had disappeared. He wondered if that had something to do with the new inner cubicle. As he approached the counter, the woman looked him up and down quizzically. Returning her gaze to his face she gave him a big, open smile and said,

"Hello David, nice to see you again. They told me you were coming. How are you?"

"Pretty good, how are you, Kate?"

"Oh, you know, same as always. You know where to go, don't you?"

"Do I need to be searched for weapons first?"

"Oh no, you were scanned as you stood in that cubicle. I can tell you are clean."

"What would have happened if I hadn't been clean?"

"You really don't want to know."

"Must be an expensive piece of kit?"

"I wouldn't know, I just operate it, but it makes reception a bit nicer without the bullet-proof screen. I feel like Clark Kent with his x-ray vision. You're to go straight to Sir's room."

"Ok, thanks."

"Good luck."

As David went through the door, which was located to the left of where Kate sat, a series of memories washed over him, some of which were pleasant, some not so pleasant. Accompanied by thoughts from the past, he walked slowly down to the end of the corridor, turned left and entered a sort of staging area. There were several doors which opened off from there, but he approached the door where his former boss had had his office when David was there. He had assumed that he must still be in the same room as Kate hadn't said any different. As he approached the door, it opened and Mark stood there, waiting for him, so either Kate had told them he was here, or they had surveillance cameras in the corridors. There was no welcoming smile on Mark's face, David noticed, not sure why that bothered him.

"Come in David, Sir is waiting for you."

David moved past Mark and saw his former boss sat behind the very same desk that had been there all those years ago. Totally unexpectedly, David felt strangely awkward and merely nodded to his former boss, before thinking to add,

"Good morning, Sir, how are you?"

"Fine, sit down David, it's good to see you again. How is life in the backwoods?"

"A bit more interesting of late."

"Yes, so it seems, judging by the reports of my operatives."

"Yes, thanks for helping me out."

"No problem; there are, however, some very good reasons why I decided to help, which I now think it's time to update you with."

"Yes, somehow I thought there might be."

"Still as astute as ever; it really was a shame that you decided to leave our little club."

Unexpectedly, he turned to Mark,

"Don't you agree Mark?"

A look of irritation flitted across Mark's face, but he said,"

"Of course, he was very good."

Although David was starting to feel a bit perplexed, he could also understand a little why Mark had been unsmiling on his arrival. His former boss appeared to be going out of his way to make Mark feel uncomfortable about David's talents. Knowing his boss, he was simply using the occasion to keep Mark nervous as to his position as number two in the department, he liked to create a certain level of insecurity in his staff. He thought it made people become more efficient if they were kept uncomfortable about the security of their job, though David hoped it didn't cause problems with him and Mark working together. On the other hand, he might also be trying to send a message to David that he could return if he wanted to, but he wouldn't ask him to come back, it would be up to David to ask.

"Now, about your little problem,"

Unaware of his actions, David leant slightly forward in anticipation, resting his arm on the desk and waited.

"Whilst the situation of being asked for help by someone who has left the department might not appear to be exactly normal, very little of what we do could be classed as normal."

The boss stopped, waiting for them to appreciate of his joke, to which they both duly obliged with a short burst of laughter, before he continued,

"I have decided that we will help you, but there is a very important rationale behind my decision, which you now need to know about."

David nodded, as much to himself as to his former boss, as his hunch was confirmed, but now intrigued, he waited for his former boss to continue with his explanation.

"When you first contacted us and described the murders at the hotel, there was a certain degree of similarity in the details you gave, with other occurrences elsewhere in the country which had come to our attention. Obviously, I couldn't be certain of a connection straight away, but I was willing to help you out in order to find out. If the two situations were not related, then it would simply have been described as a favour to you, but if they were related it would have given us more information to work with. As the situation at your hotel progressed, all the pieces fell into place and it became clear that a familiar pattern to what had happened in other hotels was being repeated. It appears that round the country, events similar to the one at your hotel were also happening, not at the same time, but in one hotel at a time. Apparently random attacks on hotel guests, the only common factor between them was that, in every case, the victims had been abusive to members of staff. So far 15 people have been killed and the police around the country are completely baffled. In all of the murders, the killer leaves some sort of memento as a clue to explain the murder."

"Like the cup of coffee in the first murder at my hotel," David commented.

"Exactly," replied Sir. "Well, the police have not been able to find a single credible suspect. There is nothing that the police have discovered that seems to connect all the different hotels and murders. In desperation, the police contacted us a few months ago to see if we could use our expertise but, so far at least, we have also drawn a blank. Because the murders took place at random hotels throughout the country, 'til now, we had no idea when or where another murder would be committed, so we were unable to make any progress. The trail, as it were, had disappeared. We, too, had come up with a plan to trap the killer but we never knew at what hotel they were operating."

"So that's where I come in, I can provide you with the chance to set up a murder to catch the murderer."

"Precisely, it's the perfect scenario for us, you know how we work, you also know the hotel and the staff there, so it should be fairly straightforward for you to set up the trap and we also know you will keep our existence secret from all but the essential staff."

"Well, yes, I don't really want them to know too much of my past either, they think I'm just an office worker who got bored and changed to become a gardener and I would like it to stay that way. I have to stay friends with them for when this is all over."

"Obviously, we won't say anything to change that, will we Mark?"

"Not a word." agreed Mark, who suddenly felt a lot happier, as David seemed to be talking about remaining where he was, rather than returning to the department.

"So, it's a case of 'I'll scratch your back and you'll scratch mine' and everyone benefits."

"Succinctly put," agreed the boss, "Now, go with Mark, as he will be liaising with you on this. You can swap information and plan on how you are going to carry out the operation. Oh, I'd also like you to do a refresher course in unarmed combat before you go back, either today or tomorrow, I think your last encounter showed you may be a bit rusty."

David looked across at Mark and could see he was grinning widely, probably at the thought of David being pummeled by some of his colleagues. Still, he had already admitted to himself that Sir was correct; he did need to refresh his skills if he was going to work effectively with his old colleagues and not put them in danger or, even worse, have to look after him in a fight.

"Ok, that's fine; I could definitely do with the practice," he admitted, "Especially as there is some evidence to suspect there might be two people working together to carry out the murders."

"Two people?" Sir Peter queried.

"Yes."

With that, he explained what had happened when he had been knocked down on the aborted murder attempt and what he had seen and heard which led him to believe that one of the attempted murderers had to be a woman. He also explained that he felt it unlikely that the woman who he had briefly seen would have been strong enough to hold down and strangle the first victim, as well as hold him down, unless, as he had considered, she might have been a trained operative. In view of that, he explained, he felt that there was a good chance that there must be two of them.

"I see, it makes sense, but it is still possible that it could be one person. I think, though, it would be wiser to prepare our plan on the assumption that there may be two people involved, that way we are less likely to be surprised. If there is nothing else, go and sort out the details with Mark."

"Ok."

With that Mark led David out of the office and into the operations room, a room which David remembered very well. The equipment in it had changed quite a lot since he had last been there, although they still used a kettle to make coffee. They made themselves some coffee and began the task of putting together all the details they had from the various murders with the information that David provided. Once all the details had been logged, they began to discuss all the various options they could think of for the operation. For several hours they debated various scenarios, discussing the pros and cons of each approach, discarding the options that were impractical or where it was too difficult to control the variables. Finally, they were left with the one option they both felt had the best chance of success, with the least disruption to the routine of the hotel. They re-assessed that option one last time and decided that it was the one to go with. Having decided on the overall approach, they then set about discussing what resources would be needed, along with the number and make up of personnel they would need to use.

At one point, when the two of them were taking a short break, David thought that the last few hours had flown by without him noticing. He wondered at how much he was enjoying himself but then, he told himself quickly, trying to bring some sense of normality back to his situation, he had always enjoyed the planning side of the job, it was some of the other, more dubious aspects that had, on occasion, tormented him.

A short time later, when they finally dotted all the i's and crossed all the T's, they had their working modus operandi.
"Well, that's sorted, then, all that remains is to decide when we want the operation to begin," David stated.
"I don't think we want to wait too long in case the murderers move on to another hotel and we lose this chance," Mark replied.
"Ok, how about the week after next, that will give you time to brief the operatives and to make sure everything is in place at this end."
"What day of the week do you think would be best?"
"I think it would probably be best to go for a Wednesday night, it's usually not too busy in the hotel then; fewer witnesses or people to get in the way."
"I always thought Monday and Tuesday evenings were the quietest."

"That's normally true, but the Lion puts on special events on Mondays and Tuesdays to draw people in, so those nights are often quite busy."

"Ok, it's agreed then, a week on Wednesday it is."

"Now that the basic scenario is agreed, which operatives are you going to send?"

"I don't know yet, I'll have to check with the boss and let you know."

"Ok, I'll discuss with Chris and Tony what the best abuse scenario would be."

"Good, now, when do you want to get your training session done?"

"I'm knackered today and want to eat first. Is there any chance we can do it tomorrow morning?"

"No problem, do you want to stay in a hotel or one of the safe houses tonight?"

"I think a safe house would be the best option; I can buy some food on the way and then spend the rest of the evening working on how we can make this work, how many people at the hotel need to know and then, who to tell and who not to tell, without any distractions."

"Ok, I'll get one of the drivers to take you. What time you want to get here tomorrow to do your training?"

"Shall we say around 10 o'clock; then we can discuss any issues we may have thought of, do a couple of hours of training and then catch an afternoon train home?"

"Fine, I'll just go and see who's available to drive you."

"Thanks."

Mark left the room for a minute or so and then returned with someone David didn't recognize.

"This is Jackson; he will drive you to the safe house and also pick you up in the morning to get you here for 10 am."

Jackson and David nodded to each other, sizing each other up in the process, before Mark left with a 'see you tomorrow' wave and Jackson led David, who had picked up his belongings, to the car, which was parked in their private underground car park. He then drove him out of the exit, which, as David remembered, surfaced about half a mile away from the department headquarters. David was in the back of the car, which was fully enclosed, with blacked out windows so he couldn't see out of the car. He wondered which safe house he was being taken to, and was considering whether to ask, however, Jackson forestalled him.

"Mark told me you used to be one of us and I didn't need to keep the location secret. I'm taking you to the safe house in Battersea, do you know the one I mean."

"Oh yes, I remember that one. I need to get some food though."

"Ok, there's one of those local supermarkets on the way, I can stop so you can get what you need."

"Thanks."

They drove in silence for a few minutes before David asked,

"How long have you been with the department?"

"Just a year; how long were you here for?"

"Too long, I think."

Jackson gave a shrewd look at the driver's camera which showed David's expression in the back of the car, but made no comment. There being nothing else really to say, they continued driving in silence for a while, before they stopped outside a supermarket. David bought food for his evening meal and breakfast and then returned to the car. Once back in the car it was only a few minutes before they arrived at the safe house. David was quite pleased that he had been given one of the pleasanter safe houses. At least he knew he would be comfortable there.

As they approached the safe house Jackson pressed the remote-control button which operated the electronic gate and they entered into the underground garage. When they had parked up, Jackson preceded David to the private lift which took them to the apartment and let him in. David had a quick look round,

"It's virtually exactly the same as when I was last here," he said.

119

Jackson just grunted; it appeared he did not talk that much, at least to someone he didn't know. Also, he must have been confused as to David's status; he would have heard from others who knew him that David used to be second in command of the department, so he was probably trying to be professional. Also, the fact that they had sent David to one of the high status safe houses would also suggest that David was still important. He might possibly have also heard a rumour that there was a chance that David might return to the department, so maybe he was also trying to impress him, just in case he did return as second in command. There were a lot of maybes.

"I will pick you up at 9 o'clock tomorrow morning. Mark said to tell you not to leave the safe house."

"I thought that would be the case. I've got plenty to keep me occupied. See you tomorrow."

"Yeah," said Jackson and he let himself out of the apartment.

David had a quick, but careful look around the apartment, noting where the hidden cameras and microphones probably were, but he tried to be casual and not make it obvious that that was what he was doing. He was only doing it out of an old habit in any case and to check on his abilities to detect them, though he knew he probably wouldn't find them all. Obviously, it didn't really matter about the surveillance as he had nothing to hide. He wasn't a foreign agent who had been picked up for questioning away from the department in a secret location, or a double agent who was being debriefed, so he could be left alone with just the cameras and microphones for company, though he also knew that, at least for some of the time, someone would be watching him.

He went into the kitchen and set about preparing himself some food as he realized that he really was very hungry. It had been a long, hard day and they hadn't really eaten all day, just coffee and biscuits whilst he and Mark were working. He had bought himself pizza for his evening meal, as it was easy to cook. Twenty minutes later the pizza was ready and he settled down to eat, following it up with a piece of coffee and walnut cake. Feeling better having eaten, he washed his plate and utensils and then he settled down for the evening. He spent his time thinking his way carefully through the plan they had come up with to see if there were any flaws that they had missed, but there weren't any that he could see; it appeared that they had done a thorough job of preparation. If it went to plan it should be quite straightforward, but how often did that happen, he thought. Something, somewhere, usually went wrong, but at least they would have the expertise on hand to deal with any contingency that might potentially crop up. At least, he hoped they would!

Eventually he decided that he would have a shower, watch something undemanding on TV and then go to sleep. He knew that Mark would get one of the department's best men to work with him during the unarmed combat refresher and he would probably end up battered and bruised afterwards. Still, despite that, he was actually looking forward to it, gardening in Derbyshire kept him fairly fit with all its hills, but he knew he needed to be fighting fit if he wasn't going to let his old colleagues down, or, and this was as equally important to David, show himself up.

Just before he was about to have his shower, he received a text message from Tony asking when he was next coming to the hotel so they could discuss his book. 'Good man', thought David, 'at least he has learnt to be cautious'. He considered how well, on the whole, Tony had actually dealt with the extraordinary situation; especially the quick-witted way he had dealt with Vicky turning up when they were trying to move the body, and thought Tony would probably have fitted in well in the department. Despite that, though, he decided, not to reply that night, but wait until he actually got back home tomorrow evening. He could then decide whether to go to the hotel that evening, or put it off until the following day. It would all depend on just how battered and bruised he was feeling after the combat training. He foresaw a situation where simply walking could be quite difficult. It all depended on how Mark set the session up. He may well think it amusing to make the session as difficult as he could. It really depended on what 'Sir' wanted, he might let Mark loose on him, or he might really want to use the training as a way of assessing David's current level of fitness, especially if he thought there was a chance that he might want to rejoin the department. If that was the case, he could expect a thorough work out, but not an all-out assault. Whatever the boss wanted, though, Mark would put it into place; he would not ad-lib for his own amusement. Either way, he foresaw a very uncomfortable session, followed by lingering and possibly excessive pain. With that less than happy thought, David had his shower and settled down for the night.

Back at the department Mark put a quick call through to his boss.
"He seems to have settled down for the night; nothing unusual."
"Did he sweep the place?"
"Very casually; if I hadn't been checking, I wouldn't have noticed."
"Good, his training is still there at least, make sure he gets a good work out tomorrow, Mark, but make sure he doesn't get too beaten up."
"Of course. In terms of the operation, do you have any preferences which operatives I allocate?"
"I want you to use Natalie as the lead member of our agents. You choose any others you feel is needed."
"Why Natalie?"
"I want to see how she copes with more responsibility. Also, David has always worked well with women, and I want him to enjoy working on this operation."
Mark took a quick breath and then asked the question that had been needling him,
"You really would like him to come back wouldn't you?"

"Oh yes. It would be a waste of his talent and our training if he didn't, he was very good, however, I don't think we need to tell him that. I want him to make the choice without any overt pressure from us."

"I see."

"Don't worry Mark, even if he did come back, he wouldn't get your job, you too, are very good and David has shown that he may have too many scruples, but it would be good if he did return, there aren't many people as capable as he is. We do work in a rather unique and specialised field, after all. Go home, and get some rest," he said, and the phone went dead.

Mark looked at the now dead phone; if there was no threat his current position, he too, would like it if David did return, he was very good to work with and this afternoon had only reinforced that view. They had both played off each other, using their different skills to come up with a very workable plan that should succeed in catching whoever it was that was murdering hotel guests.

Chapter 10.

The Mind Is Willing.

David woke fairly early the next morning and got slowly out of bed. His night had been plagued by dreams of wooden zombies attacking him and he definitely did not feel as refreshed as he would have liked. He decided he was not really looking forward to his impending physical ordeal. The idea of doing unarmed combat with some of the best practitioners in the department was less appealing than it had seemed when he was home, now the ordeal was near he was unsure whether his body would be able to deal with what was coming.

To pass the time he took a leisurely breakfast of cereal, toast and tea before clearing everything away, washing up and then packing his few belongings, ready for when his driver arrived. Knowing the way the department worked, he expected Jackson to be exactly on time to pick him up and take him back to their headquarters, so David made sure he was ready to leave the apartment for 8-55 am. Sure enough, at 9 o'clock exactly there was a knock on the door. David smiled at that and was just about to open the door to let Jackson in, his hand reaching for the door handle but, just before he opened the door, he decided it would be safer to check that it really was Jackson outside of the door. He quickly looked through the spy hole in the door.

Back at the department, the boss almost purred with appreciation as he watched the monitor displaying pictures from the safe house. Despite the fact that it was completely unlikely that David would feel himself to be in any danger, the boss was gratified to note yet another sign that David was still on the ball and remembered to apply his training before opening the door.

124

David confirmed that it was Jackson who was stood outside waiting for him; noting too, that Jackson was following departmental protocol by standing in just the right place to ensure that David could see his face through the spyhole. Satisfied, David opened the door to let his driver into the safe house.

"Good morning, are you ready sir?" Jackson asked.

"Yes, let's go."

David picked up his belongings and followed Jackson to the car, noting that Jackson did not offer to carry his bag for him, which meant he kept his hands free. When they reached the car, David again sat in the back, unable to see out, but it was only a relatively short drive to the department headquarters, so he didn't have too long to obsess about the training session or become overly nervous, wondering which of the instructors would be given the task of working with him, or possibly working him over.

When they arrived at headquarters they again entered via the underground entrance and went up the stairs to the main building, then to the operations planning room. Mark was already there, waiting for him, a small smile playing across his face. David put his belongings down on a chair and waited for Mark to set the training in motion. Mark was clearly in no immediate rush and continued to look quite cheerful as he greeted David.

"Did you sleep well?" he enquired, still smiling his self-satisfied smile.

"I'm sure you have had a report on what I got up to last night," David said, just a little testily, reminding Mark, he knew how the department worked.

"Oh, we know what you got up to, but that doesn't tell us if you feel refreshed and ready for battle," was Mark's bland response.

"I'm fine; can we get on with it?"

At that Mark, grinned even wider and David swore to himself, having given away the fact that he was nervous.

"No problem, we can begin straight away, if you are that eager," Mark agreed and led him through to the gym they used.

"Do you remember where the changing room is?"

David nodded and Mark continued,

"There is some kit in there for you. When you are ready, go to the practice room."

"Ok," David replied, noticing that although Mark had been smiling earlier, he was now very formal. David wasn't sure that that boded well for his prospects. David hoped it was simply a psychological tactic, testing his mental strength, as well as his physical capabilities.

'Ah well', he thought, 'I can't really stop now'.

He made his way to the changing room and quickly got changed. The kit fitted him perfectly and, once again, he wondered how closely they had been monitoring him, although his weight hadn't really changed in the years he had been gone, so it could simply be that they had used his old details to provide some kit for him, either that or it was a complete fluke.

'At least I will feel comfortable', he thought as he walked to the practice room.

Although he wasn't aware of it, his breathing had become quite shallow and rapid as he entered the room, but when he saw it was Andy who was to be his opponent, he breathed a small sigh of relief. If they had just wanted to really hurt him, he thought, they would probably have chosen Colin to be his opponent and that certainly wouldn't have been good. Colin always tried to hurt everyone he fought against, and he had always held a grudge against David because David had always been better at unarmed combat than him. He would have loved the chance to get his own back on an out of practice David. Andy, though as hard as nails, was fair, not that he wouldn't hurt David, but he would only do so in the interests of improving his technique, unless, David reminded himself, he had been ordered to hurt him. David fervently hoped he hadn't.

Andy gave him a brief smile of acknowledgement, walked to the mat in the centre of the room and waited for David to join him there. They bowed to each other and then the 'refresher course' began. For two hours, virtually nonstop, Andy attacked and David reacted. Initially Andy was able to beat his responses easily and his blows repeatedly thudded into David's body. After about half an hour, though, David's body and muscle memories began to remember what he was supposed to do and for about forty-five minutes he was able to give a good account of himself, repelling most of the attacks and even managing to successfully attack Andy on a few occasions. After that though, his body rapidly began to run out of steam and Andy, again, dealt with him very easily. After two hours of actual fighting, Andy called the session to a halt, the two of them bowed again and then David sank gratefully onto a chair, breathing heavily and already starting to feel pain seeping into his body. Despite the pain, David couldn't help smiling, realising he had really enjoyed the challenge of being on the mat with a trained professional. He was pleased that for a short time he had still been able to give as good as he got.

Now that the session was over, Andy sat down next to him, smiling pleasantly at him and quietly said,
"Good to see you again David. I have to say that for a man who hasn't worked out in a while, I was genuinely impressed with the standard of your responses, once you got back into the swing of it, that is. You ran out of energy towards the end, but that was only to be expected, it was a very thorough work out. It wouldn't take long for you to regain your former standard. I think you'll suffer later though," he laughed.
"Thanks Andy, I don't know about later, I'm starting to feel like I've been through a meat grinder already, so God knows what I'll feel like tomorrow. Still, I needed the refresher course."

"That you did, you were very slow at the start," and with that he rose from his chair, placing a companionable hand briefly on David's shoulder before he left.

As Andy walked off, David rose very slowly and painfully from his seat and made his way back to the changing room, clamping his teeth together to keep from groaning. Once there, he took a long and much needed warm shower, hoping it would ease some of the pain from his muscles as well as the bruises. It did, but only for the very short time he was actually in the shower. By the time he returned to the Ops room, he was walking slowly and very gingerly and bore a striking resemblance to a ninety-year-old man suffering with arthritis and severe back pain. His mood wasn't improved by seeing Mark grinning very smugly at him and clearly enjoying his discomfort. Knowing what the answer clearly was going to be, a gloating Mark rubbed it in still further by asking David how his body was doing. David mouthed an obscenity at him, which only made Mark grin even more and then David, too, seeing the funny side of it all, was forced to give a rueful grin.

"I didn't realise how out of shape I was 'til then. I thought gardening on the hills of Derbyshire had kept me fit but that hurt; well, it still hurts now."

"Actually, Andy was very complimentary about your performance, considering you haven't done this for several years. Sir is also impressed."

"Well, that's nice," said David sarcastically.

"Yes, in fact he was so impressed with how well you performed, he asked me to ask if you wanted to go to the armoury and practice with some firearms."

Watching very closely for David's reactions, Mark left it hanging for a few seconds, before asking,

"Do you?"

At Mark's offer, David's breathing had sped up in excitement and instinctively he was about to say 'yes', as he had to admit that the offer was definitely tempting. Part of him wanted to see if he still retained the skills he used to have and he was on the point of saying 'yes' when the thought hit him that this was probably just another of the boss' tests to see whether David wanted his old job back, or to tempt him into coming back. In view of that, and though it was hard to do, he shook his head and said,

"Thanks, but I don't intend shooting whoever is committing the murders, I needed the unarmed combat practice, but I need to get back and set up the operation. Mind you, I don't think I would be able to hold a gun steady with the state my body is in. Thanks anyway."

"Fine," Mark answered, apparently totally unconcerned with David's response. "I'll get Jackson to drive you to the station. I will confirm the last few details about the operation and the operatives with you as soon as possible, using secure channels, of course."

"Ok, does Sir Peter need to see me, or do I just get going?"

"I will be overseeing the operation at this end, so I can't see that there is any reason to hang about. You'd better catch your train before Rigor Mortis sets in."

David mouthed an obscenity at Mark and then he slowly, picked up his belongings and once again, gingerly followed Jackson to the car. Even though he could see that David was struggling, Jackson still did not offer to carry his bags. Despite his pain, David both respected and cursed his professionalism. Very quickly they arrived at St. Pancras station and David thanked Jackson, got painfully out of the car and slowly made his way into the station.

Whilst David was entering the station, the insider in the Special Ops department made another call to the office in Marylebone. The same person answered and listened as the informant said,

"Just to let you know, Sir Peter has decided to commit the department fully to dealing with the murders at your Hotel.

Several members of the department will be working with his old operative to solve the case."

"Thanks for letting me know, it is most appreciated. If anything changes, please let me know."

After he had ended the call, the man immediately called his second in command.

"Joshua, things have got a little more complicated at our Hotel. Sir Peter is sending in some of his operatives to try to solve the case."

"Ok, do you want me to close down the operation there and move the operation elsewhere?"

"Not this time, I think it's time we tested how robust the operation is and whether it can deal with this sort of opposition. Sir Peter's operatives will be a good test of how well our whole operation works. However, we don't want to make it too easy for them, so you might want to think about disrupting their operation."

"I see. How far can we go?"

"Nothing that would be obvious; make it something that appears purely accidental, certainly nothing terminal at this stage."

"Ok, I will get onto it."

A short while later Joshua sent a text to their source in Sir Peter's department asking for any information they had on the former operative. Once he received the information, he would be able to work out a plan to try and incapacitate him. Hopefully, if they could do that, it would derail Sir Peter's operation.

Back at the station, a very sore and hobbling David had found out the details of his train and had also noted that there were no reported delays. Thankfully, he had ample time to get something to eat before he caught the train. After a good meal, and a couple of medicinal glasses of wine, he made his way back to the platform, showed his ticket at the barrier before boarding the train, happy to be able to sit down and relax his aching body. Once again, the journey was uneventful and for most of the trip he had the seat and table to himself, except for a short part of the journey, when a business woman sat opposite him and spent most of her time on her phone, discussing business with her colleagues. During the rest of the return journey, he reviewed the past couple of days and assessed his own reactions to being back working in the department headquarters alongside former colleagues.

After he had got past the surface excitement of working there, he had to admit that his feelings were somewhat ambiguous. As he was fully aware, since his separation from his partner, his life had generally seemed to be without real meaning; he had thought he was content, if that was the way to describe it, to just drift from day to day, without any real plan or direction. But, whilst he enjoyed working as a gardener, it was a solitary working life, with few people to talk to, so a lot of his time was spent either brooding, or thinking through various ideas that he had for his writing. Add to that, going home to an empty, quiet house and he could understand why he had begun drinking at home, just occasionally at first but increasingly more often and more copiously. He didn't like to admit it, but the drink had helped him on those nights when his mood had turned sour.

However, he had to admit, since he had become involved in trying to solve the murders at the hotel, he had found that he was much less inclined to automatically reach for the wine bottle from early in the evening. In fact, he was pleased to note, he no longer 'needed' the drink anymore and he was beginning to feel more alive again. He was also glad to be using his intellect once more, other than for writing and, having been shown how far his fitness levels had fallen, was also now keen to improve that as well. However, he was still in no way certain that he wanted to return to the department, with all that that entailed. He certainly needed to seriously think the whole situation through for a while longer yet. 'At least', he told himself, 'by the end of the operation at the hotel, having liaised with the department again and working alongside some of the operatives, I will have a better idea of what I want'. At least he hoped that is what would happen.

During the journey back, firstly on the train and then on the bus home from Derby, David had received quite a few pitying looks when he had had to get up and walk and the occasional groan of pain had escaped, uncontrolled from between his clenched teeth. For some reason he could not understand, he also received a few very disapproving looks, too, so it was with a great sense of relief that he was finally able to get off the bus near to his home. Even then, it was a slow and painful walk up, what was, it had to be said, only a slight slope up to his home. It was without doubt, one of the slowest and most painful walks he had made in a while, made even worse when he met one of neighbours, who cheerfully watched him as he hobbled up the street, clearly laughing at his predicament. When David finally reached him, he said,

"Thanks for the sympathy."

"No problem. What's up with you, you old git?"

Obviously, David couldn't give the real reason why he was walking so slowly and painfully, so he resorted to an excuse he had used before.

"My bloody back's gone again. I was trying to walk it off, but it just isn't easing up."

"That's the problem when you get old."

"I'm not bloody old; I just look like I am. I'm off before you can think of any more insults."

David set off again up the hill towards his house. He had only gone a short distance when his friend called out,

"I've thought of about six more insults, and you've only gone ten feet."

"Well, keep them to yourself, git."

Laughing loudly, his friend turned away and went back into his house, leaving David to continue his slow and painful stagger up the street to his home. Luckily David didn't meet any more of his neighbours on the way and when he finally arrived at his home, he was able to climb the five steps, groaning through compressed lips at each one, to his front door, open it, and stagger inside.

The day was turning into evening by the time David had finally opened the front door to his home and, reflecting on the comments of his friend on the street, his mind and body were telling him to stop pretending he was 20 years younger and that it was, actually, perfectly acceptable to just collapse. With a great sense of relief, he did just that, but even that didn't get rid of all the pain, just some of it. At least sitting down, he did not entirely look like he had spent his adult life in some sort of hedonistic orgy, which had left him looking like someone who was 30 years older than he actually was.

After he had rested a while, he decided to have another shower and cover his body in 'Wintergreen ointment' to try and ease the pain. Ten minutes passed before his body accepted the commands from his brain to get up off the chair, but, finally, he managed to stand up and, using the banister, pull himself upstairs to the shower. It took another ten minutes, though, to get undressed and get in the shower.
'I must get a proper shower cubicle put in,' he told himself, as he struggled to get his legs over the edge of the bath that also doubled as his shower. The side of the bath had never seemed so high before, and he felt a bit like Sir Edmund Hillary trying to scale Mount Everest. After his shower and a generous application of wintergreen to his muscles, he decided that there was no way he was going to humiliate himself further by going to see Chris and Tony, or any of the other people he knew at the hotel, for that matter. Apart from the obvious pain, which was a major consideration, he thought it might not create a great deal

of confidence in his ability to deal with the murderer if Chris and Tony saw him hobbling around and grimacing in pain. He also doubted whether he could walk the mile and a half to the hotel and if he took his car, he could foresee a situation where he might find it impossible to get himself out of the low slung sports car he drove. He also wasn't in the mood for the level of mickey-taking that would also be his lot. No, he thought, a drink, followed by a good night's sleep would do him the world of good, or so he hoped.

He also decided he had better reply to Tony's text from the previous evening, so he sent him a quick message telling him that, hopefully, he would be coming into the hotel the following evening. For once, he didn't take too long deciding on which wine he felt like drinking that evening, simply choosing the easiest one to reach, though just opening the bottle caused his muscles to rebel. He decided to spend the evening simply resting, watching a film. He carried his bottle of wine, plus glass, up to his lounge. It was at this point that he decided it was a very bad idea to have his lounge in the attic of his house; climbing the three fights of stairs took him a long time. Much later, after several glasses of red wine and an evening watching his favourite film, Apollo 13, he gritted his teeth and made his way back down one of the flights of stairs to his bedroom, discovering in the process that climbing down the stairs was even more painful than climbing up them. He decided he couldn't be bothered to deal with the pain of taking his clothes of, so he just kicked of his slippers, got under the duvet, groaned a lot as he searched for a comfortable sleeping position and then gratefully fell, very quickly, into a well-deserved sleep.

Chapter 11.

The Sweet Forgetfulness Of Sleep.

The next morning David woke feeling nicely refreshed, but then made the mistake of trying to get out of bed and pain exploded in every part of his body. He had forgotten how much pain he had gone to sleep with, but that sweet forgetfulness had only been a temporary illusion. At first his muscles completely refused to unlock, but after several minutes of intense pain, he managed to reach a sitting position on the bed. After a few minutes rest, he managed to turn his body the 90 degrees necessary to get his legs over the side of the bed and his feet on to the floor. Resting again for a short while, he took in a few deep breaths, before he gritted his teeth and, with pain again erupting in every part of his body, forced himself to stand up. Then, in a move that can only be described as utter insanity, he reached his arms out sideways and, with teeth firmly clamped together, he tried to stretch his muscles. When he had managed to raise and lower his arms a few times, he then forced himself to lower his body into a crouch. Ignoring the resistance from his body, David continued to force himself to crouch, stand, crouch, stand; several times. After a few minutes, and an eternity of pain, he began to feel his muscles ease, if only slightly. It appeared his recovery, if slow and very reluctant, was nevertheless in progress.

Even though it was the weekend, Joshua was in his office in Marylebone looking through the information about David that had arrived the evening before. It was quite a detailed biography of his time in the Special Ops department, as well as his contacts and work since leaving the department. After a couple of hours sifting through the material Joshua had put together a serviceable plan to force him out of the operation, which he hoped, would cause the Special Ops department to pull out of their operation, thereby not hindering the operation at the hotel. Joshua picked up his phone and called some of his operatives, telling them to come to his office for a briefing.

With it being the weekend, there were no time pressures on David, so he didn't do a great deal throughout the day, but he did make sure that, at very regular intervals, he forced himself into exercising his muscles and, as the day wore on, he found his muscles were aching less and he was able to walk round more or less normally and less like one of the living dead. By the time he set off for the Hotel and his briefing with Chris and Tony, he was beginning to feel fairly pleased with himself; he had had his training session, taken his beating, given some in return, and had only taken one day to virtually recover. Not bad for someone his age; it seemed that gardening on the hills of Derbyshire did have its plus points, after all.

When he walked into the hotel he stopped to say 'Hi' to Nathan, on reception, spent a few minutes discussing Nathan's new garden, of which Nathan was inordinately proud, discussing with him how best to look after his vegetables, before going through to the bar to get himself a deserved pint of Peroni. With pint in hand, he went to sit in the area of the bar where the TV was, so he could watch a bit of mindless sport before he went through to the other bar area to get a pizza.

Around half an hour later, he went to ask Vicky for the next available table,

"It's quiet at the moment; you can eat straight away if you want."

"Excellent, lead on."

"Usual pizza?" she asked as he sat down.

"But, of course," he responded. "How are you, anyway?"

"Oh I'm fine, are you ok, you seemed to be limping a bit?"

"Yeah, a bit stiff, I decided to take up jogging again and my muscles are rebelling a bit. I don't think they liked the sudden burst of sporting activity."

"You should take it easy at your age, you might do yourself some permanent damage," Vicky said with a sly grin.

"Cheeky wench, go and fetch me my pizza, minion."

Vicky walked off, still grinning, and David looked around at the customers who were enjoying their food and drinks, and the staff who were serving them, finding himself wondering if possibly one, or even two of them were murderers. He found it hard to believe, but all the available evidence seemed to point to that one fact; it had to be at least one member of the staff who was killing guests.

A few minutes later his pizza arrived, brought by Hattie.

"How are you?" she asked, "Haven't seen you in a while."

"I've been in as usual, must have just missed each other, how's your new job?"

"It's good, I'm really enjoying it. I've sort of been promoted already; I'm mostly working in the lab now."

"Good, make the most of it. Don't work here too much, concentrate on a career."

"Oh, I am, I've cut down on my shifts here, but it's still nice to work here occasionally, most of the customers are nice and the staff are friendly."

When David had finished eating Tony stopped by, probably hoping for a quick update on David's plan. They shook hands as usual, to be followed by the traditional greeting from Tony,

"Good evening, my man, how the devil are we?"

137

"Fine, young man, what about you?"

"Overworked and underpaid like most of the world, but that's life."

"True."

"Any news to report?" Tony asked, trying to appear nonchalant.

"Well, I have some good news regarding your book, but it is quite complicated and will need us to concentrate on going through the details carefully. It will be better if we go through it when it's quieter later."

"Ok, that's good. See you near closing."

David finished the last of his Peroni and went to pay for his meal, which he always did as soon as he had finished eating, a habit he had gotten into ever since the time he had once forgotten to pay, having spent the evening getting drunk, before he somehow managed to stagger home. Tony had kindly paid his bill for him, a gesture that Tony often made sure to remind him of ever since, especially if he wanted David to buy him a drink. Vicky and several of the other staff, who also knew him quite well, also thought it amusing to remind him of his failings from time to time too. Having paid for his pizza, David went from the eating area and back into the TV bar where he bought himself another pint of Peroni and went back to sit where he could see the TV. After a while he got bored watching the sport and moved to sit in a quieter area of the bar, where he took out his notebook and started writing the outline of a short story he had been thinking about.

It was around eleven thirty before Tony had finished his duties and had a chance to come and join David.

"Shall I fetch Chris?" he asked.

David gave him a questioning look, but Tony didn't get it until David said,

"Does Chris normally join us when we are actually discussing your book?"

"Oh yeah, didn't think of that."

"No matter, you can fill him in with the details later."

Just at that moment, David saw Vicky approaching their table from behind Tony, so he quickly diverted the conversation to Tony's book.

"I have got an email address of somewhere where, for a small fee, we can arrange for an author or an agent to read your manuscript and then give you feedback on what needs to be done to improve it."

He looked up, as if he had just noticed Vicky.

"Hi Vicky."

"Are you two still sorting that book out, it's taking ages?"

"These things take time; it has to be as good as you can get it before it's worth trying to get it published. It's very competitive out there." David informed her.

"Well, the rest of us are getting pretty bored by now. I think we will all be damn glad when you have finally published it."

"Oh, then I'll start my next book," said Tony.

"Oh, god help us, will this torment never stop?"

"Sooo, anyway Vicky, are you just here simply to abuse us or did you want something in particular?" Tony asked.

"It's always fun insulting you but actually, Chris asked if you have sorted out the staffing rota for next week?"

"Tell him it's nearly done and I'll finish it later before I go tonight."

"Do you want me to finish it; I have finished my duties, so I've got time?" Vicky offered.

Before Tony had chance to reply, David gave him a quick kick under the table and as Tony glanced at him, he gave an almost imperceptible shake of the head to him. This time Tony caught on straight away, he was definitely getting quicker at picking up on David's hidden messages.

"No, I'll do it later; there are a couple of things that need to be adjusted but thanks for offering."

"Ok, I'll go and tell Chris," she replied as she walked off, "I'll join you for a drink in a bit; when you have finished discussing that bloody book, that is."

When Vicky had left Tony asked David,
"I suppose you had a good reason for stopping me let Vicky finish the rota, she's perfectly capable and it would have saved me having to do a very boring task?"
"I'm sure she is very capable, but we may want to change the staffing when we have finished discussing the next move in trying to catch the murderer."
"Oh, I see, I take it your 'old friends' agreed to help, then."
"They did, we are going to arrange a nice little charade, where one of them acts as a guest and insults one of the staff. Then we are going to stake out the bedroom they are in. Two of them will be in the room and I will be watching the corridor outside through the camera, that way I can tell them when the attack is about to occur. Once it is clear that the attack is about to take place I can then go to the room as cover from the outside and act as a backstop to make sure they don't escape. Hopefully, with three of us there, we should be able to capture the killer without too much trouble."
"Are you sure it will work?"
"You can never guarantee it, but we've tried to eliminate as many problems as possible and the agents will be very good at what they do, so hopefully there won't be too many problems."
"Do you know when it will be happening?"
"We've set it up for a week on Wednesday, as Wednesdays are normally relatively quiet."
"That's ok, there is nothing big on in the hotel on that Wednesday."
"Can you just go and check to make sure there really is nothing big going on that night? I wouldn't want to get it all set up, only to find that on that particular night there are hundreds of people here for the mayor's annual bash or something."

"Do you mind, I'm the Deputy Manager, I know what's happening for the next few weeks and that night is fine, no special events are on."

"If you are sure?"

"I am."

"In that case, I apologise profusely for doubting your efficiency," David replied, with a smile.

"That's ok then, apology accepted," Tony retorted, smiling in response.

"Right, can you come over to my place some time in the next couple of days, so we can discuss all the minute details?"

"Can't we do it now?"

"No, it is quite detailed, we will have to work out suitable rooms, come up with a believable charade, whether we need any particular staff on duty, all those sorts of details, and I don't want have to spend all my time checking that no one is near, or listening to what we say. We don't want to spoil the surprise."

"I can't make tomorrow, but Tuesday is my evening off, is that ok?"

"Yeah, Tuesday will be fine, shall we say about 8pm; I've got plenty of wine in."

"That's fine for you, but I prefer to drink lager when I'm thinking, after all, most of my book was written whilst I was seriously under the influence of Stella. I'll bring some bottles for me."

"Does that mean the charade will be full of swearing, like your book was?"

"Don't exaggerate, only half the words were swear words."

"Yes, and usually the same one if I remember rightly."

"Ok, ok, I let you remove them in the end, didn't I?"

"Yes, but it was very hard work persuading you."

"Sod off."

"See," David said in apparent seriousness, "when you are sober, you are much more polite."

Tony swore at him again, as both started laughing. After they had composed themselves, once more, David said,

"Ok, now we need people to see and hear us discussing your book for a while, so let's move to the main bar for a last drink."

They moved to the main bar, where a few of the remaining staff were having an end of shift drink. They discussed Tony's book, loud enough to be heard whilst they sat at one of the nearby tables, before they walked across to join Vicky and a couple of other members of staff for a final few minutes, before David left to walk home. He found he had stiffened up again whilst he had been seated at the hotel, so the forty-minute walk home helped to ease his muscles again.

It was around 1 am when he got home, but luckily he didn't have to start work until after midday the following day as he had to wait in for a delivery. All his recent activity was taking its toll on his body and so he was really pleased that he would be able to have a bit of a lie in. Another plus point was that he was now able to undress before he got into bed and, almost before he had time to arrange his body into a comfortable position and settle down, he had fallen into a deep sleep.

Chapter 12.

Plans, Plans and More Plans.

Early on Tuesday morning Mark called Natalie and Johnnie into his office and informed them that they would be working with David and briefed them on the operation. As they were finishing up, he added,

"Lastly, there are a couple of things you need to know. Firstly, Natalie will be the senior operative."

Natalie looked across at Johnnie, whose faced showed no emotion, before saying,

"But Johnnie is far more experienced than me."

"I know, but that's not an issue as David will be the one in charge overall, it's just that the boss is trying to persuade David to return to the department and, as David has always worked well with women, he wants to make the operation as enjoyable as possible, under the circumstances."

"Well, that would be a novel experience; most of the men here are dinosaurs."

"Finally, it is most important that neither of you let David know that we are trying to entice him back, he doesn't like feeling manipulated."

Both Natalie and Johnnie nodded as they got up to leave.

Later that evening, Tony had arrived at David's house. They had begun by working out a few of the easier aspects, such as deciding to use room 15 as their base of operations, as it was the most favourable location in the hotel for setting a trap.

The room was situated on the second floor and at the end of the corridor, so it would make it easier to trap the killer. Also, David would then be able to use room 12, which meant the killer would have to pass his room on the way to room 15. They could also set up the surveillance camera in the smoke detector, which was located at the junction where the corridor turned. This would enable them to see the whole corridor, whilst remaining unseen. This was vital, as it meant that David would be able to give the operatives in room 15 a heads up when the killer was approaching the room, allowing them to be fully prepared to spring the trap and, hopefully, deal with them with the minimum amount of fuss.

After that, they started to examine the more tricky aspects,
"So, the important question is, which members of staff do we want to be on duty on that night and which member of staff is going to be abused," Tony asked.
"It doesn't really matter which members of staff are on duty that night, but we need to think carefully about which member of staff would be the best one to be on the end of the verbal abuse?" asked David.
"That's tricky, obviously, it needs to appear to be a real verbal assault, but we do have real Health and Safety issues to deal with, we don't want to damage them psychologically and have them sue the hotel."
"Actually, thinking about it, we probably need to decide what the abuse scenario is going to be before we can decide which member of staff to use."
"Good point," Tony agreed.
"We don't want something that appears contrived, as that could give the game away, so what are the sorts of situations that have happened that we might be able to refine and use?"

Tony sat quietly for a few moments, dredging through his memories for a suitable scenario, trying to remember some of the issues guests had made major complaints about. However, as normally happens in these situations, as soon as he tried to remember specific situations, his mind went blank. To cover this, hopefully, temporary embarrassment, Tony asked,

"Do we want to use one of the episodes that have triggered a murder attempt already, as we know they work?"

"Possibly, if we can't think of anything else, although we had better not use the theft of jewels again as that might be too obvious, so that leaves us with things like bringing the wrong food/drinks or spilling something on a guest. The problem with both of those scenarios is that we are trying to limit the number of people who know what's going on. After all, it's always possible that the member of staff we told might turn out to be the killer."

"Actually, thinking about it, neither option is really a problem, as all we need is for your operative to say that the wrong thing has been brought, it doesn't actually have to be the wrong thing," Tony pointed out.

"True; mind you, it seems a bit flimsy. The bloke that flew off the handle before was clearly a self-important idiot. It might seem odd to have two similar people quite so soon."

"I wouldn't throw that scenario out too soon, you do get a lot of self-important idiots staying in hotels and complaining about everything under the sun,"

It was clear from Tony's disparaging tone that it really must be a major source of irritation to the staff.

"I'm glad I work with plants and vegetables," David said thankfully.

"Oh, we deal with a lot of vegetables, too," Tony said with a bitter laugh.

"I think we need to think about this a bit more yet. I will contact the department tomorrow to see if they know yet who they are sending, as that might make it easier to decide."

Hearing that, Tony gave an internal sigh of relief. His memory was still refusing to co-operate with the request for it to provide him with even one concrete example of previous bad behaviour by guests that might work as a possible scenario. At least now, he would be able to go away and think about the issue without any immediate time pressures.

"Good idea, is there anything else we can decide tonight?"

"Not really, until we decide what the scenario is that we are going to use, we can't decide which member of staff to use."

"Ok, pass the Stella, it's time for a drink and to actually discuss my book. Although Vicky takes the piss, she is interested in it and she will ask if there has been any progress on it, so I need to have something for her."

"Ok, let me just get some wine, then I will update you on the editing and possible ways to get it published."

Tony and David spent the rest of the evening drinking Stella or wine respectively, though neither of them seemed driven to drink with the same sort of frenzy that had normally happened on previous occasions. This meant that they remained sober for much longer than usual and spent much longer discussing the suggestions that David had come up with and to come to an agreement of how they should proceed. Both of them were actually very pleased with what they were able to achieve, though neither of them actually said so aloud, as that would also be an implicit admittance of their past failings. About 11-30pm Tony decided it was time to call it a night and so he set off to catch the bus home. Unlike David, he couldn't be bothered to walk all the way to his own home. As far as he was concerned, buses wouldn't have been invented if people weren't meant to use them.

David decided to go to bed not that long after Tony left and pretty soon was snoring quite contentedly in his sleep, before descending into a deep and undisturbed sleep. The next morning dawned bright and clear and, as David had not overindulged on the alcohol front and gone to bed fairly early, he was actually quite alert and cheerful as he got out of bed. For the first time in a while, he was almost looking forward to a day doing a bit of good honest, physical labour.

Feeling even more cheerful after eating a good breakfast, he set off for work with a light step, pleasantly aware that all his aches and pains had fully gone. He collected his tools and drove to one of his newer clients who lived near Middleton. After a pleasant drive through the back roads of Derbyshire, he worked steadily throughout the morning, doing the myriad tasks that a garden required to keep it looking good.

About halfway through the morning, whilst taking a quick break, David abruptly realised that he had been so immersed in his work, he had forgotten to ring the department to find out which operatives were going to be sent to assist him.

With a cup of coffee in one hand, his phone in the other, David rang the department. He went through the usual protocols and was put through to Mark.

"Well, well," said Mark, "you're not missing us already, are you; it's only been a couple of days since we met?"

"Oh, shut up," was David's less than sarcastic response, "I am trying to plan how to set up the actual scenario of causing a scene and I need to know which operatives you are sending so I can tailor it to one of them."

"Right-ho," Mark responded, smiling to himself; he always liked to wind David up when he could, "We are sending you Natalie and Johnnie. Johnnie is there primarily to do the physical stuff and Natalie to do the organising and acting, which she's good at. She is also very good at the physical stuff too. Is that ok?"

"Yes, that's fine, I can certainly work with that. Obviously, we will need to meet beforehand to go through the details, so when would be the best time?"

"We thought it would be best if they were to come to your home for a review meeting on Sunday evening, just to check in with you. Are you going to be there about 7-30pm?"

"Make it 8pm and there's no problem. If me and Tony work out the scenario early enough, I'll let you know so you can give them the basic details."

"Ok, I'll tell them. Have fun."

"Thanks," said David, somewhat wryly, before Mark rang off.

David looked at his phone after he had finished talking to Mark and, worryingly, noted to himself that he was not finding holding such conversations with Mark at all disturbing, they were even starting to feel commonplace. He reminded himself he needed to be careful not to allow himself to be sucked back into the department by default rather than choice.

He returned his thoughts to the problem at the hotel.

'So, the guest will be a woman', thought David, finishing his coffee and then returning to work in the garden. His mind turned toward finding a scenario that would be convincing enough to create the situation he needed to draw out the killer/s. He thought seriously for half an hour, thinking up different scenarios which he hoped would be appropriate, but failed to come up with a really foolproof and acceptable one. In some desperation, he decided that when he stopped for lunch he had better text Tony to see if he could come up with any ideas of what sort of situation to set up, after all, it was Tony that had had actual experience of that kind of thing.

Two hours later, David stopped work and went to sit in his car to eat his lunch and text Tony. In between bites of his ham and salad sandwiches he wrote,

'Hi Tony, as the guest will be a woman, can you think of a suitable situation we can create'?

Before sending it he thought he had better add, 'so that the scene in Ch 10 is more realistic'. After all, you never knew who might read the text and he definitely didn't want to give Tony the opportunity to tell him he had made a security cock-up. A couple of minutes later he received a short response,

'A bit busy. Will get back to you later tonight'.

David swore, but then realised that his initial expectation had been totally unrealistic. After all, he had just spent about two hours trying to come up with something and had failed, so it was a little unfair to expect Tony to come up with a scenario in two minutes. Anyway, there wasn't any real need to have the scenario in place that night; the only important thing was to make sure that they had a viable plan in place by the Wednesday night, though he would obviously feel better if he had an actual plan to discuss with Johnnie and Natalie when he met them.

At the hotel, Tony was busy dealing with some new arrivals, so he was not able to give the matter any detailed thought. He knew he would be able to set aside some time before the evening was out to give the matter greater attention. It made no difference that the guest would be female as he had found that women were just as likely as men to complain about nothing.

Throughout the evening, whenever he had a bit of time, Tony tried to think of a convincing scenario for the set-up, but everything he thought of simply would not work practically. The main stumbling block centred on whether or not the member of staff was going to be informed about what was going on or whether they were kept in the dark. If the member of staff was fully up to date with the situation there were any number of possible scenarios, but, as David did not want to tell any more people than absolutely necessary, it meant that, in that case, it had to be either Tony or Chris that was the victim of the verbal abuse, as they were the only ones already fully aware of the situation, apart from the killer, obviously. The problem with that was Tony could think of no credible situation where either of them would be directly in a position to help create such a situation, as they spent most of their time in the background, overseeing operations and only dealt with problems with customers after they arose. The only member of staff that Tony was completely sure of was Vicky, who he had known and worked with for several years, so he thought that if they decided that they needed to tell someone, she was the only viable possibility.

There was, however, another problem of using a member of staff who was in on the set-up and that was making the whole situation look convincing. Obviously, the female from the department should be able to carry the situation off convincingly, but would a member of staff be able to act the part appropriately, if they actually knew what was going on. Tony was unsure; he didn't think that he would be able to act convincingly if he was in that position and he thought others would struggle, too. That meant it would be much better if they were able to come up with a scenario where the staff member had no idea it was all a put-up job and therefore, simply reacted naturally. That meant he had to choose a member of staff who was fairly thick-skinned, so they wouldn't be too traumatised by the event. However, Tony had to admit that most of the staff had probably received some sort of abuse from a guest; it went with the job, so you had to be fairly thick skinned, just to get through most shifts. Despite that, the identity of the member of staff would definitely still need some serious thought though.

As the evening wore on, the germ of an idea began forming in Tony's mind and so, later that evening he rang David and went through his thought processes on the issue to see if David agreed.
"Yes, I had come up with the same initial problems myself. Have you thought of any workable scenario, so far?"
"I have got one idea, but it needs thinking through a bit more."
"Can you give me some idea, just in case I can see an immediate problem?"
"Sure, your operative will be in the toilet opposite reception and a male member of staff will go in for some reason I haven't thought of yet and your operative will get upset and complain."

"Well, the basic idea could work, but make sure you think of a very practical and viable reason for sending a male member of staff into the women's toilets."

"I know, also I still need to think about which member of staff to use, too."

"Mmm, yes," David agreed, "think it over tonight and let me know what you have come up with tomorrow, can you? I'll leave the details to you, as you are much more likely than me to come up with something convincing related to the hotel."

"Ok, I'll ring tomorrow. See you."

"Yeah, see you."

Around one o'clock in the morning, Tony had been home for around half an hour, mostly spent lounging on his sofa, trying to wind down from work and think of a suitable scenario at the same time, but, so far, nothing was coming. 'Oh, stuff it', he thought after a few more unproductive moments, 'I'm too knackered to think straight, I'm going to bed. No point in trying to force it.'

Snuggling well down into his bed, his mind still groping for an answer to their problem, it was only a few moments before his tired mind closed itself down and he drifted into a deep sleep. Some time later, he came abruptly awake, momentarily confused as too what had woken him, until he realised that he had a viable plan fully set out in his head. He picked up his mobile to get the time. It was 5am; too early to get up, but he didn't want to go back to sleep because he knew, if he did, it was possible that he may well forget what his idea was. He switched on the bedside light and picked up the notebook he kept next to the bed, as most writers do. Quickly, he wrote down his idea and having recorded it, he felt he was then fully justified in switching the light off again and curling up under his duvet once more. Lying there, he felt a sense of satisfaction at his solution, and, basking in the warm glow of his idea, as well as the warmth of his bed, it didn't take him too long to slip back into sleep.

When he awoke, some time later, his mind was worrying about his solution, so the first thing he did was check his notebook to make sure he hadn't just dreamt he had found the solution. Thankfully, there were his words, scrawled on the page, briefly detailing his idea, and even better, he could actually read them. Over a leisurely breakfast he reread his idea and checked it for problems. Closing his eyes to think, he failed to notice the jam dripping from his toast, which he then managed to spread over half the sheet as he tried to wipe it away. Luckily, by now the main points were lodged in his brain so when he finished his breakfast, he was able to pick up his mobile and phone David.

"Hi," David greeted him when he answered his phone, "do I take it by the early timing of your call that you have come up with a solution for us? Mind you, when I use the term 'early', I mean early for you, I have been at work for a couple of hours already,"

"Good morning, my good man," Tony said, ignoring the sarcasm," I have indeed got a workable scenario for you,"

"Good, let's hear it then."

With that, Tony explained the proposed scenario whilst David listened and tried to find possible flaws in the explanation. Finding none, he congratulated Tony and told him he would inform the Department, so they could inform the operatives what was going to happen and to help Natalie, in particular, prepare for her scene.

Before he rang the department, David went over Tony's plan in his mind some more, just in case he could uncover any hidden problems. Confident that the plan was viable, an hour or so after he had finished discussing the plan with Tony, he rang the Department and was immediately transferred to Mark. He explained the plan and asked Mark to inform the operatives. His heart missed a beat and he did wonder what he was letting himself in for when Mark said,

"Oh, Natalie will enjoy that; she can be very theatrical when the mood takes her. I'm sure she will give a very convincing performance. It's almost a pity I won't be there to enjoy it."
Swallowing hard, David hoped that Mark was merely trying to wind him up, but there was something in Mark's voice which seemed to border on awe, convincing him Mark was telling the truth.

Whilst he was on the phone David also confirmed with Mark that the operatives were still going to visit him on Sunday evening to check on any last-minute details or changes. Confirming the arrangements, Mark seemed to be trying to keep some amusement out of his voice, and, as he rang off, though, David was certain he had heard Mark laughing out loud.
"Git," he shouted at the phone, though too late for Mark to hear; but David was now seriously worried about Natalie's upcoming performance.

Now that everything was pretty much organized, David was feeling more confident that they would be able to capture the murderer or murderers. He went back to work and spent the rest of the day weeding and cutting the grass for a client in Duffield, singing to himself as he worked, as well as going over the plans in his head. Everything seemed to be falling into place; however, just as David was finishing his work and was putting his tools back into his trailer, one final problem struck him. He would have to stay at the hotel during the period of the entrapment and so he would need an acceptable reason for being there for several days. He felt he needed to be in the hotel from early afternoon Tuesday onwards, at the latest. Whilst pretending to be drunk might be ok for one night, it wouldn't explain why he was there so long. Also, he had to be sure he had the use of room 12 and so couldn't leave it to chance, or the last minute; after all, the room might be given to another guest by one of the receptionists earlier in the week and so be unavailable. It would probably be best, therefore, he decided, that he booked into the hotel sometime on Monday. He had to make sure, therefore, that he came up with an acceptable, nonsuspicious reason for his being there for an extended period.

As he drove back to his rented garage, he tried to think of a good reason for being at the hotel, but still hadn't thought of anything concrete by the time he got home. Once home, he decided to shower before eating. Having turned on the shower, he undressed in his bedroom and returned to the bathroom. Stepping into the bath and under the shower, a blast of freezing water hit him. Swearing, he jumped back out again, wrapped his towel around his torso and went to look at the boiler. As he thought, there was a notice on the boiler's read out which said, 'Water pressure low'. Low water pressure stopped the boiler from firing up. Whilst it was a quick thing to fix, it gave him his idea for an excuse to stay at the hotel. He decided to say that his boiler had broken down and that his plumber had said it would take a few days to get the necessary part to fix it. He got dressed again and rang Tony straight away, hoping to catch him whilst he was still at home, so that their conversation would be private. He told him of the slight alteration to the plan and the need to make sure to keep room 12 available for him from Monday. Tony said it wouldn't be a problem; he would monitor the issuing of rooms over the weekend and make sure no-one was given room 12 before he arrived on Monday morning. David also reminded him that he had to keep room 15 available for Natalie.
"Really," Tony replied, sarcasm dripping from his voice, "I didn't know that, it's a good job you told me."
"Ok, ok, sorry about that. I was just thinking aloud."

Having apologised, David rang off and decided that he needed to try and forget about the operation for the rest of the evening. Instead, he thought it would be good to pamper himself and recharge his flagging batteries. His first act of pampering would be to take a long, hot shower, which meant he had to fix the boiler first. He climbed the stairs to the third floor where his

154

boiler was housed and reached under the front panel of the boiler to make the necessary adjustments. Opening the two feeder valves, he bled some water back into the system until it reached the correct pressure. Having done that, he returned to the bathroom, turned on the shower to make sure it was working, before getting undressed again. Stepping into the shower he took a long time over his shower, enjoying the heat relaxing his body, before he got out. Having toweled himself dry, he then rubbed liniment on his muscles to keep them loose. Feeling relaxed and clean, he turned his attention to his evening meal, deciding to heat up one of the meals he had previously cooked and kept frozen. After a moment's thought, he chose to eat a vegetable chili which, after he had thoroughly defrosted it, he then warmed it to eat as a burrito with cheese, tomatoes, lettuce, salsa and sour cream, accompanied by a very pleasant glass or two of Ripasso and some good music. Fortuitously, he even found that he still had a portion of ice cream in the freezer, which, when augmented with some Frangelico and wafers, made a very appetizing dessert. In this way, a very pleasant evening ensued, until David decided it was time he went to bed.

Over breakfast the next day, he decided that, as he still had four days to wait until the whole thing kicked off, he would keep himself occupied by working at his gardening jobs all through the weekend. That way he would keep his days occupied and help keep his mind off the upcoming operation. However, it also had the benefit of allowing him to take the following Tuesday to Thursday off from his gardening jobs, if he needed to, without having to worry about leaving work undone. David did find it rather bizarre, though, that he was so concerned about his gardening clients, in view of what was about to happen, but he had always believed in doing a job properly and he saw no reason why he should change his outlook now.

With that in mind, he checked on the weather forecast for the weekend, just to get a rough guide only, as the forecast often changed drastically overnight, let alone over a few days. He worked out whose gardens he would be able to work on over the weekend. After all, not all of his clients wanted him working at the weekend; especially if that was the only time they themselves got to spend enjoying their garden. Luckily, a couple of his clients had already told him they would be away over that weekend and so it would not be a problem if he worked on them.

For Chris and Tony, however, the whole situation was completely out of their comfort zone and the days seemed to be crawling by until the operatives were due to arrive and, potentially, they would get their hotel back. As each hour passed slowly by, they were becoming more and more anxious, constantly thinking of potential disasters and the possibility of losing their livelihoods and any raised voices set off a sense of panic in them. It was no surprise, therefore, that Tony texted David several times to make sure everything was still ok. Even understanding why they were so anxious, it still began to annoy David, until he could contain himself no longer and sent him a text telling him to chill; everything was fine and going to plan. Whilst this may have had the effect of stopping the texts, it, naturally, had no effect on their steadily escalating levels of anxiety.

"Are you sure we're doing the right thing?" Chris asked Tony for about the twentieth time in two days,

"David says it will be fine, and anyway, what else can we do now? We need to catch whoever is doing this and we can't go to the police now."

"Yeah, I know, but I wish it was all over, don't you?"

"The sensible, practical part of me does, but the hidden, darker part of me is finding it all kind of exciting."

"Yeah, well, I can do without it, I can tell you. My heart is thumping already and there are still a few days to go. God knows what state I will be in by Wednesday."

As for David, he quietly went about his gardening duties, keeping himself occupied during the day, working at a variety of gardens in the local area, though that didn't stop him from regularly finding himself absently reviewing the plan and going over all sorts of possible scenarios for how the trap might play out. When he caught himself, he would cough quietly and sarcastically compliment himself for his thoroughness, then tell himself to concentrate on his gardening and leave the plan alone. Not that these self recriminations worked too well in stopping his wandering mind as, more often than not, only a short time later he would catch himself thinking about the plan again. In the evenings he would try to keep himself occupied by carrying out his household chores, watching some of his favourite DVD's and having the odd drink of wine. The one thing that did surprise him, though, was that he didn't seem to dream about the upcoming operation, but actually slept rather well, which was pleasantly surprising, although working in the fresh air all day definitely had a soporific effect at night.

He did a full day's gardening on Sunday, back at his client in Hazelwood, and set off for home around 5pm. As he hadn't needed to bring his trailer that day, he decided to enjoy himself by throwing his car around the twisty corners as he had been trained to do. He was approaching one particularly tricky corner when he noticed a young woman standing by the road talking on the phone. At first, he was sure that the woman was his ex-girlfriend and turned to look at her as he passed. With a mixture of relief, tinged with sadness, he saw it wasn't her, just a very close resemblance. Momentarily unfocussed, he forced his mind back to the road, just as a black Range Rover came round the bend, on his side of the road.

"What the fuck," he swore as he wrenched at the wheel to avoid the car which appeared to make no effort to get back to its own side of the road. Without conscious thought, his past training took over. Changing down, he braked hard, before hitting the accelerator again to try and regain traction on the front wheels.

Pulling at the steering wheel, he tried to swerve back towards the road so as to avoid the ditch which he knew ran along the left-hand side of the road. Gravel and grass spewed from the tyres as they fought for grip. Still accelerating, David sawed at the steering wheel as his car jolted over the rough grass. After what felt like an eternity, one front wheel managed to find traction on the tarmac at the edge of the grass, giving him some control. The rear though, was still fishtailing as the car lurched back on to the road. With all four wheels now back on the road David quickly brought the car under full control. Braking to a halt, he saw the Range Rover disappearing in his mirror. Swearing again, instinct made him decide to chase after it, lunatics like that should not be allowed on the road. He quickly found a wide drive to turn round in and swerved into it. As he spun round in the drive, a large lorry drove slowly past, making him wait. Every nerve end was screaming at him to get after the Rover. After what seemed an age of futile fuming, he pulled out behind the lorry, following it round the sharp bend in pursuit of the Rover. Cursing the lorry's slow speed, he had to wait until he was completely round the corner before he could pass it and then go in pursuit. However, the delay meant there was now no sign of the Rover and after a minute David arrived at the junction near the Bridge Inn. He pulled into the pub car park to take stock. It was a three-way junction and he had no idea which way the Rover would have gone. Reluctantly, he decided he may as well go home. Driving slowly, he approached the corner where he had nearly crashed, noticing there was no sign of the woman who had been standing there earlier. He didn't see her on the road anywhere nearby and idly wondered where she had gone, as he continued his drive home.

When he had parked up, for once finding a space outside his house, he sat for a few minutes thinking about his near miss. Initially he had thought it was just another of the many idiotic drivers, going too fast round the corner, but some little details were concerning him, particularly the disappearing woman who looked so much like his ex and had distracted him just as the Rover came round the corner. Secondly, there was the look of the black Range Rover, which was very much standard issue for operatives in his former line of work. He also remembered the look on the driver's face as they passed. He had looked cool and collected as he had stared at David, with no sign of fear or panic. He decided the incident might not be as innocent as it seemed and it would be good to be on his guard over the next week. With that, he got out, quickly checked his car for damage and finding nothing other than dirt, he unlocked his front door and went into his house.

As David was checking his car, Joshua received a call telling him that the attempt to disable David had failed. After swearing quietly for a few seconds, he put a call through to his boss,
"Good evening Sir, it seems our operatives failed to disable David. Apparently, he was good enough to take effective evasive action and avoid crashing. The operative did not want to deliberately hit him as that would have been too obvious."
"Damn."
"Do you want me to try something else?"
"No, that would certainly be too suspicious; we don't want Sir Peter to know that someone is trying to interfere with his operation."
"Ok, do you want me to warn the operatives dealing with the Hotel?"
"No. Let them take their chances. I still think it will be good test at this stage to see how robust the operation is. Oh, and let's have a few contingency plans in place to deal with whatever happens."
"Very good, Sir."

After showering, David cooked himself some pasta for his evening meal and tidied the house a bit before Johnnie and Natalie arrived. He particularly made sure the bathroom was clean and looked presentable. He may be a single male living alone, but he always made sure his home was basically clean and tidy, but not spotless. He believed that too clean a house was unhealthy, you needed a certain number of germs to keep up the immune system and, anyway, there were other, more interesting, things to do in life than constantly cleaning.

So it was that on Sunday evening both he and his home were ready for visitors when there was a knock on his door. On checking the spy hole, he saw that it was Johnnie and a woman he presumed was Natalie. As he recognized Johnnie, he let them into his house. He had lit a fire in his old-fashioned range and the kitchen was pleasantly warm and welcoming.
"Very domestic," Johnnie said, somewhat sarcastically, though David thought that he detected a hint of wistfulness underlying his comment. Johnnie vaguely waved his arm in Natalie's direction, saying,
"This is Natalie, as you probably gathered; Natalie, David."
David looked at her, noting the confident way she held herself as she looked back at him. She took a moment to look around the kitchen, before commenting,
"Charming old-world ambiance. Pleased to meet you after all this time."
"Thanks, I like it," replied David, "it suits my personality, a mixture of solid, old-fashioned functionality and those few modern gadgets that are actually useful."
"Do those modern gadgets include an electric kettle? I could do with a cup of coffee?" Johnnie exclaimed.
"No, the kettle is on the range, that's where I do a lot of my cooking when I have the fire going. It's nearly boiled, anyway. Sit down."

With that he moved the kettle to the hottest part of the range and got some mugs ready for some drinks as the other two sat down.

"Tea or coffee?" he asked Natalie.

"Tea, please."

By the time he had got everything ready, the kettle had started to boil, so he quickly made coffee for Johnnie and tea for Natalie and himself. Then, without any conscious thought, they all moved their chairs closer to the fire and arranged themselves comfortably and began to discuss the final arrangements of the operation.

Although Johnnie and Natalie had been briefed by Mark, David went over the basic plan that he had agreed with Tony and went through the timings of how it would work. Natalie was confident she could carry off her role but added that she would check out the site when she had checked into the hotel. After that the discussion turned more towards the set up for how they were going to with the killer/killers, should they take the bait. David confirmed that both Johnnie and Natalie would be together in the room awaiting the arrival of the killers, whose modus operandi, up to this point anyway, appeared to be striking in the early hours of the morning when the hotel was quiet.

"Where will you be?" Natalie asked.

"In room 12, three doors away down the hall, watching through the camera. Once the killer or killers have passed my room, I will alert you by radio and then, when they have rounded the corner of the corridor, I will follow to block off any escape. Your room is at the end of the corridor and the only way out is back the way they came, so they can't escape without passing me."

"Sounds good, is the camera in place."

"Not yet, I will be staying at the hotel from tomorrow, so I will be able to set it up and check that it all works. Tony knows to keep that room available for me so there shouldn't be any problem there."

"When do I create my scene at the hotel?"

"I have arranged with Tony for it to be sometime around 4pm on Wednesday."

Natalie thought for a moment and then said,

"In that case I think I need to get to the hotel on Tuesday evening. "It would be highly suspicious if I were to arrive on Wednesday and get involved in the altercation straight away. Arriving on Tuesday will also give me time to get the lie of the hotel, so if anything does go wrong with the plan, I would know what's where and can improvise."

"Good idea," agreed David, "I have told Tony to provisionally reserve your room from Monday night anyway, to make sure it was available. Once you arrive you can get yourself set up and become known to the staff."

"Fine, do I need to ring up and tell the hotel it will be Tuesday?"

"Yes, you are booked in the name of Ms Wilson."

"Ok, what's the number of the hotel?"

David told her the number and she rang the hotel and confirmed her booking for the following Tuesday evening under her cover name.

"What time do I need to get there on Wednesday?" asked Johnnie.

"You don't want to be hanging around and stuck in the room for too long, so shall we say about 9 pm. There is a corridor between the bar and the toilets so, if you have a drink with me in the bar, Natalie can walk past you to the toilets. Give her a few minutes and then you can go to the toilet also, that way you can pass in the corridor and she can pass you the key to the room. You go up to the room and wait there and Natalie can join you around eleven."

"Sounds good, what about you?" Johnnie enquired.

"I will go to my room a few minutes after Natalie. I will monitor the bar to see if anybody appears to be keeping an eye on her. Once I get to my room, I will be able to use the camera and monitor the corridor to see what's happening and warn you if anyone suspicious heads towards your room. Have you got the radios?"

"Yes, they're in my bag. Do you want to test them now?

"No, just give me mine and Natalie can have the other for when she arrives at the hotel, that way we can check them out on Wednesday evening for when we need them."

"Ok," Johnnie said, getting a radio out of his bag and handing it to David.

"Make sure you are in your room at seven o'clock Wednesday evening so we can do the test," David told Natalie.

"Ok."

"Oh and put your 'Do Not Disturb' sign on your door on Wednesday, we don't want the cleaning staff finding the radio."

"No problem, would you also like to give me instructions on how to breathe, as well?" Natalie asked sarcastically.

David looked at her quickly, noting she was smiling at him. He gave a quick self- deprecating laugh,

"Sorry, I've been out of the game for a few years; it was a bit obvious wasn't it. I'll shut up now and let you get on with your job."

"Don't worry about it," Natalie responded, "I just wanted you to know I'm a professional."

"Right, is there anything else we need to discuss?"

"I don't think so."

Whilst he had been talking to them, David had decided he would tell them about the incident earlier; it wasn't that he trusted them yet, but he wanted to watch their reactions to see if he could detect any suspicious response.

"There is one other thing I want to discuss," he said and went on to detail the near miss earlier, along with his suspicions. As he was speaking, he watched them both as they processed the information, before asking,

"Is there any reason that I might be a target of inter-departmental rivalry?"

"Not that I know of," said Natalie, but then I am only low level, but it is always possible that another department is also working on this."

Turning to Johnnie, she added,

"Have you heard anything?"

Johnnie shook his head, saying,

"No; nothing."

David had watched them both throughout the exchange and was convinced that they didn't know anything about it, but that could just mean that they hadn't been told.

"The other option is that it was the killers from the hotel, but if it was them why didn't they just kill me, they have had plenty of chances, especially when they let me go before."

"Let you go?" both Natalie and Johnnie exclaimed simultaneously.

"Yes, they jumped me when I went intervene once, but they let me go, saying I wasn't the one they had been sent to kill."

"Interesting," said Johnnie.

"Yes, very, but if they let you go then, why would they try to kill you now?" asked Natalie.

"I don't know," David was forced to concede. "I suppose there is the possibility that it was simply an accident, though my instinct tells me it wasn't."

"Oh well, all we can do is continue and be on the look out," said Natalie.

The other two nodded before Johnnie asked, "Have you told Mark about it, he might know more, but if he did, I am sure he would have warned us."

David wasn't completely convinced about that, but said nothing apart from saying he hadn't had chance to talk with Mark yet.

As there did not seem to be any other business to discuss, David asked,

"Ok, do you want to get off or do you fancy some alcohol?"

Natalie and Johnnie looked at each other and Natalie raised her hand in the universal gesture of someone miming a drink. Johnnie nodded and Natalie said,

"Ok, alcohol it is, what have you got to offer?"

"I have quite a well stocked drinks cabinet. You can have beer, wine, white, red, even sparkly, or a range of spirits."

"Who needs a pub," Natalie laughed, "I'll have some red wine to start with."

"To start with?" queried Johnnie.

"Yes, to start with. You're driving and the hotel we're staying at tonight is cheap and not particularly cheerful. Anyway, you don't drink much so I'll have your share."

"Ok," Johnnie laughed, "be my guest. Have you got any lemonade so I can have shandies?"

David nodded and rose to get the drinks. He found glasses, opened wine and beer bottles, as well as putting some snacks in bowls. He put some logs on the fire and then settled down with the other two.

Now that they weren't discussing the details of the job, conversation was a little stilted, at least to start with, as they looked for the boundaries of what they could and could not discuss but, as is usually the case, it got easier as the night progressed, and the relaxing influence of the drink kicked in. Whilst Natalie and Johnnie were willing to discuss their work and the Department, it was only in generalities, nothing specific but they were interested in David's story, as Natalie had joined the department after he left, and had no real understanding of who he was, whilst Johnnie had only known him for a very short time before he left the department. David, in his turn, also only talked in generalities about his time there but was slightly more forthcoming about his reasons for leaving.

"It was a slow process. I started to think that some of the jobs we did were not really our province and maybe our solutions were a bit drastic and possibly unnecessary. Then, one of the jobs I was overseeing got a bit messy, due to some incorrect intel from another department. After that, I decided I needed a break. When I left, I wasn't sure how long it would be for, or whether it was going to be permanent."

"Do you ever miss it?" Natalie asked.

"Some of it; I always enjoyed the planning and problem solving."

"Have you ever thought of going back?"

"No," David lied. He wasn't going to tell them what he had been thinking, after all, they would probably report back and David didn't want the boss to think he had an edge over him, because David knew he would not hesitate to try to use it somehow.

When David finished, there was a companionable silence, whilst they all thought about what he had said, until Natalie asked if she could see the rest of David's house. David just waved his hand and said,

"Help yourself."

Natalie went off to look at the rest of the house whilst David got some more drinks. When she had left the room, David asked Johnnie how long she had been in the department.

"Two-three years."

"How come she is leading your side of the operation and not you? You are the more experienced, after all."

Johnnie shrugged, before saying,

"Mark put her in charge; they want her to get experience making live decisions in the field."

"They must have a lot of faith in her."

"They do, but some of the older operatives weren't so welcoming."

"How did Natalie deal with that?"

"Oh, she quickly changed their minds for them." Johnnie laughed. "She doesn't take crap from anyone, and the boss clearly respects her, so they keep their views to themselves."

They both relapsed into silence as they thought about what Johnnie had just said. After a couple of minutes though, Johnnie asked,

"Where did you learn about gardening, it's not something that is used a great deal in our line of work, except maybe the digging part?" Johnnie noted.

David laughed in agreement, then added,

"When I was young, I used to help in the garden, particularly in the vegetable plot. I learnt all the techniques there. When I left the department, I sort of got into it by accident. When I moved here, I would advise the neighbours how and when to plant seeds or plants, that then expanded to talking to them about when and how to prune them. It wasn't long then before I was asked if I would like to do some gardening for some of their friends and then it just sort of escalated. Obviously, I had to do a bit of rebuilding of my skills, but 'YouTube' has been very helpful in that aspect."

Just then Natalie returned from her inspection of the house.

"Very nice," she complimented him, "I loved the attic. Did you do all the shelving yourself?"

"Indeed I did, I can turn my hand to almost anything. I built all the units in this kitchen as well. Did you want another drink?"

"I thought you would never ask."

"Sorry, I don't entertain very often these days. Anyway, don't wait for me to ask, just help yourself when you want one."

"I heard you ask Johnnie about me, is there anything else you want to know?"

"Nothing special, I was just curious why he wasn't in charge."

"Do you have a problem with female operatives?"

"Not in the slightest, why do you ask?"

"I've found that many blokes have a real problem, they see it as an affront to their masculinity or something. If it's a problem I like to sort it straight away."

"If you can give and take serious banter, we will be fine."

"Oh, that's no problem I can assure you."

"Good. Now, let's settle down to some good drinking."

"Amen to that," agreed Natalie.

After that the evening continued pleasantly with alcohol and desultory conversation. The thing that pleased David was that none of them were bothered if there were periods of silence. In some way, each of them with their similar experiences, were able to enjoy each other's company without the need for constant conversation, much to David's approval. He had never been one to talk just for the sake of talking, or to cover the sound of silence.

Sometime later Johnnie stirred himself and said it was time to go. Natalie and David stirred themselves from their reveries too and David went to turn the outside light on for them, as Johnnie and Natalie collected their gear.

"Thanks for the drinks, see you on Wednesday," said Johnnie.

"Yeah, thanks," added Natalie, "I'll see you Tuesday but, don't worry," she added, a smile passing fleetingly across her face, "I won't talk to you."

Chapter 13.

That Should Get their Attention.

Once they had gone, David decided not to bother tidying up the few glasses, bottles and bowls they had used, they weren't going anywhere after all, deciding to just go to bed, where, very quickly, he fell asleep.

David woke with the alarm next morning and, after a few moments lying in bed reflecting on the night before, he metaphorically girded his loins and clambered out of bed. He dressed for work, before he opened the curtains to look out the window and check on the weather. The sky was filled with dark clouds, but, at the moment at least, it was dry, so it appeared that the weather forecast was half right, which made a pleasant change. He had lost count of the number of times he had gone to bed expecting sunshine, only to find it throwing it down, or vice versa, in the morning. After a good breakfast, he set off for work at a garden in Milford, safe in the knowledge that he only had the morning to work, so if it rained later, it wouldn't be a problem. He worked for four hours before returning his trailer to its garage and driving home to have some lunch.

Before setting off for the hotel, David called Mark at the department, having decided to report his suspicions regarding the accident. After the usual routine he was put through to Mark.
"Good afternoon David, I didn't expect to hear from you. Is there a problem?"
"Not necessarily, I just wanted to let you know about something suspicious that happened yesterday."

With that David explained the events surrounding the near accident, making special mention of the vehicle and the disappearing woman. Mark listened carefully and when David had finished, asked,

"What do you think? Do you think it was just an idiot driver or an attempt to take you out?"

"I don't know for certain, but I think we need to take the chance of it being deliberate seriously."

"Ok, I will tell the boss. Do Johnnie and Natalie know?"

"Yes, I discussed it with them last night."

"Well, make sure you stay alert until it's over."

"Oh, we will, don't worry."

"Good."

With that they ended the call and David got his car keys and set off. He arrived at the Hotel at around 2-30 pm, knowing that Tony would be loitering in the office behind the reception.

Whist David set off for the hotel, Mark went to see his boss.

"David has just called, he thinks someone might have tried to take him out."

Sir Peter looked thoughtful,

"Thinks, or is certain."

"He's not sure," said Mark, giving the details. When he had finished, Sir Peter sat quiet for a few moments before commenting,

"I think we need to take it seriously, David wouldn't have said anything if he wasn't pretty sure. That means what is going on at the hotel must be part of the larger operation we have had vague hints about. It also means that it must be some large government organisation running it."

"I agree, but what concerns me is that to set up the attempt on David, they must know a fair amount about him, which they shouldn't," said Mark.

"Mmm, yes. That means they had to get his details from our records. I think you need to do some careful investigating in case we have a leak."

"I'll get straight on it. We don't want other people knowing our secrets."

"No, we don't. However, if you find do find a leak don't take precipitate action, we might be able to use the situation to our advantage."

"Yes Sir."

When David arrived at the hotel, he saw Nathan was on reception, which made things easier, as he wouldn't ask a load of possibly awkward questions.

"Hi," greeted Nathan, "how are you?"

"Me, I'm fine, however, my boiler isn't. Have you got a room I can use for a few days until it is repaired? I haven't got any heating or hot water. I'm not bothered by the heating, but I do tend to need a shower at the end of the working day."

As arranged, just then Tony emerged from the office.

"I thought I heard your dulcet tones, how are you my good man?"

"David says he needs a room for a few days."

"Yes, I heard. Let him have room 12, that's not needed for a few days."

"No problem," said Nathan, turning back to his computer to register David onto the system.

"Thanks," said David, "I really didn't fancy spending a few days without being able to have a good shower. Now I know I have a room, I'll just nip home and get a few clothes; I'll see you later this evening."

"Ok, see you in a bit," said Tony.

Nathan gave a perfunctory wave as David turned to leave.

David drove the 10 minutes home and, after making a cup of tea, went upstairs to pack his travel bag before settling down for a few hours until it was time to return to the hotel. He decided to have his evening meal at home before going back to the hotel, not wanting to spend too much time in his hotel room; or in the bar either. Around eight o'clock that evening that he arrived at the reception and told the evening receptionist that he was booked into room 12. Although he couldn't remember the name of the receptionist, he did recognise her and she obviously knew him.

"Hi David, Tony said you would be in sometime. Boiler problems, I hear. That happened to me not long ago, too. It's a real pain, isn't it?"

"Yeah, it is, I'm just glad all the rooms here hadn't gone, otherwise I would have had to spend a few cold nights at home, and probably have gotten very smelly too."

The receptionist laughed, sniffed a couple of times, wrinkled her nose and handed him his key.

"Well, at least you can have a shower now, if you want," she exclaimed laughing.

"That's just what I intend to do."

David picked up his bag, smiled at the receptionist, before he walked up the two flights of stairs to get to his room. Once there, he quickly unpacked his few belongings, had a quick shower to maintain his cover story before he returned to the bar for a drink and to check in with Tony.

A short time later he made his way back downstairs, passing the reception where the receptionist smiled and asked,

"Do you feel better now?"

"I feel cleaner, I will feel better when I've had a drink or two."

The receptionist gave a pleasant laugh, then said,

"Enjoy."

"Oh, I will," David replied, before making the short walk to the bar.

He walked to the bar and one of the barmen, whose name he thought was Simon, said to him,

"Boiler problems, I hear."

"Bloody hell," David burst out, "has Tony told everyone in the hotel about my boiler problems?"

"Probably not everyone, but quite a few," responded Simon, "is it a Peroni, as usual?

David nodded.

"Are you paying now, or shall I put on your room?"

"You may as well put it on my room tab; it will be so much easier when I only have to pay once."

"No problem, what number?"

"12."

David spent the next couple of hours drinking sparingly from his Peroni and sporadically watching the TV screen in the corner of the room. As the evening progressed, Tony joined him briefly for a drink before resuming his duties. Around 11-30 pm. David decided that he would go up to his room, watch a little TV and then get some sleep. He was pleased to note that he was not at all interested in consuming a large amount of alcohol, so staying in the bar seemed rather pointless. Once in his room, he half watched the TV for about an hour, though, if anyone had asked him, he would have been hard put to remember what programme he had actually watched. As silence settled on the hotel, David undressed, got into bed, hoping for a good night's sleep.

The next morning dawned, bright and clear and he went down to breakfast fairly early, before preparing to go to work, not wanting to hang around at the hotel as it would have driven him crazy. He drove home, put his work clothes on and set off, intending to work until around 4 pm. He decided to work in the garden at Middleton, a drive through the back roads, of around 20 minutes. The weather stayed dry throughout the day and so David was able to get a lot of the preparation work done on the path he had to lay next to the house. He set out a wooden frame to work within, put down the hardcore and tamped it down firmly. After having a quick lunch, he made a concrete mix and then carefully started to lay the eight slabs that formed the path, ensuring there was a slight slope away from the house for rainwater to run off. It took a couple more concrete mixes before he had laid all eight slabs. When he had finished laying the slabs and checking they were level with each other, he loaded his trailer before driving back to Milford and returning his trailer to its garage. He went home for a drink and to pick up some clothes, before returning to the hotel around 7 pm.

Before he went up to his room to shower, he went to ask Vicky if there would be a table in the pizza bar around 45 minutes later. Vicky nodded that was fine and so he went for his shower. He enjoyed a hot and quite lengthy shower, before getting dressed to go down for his pizza. He had thought about going to the restaurant, but in the end, decided on a pizza, as he thought it would be better not to eat in the restaurant, as he didn't want to be there if Natalie was. Not that he doubted her professionalism; it would just be easier for Natalie to be there on her own. He wanted to make sure that there was no chance of anyone making a connection between the two of them.

As usual, Vicky had given him a table at the edge of the room, so he was able people watch. When he had finished his meal, he went to the pay station to pay for his meal as usual, but Vicky just laughed at him, playfully chastising him in mock serious tones,
"David, you are a guest at the hotel for a few days, so I have put the meal on your room tab, go and enjoy a drink in the bar, where the barman will also put your drinks on your room."
Realizing she was right, he grinned and took himself to the bar, saying as he left,
"Thank you, thank you, thank you, oh glorious one."

As he reached the bar, the barman was talking on his radio headset, so David waited until he had finished. He was just about to order his Peroni when the barman held up his hand to stop him, whilst walking to the pumps to pull a pint. When it was full, he placed it on the bar in front of David, saying,

"Vicky asked me to tell you that I have put this, and will put, all succeeding drinks on your room."

David mouthed a silent obscenity at him and at Vicky, before walking off with his pint. As he walked away, he heard the barman laugh, which just made David laugh too in response. As he sat down at a free table, he found himself thinking 'how can any one of them be a murderer, I just don't believe it'.

He was halfway through his pint when Tony came over to join him, bringing another couple of drinks with him. He sat down and looked enquiringly at him. David, noting the proximity of some of the customers, almost imperceptibly shook his head and then asked, loud enough to be heard at the nearby tables,

"Is there anyone here you haven't told about my boiler?"

Taking his cue very quickly Tony responded,

"I did miss one or two members of staff, but I have put a message on the notice board for those I missed. I didn't want you to be bothered by curious staff asking why you were staying here, especially when you weren't drunk."

"That's so kind of you; I am overwhelmed by your solicitousness."

"Don't mention it."

"Ok, I won't." David said with a laugh.

"Cheers," Tony raised his glass.

"Cheers." David responded, raising his glass in salute.

Just then, the couple at the next table got up to leave and once they had gone and there was no-one else seated near them, David asked if Natalie had checked in.

"Oh yes, she checked in around six o'clock. Is everything set for tomorrow?"

"Yes, it's all in place from our side. Are you still ok with what you have to do?"

"Oh yeah, it's not going to be a problem."

"Good; make sure it's in place for around four o'clock tomorrow afternoon."

"Yeah, it's sorted. Don't worry."

"Look, a lot of things could still go wrong, so I will continue to worry until it's over."

"What can go wrong?"

"Do you want me to give you a list? Have you got an hour spare?"

Tony looked at David to see if he was joking, but quickly realising he wasn't, he gulped and said,

"Bloody Hell."

"Indeed," was David sparing response.

Tony finished his drink, a little chastened and then went back to his duties as was his normal routine, before he would rejoin David at the end of his shift, though the timing of that did tend to be a bit flexible, David had noticed. Sometimes it seemed that Tony worked almost non-stop when he was at the hotel, often even when he was supposed to be off shift. David was very glad he didn't work in the hotel trade; it appeared to be very hard work for not a lot of pay. Managers such as Tony had to deal not only with customers who could be complete and utter assholes but also with a lot of staff who were transient, uncommitted and only doing the job to get them through college or university. David sighed in sympathy with the absent Tony and thought, 'rather you than me mate.'

A little later, Natalie walked into the bar and sat at one of the free tables in the section reserved for waiter service. She ignored David completely and waited for a waiter to take her order. When he came to her table to ask what she wanted, she turned a disdainful face to him and answered,

"I'd like a large red wine, please; a good one, and hopefully I'd like it a bit quicker than it took someone to come and take my order."

She didn't speak loudly but somehow her voice carried to most of the bar. Several of the customers and staff looked up, sizing her up briefly, before returning their focus to what they were doing, either serving in the case of the staff, or dealing with the results of being served, for the customers. David surreptitiously watched her out of professional interest.

"Of course, madam. What wine would you like?" the waiter responded, though his words were a little unclear as they appeared to be spoken through gritted teeth.

"I will let you choose for me, as long as it is full bodied." Natalie said.

"Of course, madam," I will see what the barman recommends."

The waiter walked over to the bar, where the barman was already pouring a large glass of red wine. He spoke quietly to the waiter, who then returned to Natalie's table and placed the wine in front of her.

David waited rather nervously for how Natalie would respond to the wine, hoping she wouldn't make a fuss. The last thing they needed was for Natalie to make a scene just then, as they obviously weren't set up to deal with a situation that night. The waiter informed her,

"The barman has recommended this for you, it is a Chilean Carmenere; he hopes you like it, but will willingly change it if you don't."

'Don't make a fuss, please, don't make a fuss, please, don't make a fuss, please', David was trying to send his thought telepathically to Natalie as she picked up her glass in something of a studied way, swirling the wine around the glass a couple of times. She paused a little, seemingly intent on increasing the tension, before sniffing at the aroma of the wine. David found himself leaning forward, drawn into her performance. He forced himself to sit back in his sofa, whilst Natalie finally put the glass to her lips and took a sip of wine. After a moment, she turned to the waiter and gave him a warm smile,

"Thank you; that is a very pleasant wine, the barman made an excellent choice."

As she spoke, David could almost see the waiter visibly relax, as did the barman, who had been anxiously watching to see what happened, though in his case, from behind the relative safety of the bar. David pursed his lips and quietly blew his breath out, feeling himself relax too.

"Very good madam, are you a guest here?"

"Yes, I am."

"Shall I put it on your room then?"

"Yes please, room 15," Natalie replied as she took another sip of wine before adding, "You know, this really is a very good wine, thank you."

As she said that, she smiled slightly and looked round the room, her smile lingering fleetingly on David before passing round the rest of the room. As the waiter left, smiling once more, David noted that Natalie's performance had been exquisitely subtle. He understood that, not only had she created the persona of a demanding guest, on the one hand, but had also shown the staff that she appreciated good service. Interestingly, David was certain that the performance had also been for his benefit, to make it clear to him that she was very professional. 'Not bad for one small scene,' David thought to himself, taking another sip from his pint to hide his small smile of appreciation.

The rest of the evening passed quietly, Natalie finished her drink and went up to her room, without looking at David. David was busy checking whether any of the staff or customers appeared to pay her more than usual attention, but, as far as he could tell, it didn't appear that anyone was watching her.

Tony joined David around 11 O'clock and, for once, they both drank sparingly, talking little and only tending to make each other more nervous than if they'd been on their own, until David, still sober, stood up to go to his room around 11-30pm.

There were two good reasons for this, he was, after all, only supposed to be at the hotel whilst his boiler was broken, so he still had to be at work relatively early in the morning, treating the day as a normal working day. The second, more important reason, was that he still had to install the secret camera in the corridor outside his room and he wanted to be sober when he attempted that.

Whilst he was waiting in his room for the hotel to quiet down so that he could install the camera, he carefully went through the instructions he had been sent, both in terms of installing the outside camera into the smoke alarm, and also how to use the monitor to get the best camera pictures. After that, he waited for Tony to arrive to keep watch whilst he fitted the camera, spending the intervening time thinking about the scene that Natalie had to create the following afternoon. He decided he didn't need to be in the hotel when Natalie had her little scene. She had fully convinced him of her professionalism, so he wanted to maintain a clear distance between the two of them so that any prospective killer had no reason to connect the two of them. He now trusted her theatrical skills completely after the subtlety of her little performance in the bar and he was also sure that Tony would do his part competently. In view of that, he decided he would put in a full day's gardening and get back to the hotel around six in the evening. The weather forecast was pretty good so he should be able to get a full day's work in. The forecast suggested there was some chance of rain, but for most of the day they put the percentage at somewhere between 10-20 %. Mind you, it had to be said, he had often found that it often seemed to rain more when the percentage was 10 than when it was 60.

As arranged earlier, Tony came up to David's room when everyone had either gone to bed or left to go home. He was going to guard the end of the corridor to make sure no one interrupted David whilst he was busy with the surveillance camera. Tony arrived about 12-30 am, knocked quietly on David's door and then waited. David picked up his equipment and went outside to join him. He handed Tony the bag containing the equipment, then went back inside his room to get the chair he needed to stand on. Carrying the chair, he placed it underneath the smoke alarm and fetched his bag from Tony. It was a very simple operation to replace the smoke alarm with the equipment the department had lent him, which incorporated a spy camera into a functioning smoke alarm. All David had to do was undo a couple of screws, replace the unit with the new improved version, retighten the screws and the job was done. Only five minutes after he started, David returned to give his bag to Tony, who looked worried at David's speedy return, asking quietly,

"God, is there a problem, won't it fit or something?"

"Calm down, it's done. It's ready to test."

"Bloody hell, that was quick," relief clear in his voice.

"Yes, it was a very impressive piece of kit I have to admit."

David went back to reclaim his chair and return it to his room as Tony followed him in, still carrying his equipment bag which he put down on the table.

"OK, let's test it to make sure everything works."

With that David withdrew a small, phone like device from the bag. He handed it to Tony, saying,

"Hold that whilst I try and remember the activation code."

"So how do you set it up?"

"Easy, just let me put the security code into this, then, all I need is the hotel's wi-fi code. Do you know what it is?"

"Hang on," Tony said, as he took out his wallet and extracted a card, which he passed to David. "That's the code, though, actually, it should also be in the draw of the unit the TV is on."

David, put the wi-fi code into the monitor, pressed the enter key and waited. After a few seconds, they were rewarded by seeing a clear picture of the corridor outside.

"Excellent picture," Tony admitted. "I didn't expect that quality."

"I think that's because the two pieces of equipment are so close together," David replied airily, though he was just guessing.

"I'm going to practice a bit; I want to make sure I can use it properly. Can you watch as well, it would be good if you also knew how to use this thing, should you need to take over for any reason? I don't expect you will need to use it, but I want you to be able to act as backup, just to be on the safe side. It's always better to have someone capable of taking over, if necessary, in these things."

David spent a few more minutes learning how to operate the system properly, explaining how it worked to Tony as he watched, taking in the various operations that David did. When David was satisfied he knew what to do, he checked with Tony that he, too, could operate it if necessary. Tony gave a confident nod and David smiled, pleased it had gone so well.

"Well, now that's sorted, I think I'm going to get some sleep. Tomorrow promises to be a day to remember." Tony said.

"Yeah, me too. Ok, see you tomorrow," though after he looked at his watch, he changed that statement to, "I mean, later this morning."

Tony gave a quick laugh and a brief wave as he walked to the door and let himself out, pulling the door quietly shut behind him. Yawning and stretching, David then undressed and got into his bed; hoping sleep wouldn't take too long in overtaking him. His last thought before he slipped away into the arms of Morpheus, was a rather prosaic, 'shit, I haven't set the alarm', not that he made any effort to do so.

The lack of an alarm did not prove to be a problem for David as he woke early in the morning. Being in a strange bed, combined with the unusual routines and noises in the hotel encroached into his sleep. The morning dawned cloudy and wet, very wet, the forecast of 10% chance of rain had obviously been for somewhere else in the country, or another day, or even some other country rather than the one he saw out of his window. He got dressed and as it was raining, he decided there was no need for him to rush about, so he went down to the restaurant and had a very leisurely breakfast in the hotel, lingering over each course. Whilst he was eating his breakfast, he decided that, rather than mooch around the hotel all day, it would be a better option to spend the day out of the way at home. When he decided that he had eaten enough, he went back to his room to get his coat and his car keys before heading out again.

When he passed reception on his way out, it was Nathan sat at the desk. When he saw David he smiled and asked,
"Not going gardening, are you?"
"Nah, I think it might be a bit wet," David responded ironically, before adding, to maintain his cover story. "No, as I can't garden today, I have decided to go home and check up on the state of the boiler. I want to know if they have got the part they need and to get a better estimate of how long it will be before I can go home. If it's going to take a bit longer than expected I will need more clothes."
"I'm sure we are all collectively hurt that you want to leave us so soon," Nathan retorted, scowling whilst pretending to be hurt.
David smiled,
"I have found some of the staff very pleasant, but the receptionist staff can be very abrupt; terrible customer service."
"Oh, I'm sure they will be mortified to know that, we always aim to please."
"Sod off."
David and Nathan both laughed, before Nathan added,
"Well, I hope he does have the part he needs, but I bet he screws up his face and says, 'It's not been easy to get, I might have it in a couple of days', knowing he forgot to order it yesterday."
"You are a true cynic, but, yeah, probably. Still, I can only live in hope. How's Hattie?"
"Oh, she's fine, she'll be in later to do her shift, just as I finish."
"What, you finish a shift and then she starts. Isn't that a bit of a pain?"

182

"It doesn't happen a lot, Tony is very good with the rotas. Mind you, it is nice occasionally to have some time to myself."

"Ahh, what are you going to do with your time, today then?"

"Depends on the weather. If it's dry later, I was going to do some shooting. I don't think there's much chance though."

"No, neither do I. Anyway, I'd better be getting off. See you later."

"Yeah, see you."

David set off towards the outer doors, but stopped, realising he had forgotten something important and turned back towards the desk. A laughing Nathan was ready for him, holding the token he needed to get out of the hotel car park.

"I think you might need this," he said, tossing the token to David, "I was hoping you'd get all the way to your car before you remembered it."

David simply mouthed a swear word at him, caught the token out of the air with a flourish and set off back to the exit. He could hear Nathan laughing as he went out the door and thought, 'It's always good to be cheerful in your work'.

David got his car out of the car park and drove slowly home. He had a day to fill before he went back to the hotel. Because of the weather he couldn't think of much else to do other than potter around doing some cleaning, practicing his guitar and doing some writing. Oh, and also lubricating his throat with lots of cups of tea. Just after midday he had a light lunch and then pottered around for a bit longer to make sure that his lunch had settled. Around 1-30 'ish he decided it would be a good idea to try and have a nap in order to make sure that he would be awake and alert later because, if events followed previous experiences, he would be up most, if not all, of the night. He went upstairs to his bedroom, set the alarm for 5-30pm and lay down. He was still mulling over possible scenarios when, much quicker than he thought possible, David slipped from drowsy wakefulness to deep sleep.

Whilst David was busy sleeping the afternoon away Natalie and Tony, in their separate environs, were preparing for their parts in the upcoming drama. In her room, Natalie was making her final choice of clothing to wear for the fake drama. Her first choice had been to wear practical clothing but, eventually, she decided against jeans, in favour of a shortish dress. She felt she would appear to be much more vulnerable dressed that way, and her portrayal of a woman afraid of assault would be more convincing, particularly to any male observers who were there.

That, along with her intended verbal broadside against the hotel should ensure she certainly got the attention of any potential murderers. A thought struck her, 'if they were in the hotel at the time'. Stopping dead in her tracks, that last thought crashed in on her mind. What if the killer wasn't in the hotel when their staged verbal assault took place. She thought this was a genuine concern and desperately searched her mind to recall the details of the murders that had previously happened. To her relief, she remembered from the file she had read that although two of the disputes had occurred in the late evening, the other one had occurred at around the same time that her act had been set for. She also thought that David would probably have already taken that into consideration, he did appear to be very thorough in his approach. Anyway, there was nothing she could do about it.

With a sigh, but also with a sense of 'que sera, sera', Natalie resumed her walk to the bathroom to check how her ensemble looked. Having decided that her attire was just right for the effect she wanted to make, she finished getting ready before looking at her watch to see how long she had to wait until she could go downstairs. Whilst she waited, she thought about what she might say to the staff member but decided that she wanted it to be as spontaneous as possible and so it would depend, to a certain extent, on how the staff member responded, so she just thought in generalities of the main accusations she wanted to get across. At 3-50pm she decided it was time to begin the show, and, with a sense of anticipation, she left her room, making sure that the door was locked, the 'Do Not Disturb' sign in place and then made her way down the stairs to get in position for the drama.

A little earlier, at around 3-30 pm Tony had begun his part in the proceedings. He told Nathan, who was still on reception, having volunteered to do a double shift as his supposed replacement, Sally, had called in sick, to go and get a break. Pleased to have a break, Nathan wandered off.
"That is so kind of you, Tony," he said, with a touch of exaggerated servility.

A minute or so after Nathan had left, Tony checked to make sure the foyer area was empty and then he quickly went over to the ladies toilets, knocked loudly on the door and waited a few seconds before knocking again. When no one answered and he was sure there was no one inside, he slipped inside the door. This was the tricky part of the operation because he needed to do the next part without being seen. Once inside, he quickly went over to one of the cubicles, went inside and took the top off the cistern. He then quickly unhooked the lever arm from the flush control so that the toilet couldn't be flushed. He put the lid back on the cistern and made his way quickly back to the door. Opening the door a fraction, he saw that Leah, one of the waitresses, was just heading across the foyer, towards the bar. He pulled the door to without closing it completely, waited a few seconds before opening it a fraction and carefully checking again. The coast was now clear, so he quickly exited the ladies toilet and, with a puff of his cheeks, he made his way casually back to reception. He sat at the reception desk and waited for Natalie to come down and go into the toilet so that the fun could begin.

Almost immediately after Tony had returned to the reception desk, Natalie came down the stairs and, without seeming to look at Tony, checked he was at the reception desk before entering into the ladies toilet. Tony got up quickly, retrieved the 'Out of order' sign from where he had put it in his office, which was located right next to reception. He crossed the foyer and hung the sign on the toilet to make sure no-one else entered the toilets whilst he set up the next part of the drama.

He waited another few minutes to make sure that Natalie would be ready and then used the radio to call the porter who also did odd jobs around the hotel.

"Hi Tom, are you around?"

There was a brief pause before he received a reply,

"Hi Tony, Tom here, do you need me?"

"Yes, I've just been told that one of the toilets in the ladies loo next to reception won't flush. Can you bring your tools and check it out?"

"Sure, be there in a few minutes."

Just then Nathan returned from his break, as Tony knew he would, he never took more than twenty minutes or so. As he passed the ladies toilet, he saw the 'Out of order' sign hanging there and looked inquisitively at Tony.

"I only leave you for a few minutes and you start to break the place. What's up with the loo?"

"A woman just told me that one of the loos won't flush."

"Do you want me to send for Tom?"

"No need, he's on his way, I do know how to use the radio, you know." Tony countered with a smile, wondering at himself for still being able to banter when his heart was beginning to pound so hard he felt sure that Nathan must be able to hear it. Before Nathan could reply, Tom appeared at reception.

"Is anyone in there?" he asked.

Nathan shrugged his ignorance, but Tony said,

"There shouldn't be, but knock before you enter."

Tom went over to the restroom and knocked on the door, waited a few seconds and then knocked again. He looked back at Tony, who nodded, so Tom opened the door and entered. Trying to remain calm, Tony waited with bated breath for the explosion, which, sure enough, came very quickly. A loud scream pierced the afternoon and a flustered Tom burst out of the restroom; rapidly followed by an apparently enraged guest.

"How dare you sneak into the toilet when I'm in there? Are you some kind of pervert?"

Tom just stood there, looking nonplussed, but Tony swiftly intervened as he had planned to do. He wanted to try and divert most of Natalie's supposed vitriol away from Tom. He didn't want him to feel too bad over what happened, but he had chosen him because he was very practical and pragmatic and wasn't likely to get overly stressed about the incident, once it was over. He also had to work with Tom after all this was over, so he needed to support him in any case.

"I'm sorry, madam. I sent him in there."

"What, are you some kind of pervert too, do you both get some kind of pleasure from scaring women? I thought I was going to be assaulted." Tony opened his mouth to reply but Natalie's voice overrode his,

"Do you plan all these situations between you and take turns over who goes in? You're sick, both of you."

Natalie, who was enjoying herself tremendously, looked around to make sure that people in the hotel could hear her, which they obviously could, as little clusters of guests and staff were looking on from various places, though ensuring they did not get too close to the action. Natalie was also conscious that Tom was completely innocent of anything, so she decided to concentrate most of her apparent ire on Tony. Satisfied that enough people were taking notice, Natalie returned a scornful gaze to Tony and Tom. Tony noted the scornful look and the tone of voice Natalie had used and he was suddenly glad that all this was just a set-up.

He decided he wouldn't like to face her if it was for real. However, there was no time for such musings; he needed to get on with his side of the performance.

"Again, I can only offer our apologies but there is a problem with one of the toilets and I sent Tom here into the toilets to fix the problem. We didn't know you were in there."

"Rubbish, all he had to do was knock."

"But he did knock madam, I heard him do so myself."

"No, he didn't, I was in there and no one knocked."

"I can assure you he did knock, madam."

"Are you calling me a liar? No one knocked. He just wanted to catch me undressed in there."

Natalie said this last retort very loudly.

"There was an out of order sign on the door, madam, as you can see."

Natalie turned and looked at the door and saw the sign there. This had been arranged between them in the preparation stage and Natalie had already decided her response.

"Obviously you put that there once I had gone in to make sure I remained on my own."

"I can assure you we thought the toilet was empty."

"I've had enough of this; I want to see the owner, straight away."

"I'm afraid he is not here at the moment."

"How very convenient for the two of you. In that case, I want to see him as soon as he gets here."

"Of course, madam, I will let you know as soon as he arrives."

"Good, now I'm going to my room, and I hope neither of you bursts in there."

With that Natalie turned and stormed off to her room upstairs without a backward look, which was lucky as she was smiling quietly to herself, pleased with how the whole performance had gone.

It wasn't entirely acting that led Tony to mop his brow. He really did feel brow beaten, even though he knew it was just an act by Natalie. Tony turned to Tom,

"Sorry about that, are you ok?"

"God, she's a scary one, but I'm ok, you took the brunt of that. Thanks."

"Well, I did send you in there."

"Yes, well, I'd better get back in there and fix that toilet."

"Ok, I haven't seen anyone else go in there but I'm not going to take any chances, I'll send Vicky in there to check."

"Good thinking."

As Tony had noticed, Vicky had been watching from nearby and hearing Tony, she went into the toilets to check for them. A few seconds later she came out and gave the 'all clear', so Tom entered the toilet with his tools and all the people that had been surreptitiously watching now pretended that they hadn't been watching at all and returned to what they had been doing before the confrontation began. As he watched the people move away, chatting amongst themselves; Tony did wonder how the whole scene which had just unfolded would embed itself in people's memories. In a moment of prescience, he foresaw a new myth that would be created out of the fragments of people's memories. In years to come people would start conversations with,

"Can you remember when that bloke went into the ladies loo and that woman…."

He hoped he wouldn't become remembered as one of the participants.

A few minutes later Tom emerged from the toilet, removed the out of order sign and returned it to reception.

"All fixed," he told Tony.

"What was it?" Tony enquired.

"It was very odd, somehow the hook had come loose between the flush control from the lever arm. I've never known that to happen before."

"Maybe the gods were playing tricks on us," Nathan said.

Tony silently thanked him for taking Tom's thoughts away from the broken toilet.

"You could be right, they say the gods move in mysterious ways," Tom replied, "anyway, I'm going for a sit down and a cuppa."

"I don't blame you," said Tony.

Tom went off for a break and Nathan and Tony looked at each other for a moment, before Nathan said,

"One scary woman that."

"You're right there," replied Tony, "I think I need a drink, too."

"Yeah, I bet."

With that, Tony went off to the bar as he really did need a drink. Natalie's performance, and the ending of the adrenaline rush that had sustained him throughout the afternoon, had suddenly left him feeling drained. Nathan turned back to the reception, silently thanking the gods that he hadn't been the target of Natalie's verbal assault.

Chapter 14.

And Now We Wait.

An hour or so after the dramatic scene at the hotel, David was starting to stir in his bed. The alarm went off, bringing him fully awake, but somewhat disorientated and temporarily unsure of the time of day. He vaguely recalled a dream he had been having when he was in the last moments of waking, where he was being chased by an unseen monster down an unending corridor, running as fast as he could but hardly moving. He then remembered what day it was and what was supposed to happen that evening and fervently hoped the dream wasn't an omen. As it was getting on towards 6 pm, he felt he could legitimately go to the hotel, have a shower and find out whether or not everything had gone as planned. He picked up the two-way radio that Johnnie had left him and put it in a rucksack to take into the hotel. For once, he didn't stop to make himself a cup of tea, but simply went downstairs, picked up his car keys and his rucksack and drove to the hotel.

Back at the hotel, Chris had arrived, feeling coiled up and tense, but managed to calmly ask Nathan if everything in the hotel was ok. Nathan began to explain the incident with Natalie, adding many garish details about what happened, as Tony came out of the office to join them.
"Was she alright in the end?" Chris asked him.
"No, she wants to speak to you as soon as you get here."
"Shout at you more like," Nathan added with a great deal of relish, glad that he would be sat safely in reception.
"Probably," agreed Tony, frowning at Nathan.
"Ok, I'd better go see her," Chris said, adding a sigh.

"I think it might be a better idea if we went to her room together."

"Good idea, ok, let's get it over with."

With that Chris and Tony went up to Natalie's room. Natalie opened the door at their knock. In case anyone was listening, Chris said,

"I'm the owner of the hotel; I believe you wanted to see me."

"I most certainly do, your staff tried to assault me," Natalie almost shouted.

"May we come in," Chris asked.

"If you must," Natalie said, apparently very grudgingly, but she moved back into the room so the two of them could enter.

The two of them went passed her into the room and Natalie shut the door behind them, before turning and smiling at the two of them. They chatted for a few minutes before Chris and Tony left the room, both assuming the faces of people who have just undergone a difficult ordeal. They returned to their office behind the reception and Nathan, seeing their faces, said,

"That didn't go well, then, I take it?"

"Well, she was a little difficult," Chris said diplomatically as they went into the office. Once there, the two of them smiled at each, simultaneously sitting down and sighing.

"Well, now we wait," stated Chris.

Whilst Chris and Tony were talking to Natalie, David arrived at the hotel and parked in the staff car park. He knew that, technically he wasn't staff, but it made it easier to get out and it was where he usually parked when there was space. He purposively went in through the main doors which took him passed reception. Nathan was sat behind the reception desk, eyes on the computer, though he was probably only pretending to be working. He looked up as the door slid shut, saw it was David and smiled in welcome.

"Hi David, still residing here, I take it."

"Yep, still no boiler. What are you doing here anyway; I thought you finished at lunch?"

"Yeah, I was supposed to but Sally called in sick, so I agreed to stay on. It was chucking it down and Hattie is doing the afternoon/evening shift, so it seemed a good idea at the time."

"What do you mean, 'at the time'?"

Nathan looked round to make sure no one was about and then said in a very soft voice,

"Well, one of the guests had a right old ding dong with Tony. She was in the toilet over there," he said, pointing at the toilets in the reception area, "and Tony sent Tom in to do some repairs. She went ballistic, accusing them both of being perverts."

David silently thanked Nathan for introducing the topic as now, he wouldn't have to try and maneuver the conversation that way, he just said to Nathan,

"Didn't Tom knock before he went in?"

"He did, but she said he didn't and said she thought she was going to be assaulted."

"Did she shut up in the end?"

"No, she wanted to see Chris when he got in, they are with her now."

"I miss all the fun."

"It wasn't fun, I can tell you, she is one scary woman."

"Oh well, at least it seems peaceful now. I'm off for a shower, and then a pizza and a pint or two."

"Lucky you, see you later."

Nathan handed David the key and he made his way upstairs to his room. When he was settled inside his room he sat on the armchair and wondered about what Nathan had told him. Whilst he was pleased that the altercation had gone to plan, he was a bit worried by Nathan's comment that Natalie was a scary woman and hoped she hadn't overdone it.

At 7pm David got the two-way radio out of his rucksack and called Natalie. She answered immediately.

"Ah, David, so nice of you to call."

"Evening Natalie, I think we can say that the radios are working. I hear you gave a good performance this afternoon."

"One does one's best."

"Yes, well, it appears that you are now 'one scary woman' to the staff."

"That's nice; maybe they'll put that on my gravestone, one day."

"Hopefully, not too soon."

"How sweet of you to care. Well at least I should have caught the attention of the 'would be' killer. I think we can safely say I should be a potential target now."

"Yes, I think that's a certainty; what are your plans for the evening?"

"I don't think tonight's the night for a date, do you, we might get interrupted?"

Enjoying the bantering tone, David joined in lighthearted conversation,

"Oh well, I'll just have to rein in my baser instincts then. However, what I meant, as you well knew, was, will you be staying in your room or spending time in the bar and restaurant?"

"Until Johnnie gets here, I think it would a better idea to be in company, just in case the killer simply can't wait to embrace me. I will go and have a meal in the restaurant and then sit in the bar."

"Good idea, I will be down there as well. Did you sort out your arrangement to pass Johnnie the key to your room?"

Natalie gave a frustrated sigh and then added,

"What did we say about me being a professional?"

"Yeah, sorry but I'm used to dealing with Tony and Chris."

"Apology accepted, I'll let you buy me a drink when this is over."

"If we catch the killer, I'll buy you a meal."

"And drink as well, I hope."

"Of course," David said laughingly, enjoying the banter.

"Right, put the radio down, I'm going to make myself look good for tonight."

"Is that wise, shouldn't you... forget it, you know what you're doing."

"Ah, progress. Bye."

Around 7-30pm David went downstairs, waving negligently to Nathan as he passed the reception and made his way to the pizza bar. Hattie was on duty at the pay station and, after a few pleasantries, he asked her if there was a table free.

"There will be in a few minutes, if you're in the bar I'll come and fetch you."

"Thanks."

David passed through the archway into the main bar and, seeing him approach the barman was already pouring him a Peroni. Although he regarded that as perfect service, after the banter of the night before, David decided it was his turn to have a bit of fun, saying in a serious tone,

"A large red wine, please."

The barman, caught unawares, looked up from pouring the pint with a very surprised look on his face. When he saw that David was grinning hugely and clearly not being serious, he mouthed an obscenity at him, before topping the pint off.

"Here you are, you git," he said to David, placing the pint on the bar.

"Many thanks, my good man, I hope you are well?"

"I was until some git took the piss," he said quietly, smiling at David.

"What goes around, comes around," David said serenely. "That's what life is for," he continued expansively, "drinking and taking the mickey out of barmen. Thanks, put it on room 12, will you?"

"But of course, and my drink too?" he enquired.

"It would be a pleasure to buy such a noble barman a drink," said David, picking up his pint, raising it to the barman in salute, before finding himself a table.

After about 10 minutes, Hattie came to fetch him for his pizza, making small talk as they walked back through the archway to the pizza bar.

"Did you get any gardening in today?" she enquired.

"No chance, much too wet, I spent the day checking up on the plumber. At least he thinks he should get it repaired by the end of tomorrow, so I should be able to go home."

"That's good, I bet you will sleep better tomorrow night when you are in your own bed rather than here."

"How true," David agreed, fighting hard to keep the irony out of his voice as he thought what might be in store for him that night and how little sleep he was likely to get.

Hattie showed him to his table and asked if he needed the menu. David shook his head and said,

"Just the usual please."

"Ok."

Hattie walked off to give his order to the pizza chef, who looked over at David and waved. A few minutes later, his pizza was ready and was delivered to his table. As usual, he thoroughly enjoyed it and it filled him up ready for the evening ahead, or at least, he hoped it would.

Hattie came to collect his empty plate and asked if he wanted another Peroni. David thought it wise to drink slowly so said,

"You know what; I think I really fancy a coffee just now."

"No problem, which one?"

"An Americano, please, black, no sugar."

"I think we can just about manage that," Hattie said, as she walked away.

A few minutes later, one of the other waitresses brought his coffee and David made sure that he dawdled over drinking it. Whilst he was sitting there, Tony came and joined him, he had a smile on his face, which David found surprising, especially with what lay ahead of them.

"You look happy," he said enquiringly.

"Yes, well, that's why I thought you might be interested. I was overseeing the restaurant for a few minutes while Vicky was taking a break. Natalie was eating in there and it seems that she has made a serious impression on the staff with her antics earlier. I have never seen the staff give such excellent service. They were almost falling over each other, to give the best service, though whether that was to impress her or because they were afraid of her, I am not sure."

"I bet she enjoyed that."

"I imagine she did, but you couldn't tell. She looked as if that was how she was normally treated. I think the staff were even more intimidated by that than when she shouted, she just oozes self-possession."

"Where is she now?"

"In the bar."

"I think I'll go in there as well, I want to make sure that Johnnie gets here ok."

"Ok, I'll see you later," Tony said.

David sat for a few more minutes finishing his coffee before he got up from the table to go through to the bar. On the way, he passed the pay station, where Hattie was standing. He was just about to offer to pay for his pizza again, when he remembered it would be put on his room. Not wanting the staff to have another opportunity to laugh at his expense he simply said to Hattie,

"I do like this not having to use actual money, it almost makes it seem like you aren't actually paying."

"Until you get the bill for your room."

"That's true."

"Are you going to be in the bar later?"

"For a while, but I won't be drinking late, I have to go to work tomorrow," David lied.

"Wuss! What happened to the hard drinker?"

"About 20 years, I can't keep up with you youngsters anymore," he sighed.

"Oh, you poor old man."

"Such sarcasm ill becomes one so young," he said huffily as he walked off.

He could still hear Hattie laughing as he left the room. 'Disrespectful wench' he laughed to himself. As he entered the bar, David casually glanced around the room to see where Natalie was sitting. He noticed she had chosen a table where she could easily see both entrances to the bar and he metaphorically nodded to himself in approval. He'd heard from Mark how good she was and the more he saw of Natalie in operation, the more confident he was that they would be able to catch the killer; or killers, he reminded himself.

David took his pint and found a quiet table, where he could drink slowly and wait for Johnnie to arrive. He would worry until then, as things could always go wrong and it was possible that, for some reason, Johnnie could fail to show. It was unlikely, but possible. So, it was with a sigh of relief, that David noticed Johnnie entering the bar from the main entrance a short time later. He observed where both David and Natalie were sat, waved at David and went to the bar to buy himself a drink. When he had got his pint, he came over and sat with David.
"How goes it, David?" he asked.
"Fine, we don't see you here very often."
"I've had a job in the area, so I thought I would come and see if you were in and check to make sure my previous work here was ok at the same time."
"Oh, well it's good to see you anyway. Cheers."
"Cheers."

David and Johnnie continued to drink slowly and occasionally engaged in desultory conversation until David asked, when there was no-one near their table.
"When have you arranged to get the key to Natalie's room?"
Johnnie looked at his watch before saying,
"In about five minutes."

A few minutes later, as planned, Johnnie got up to go to the toilet. He passed Natalie but didn't look her way. A few minutes later, Natalie also made her way to the toilet and as the two of them passed in the corridor, Natalie surreptitiously passed the room key to Johnnie, who quickly pocketed it and then returned to sit with David, hiding the key in his shirt pocket.

Natalie returned to her table a few minutes later and resumed sipping at her wine. David and Johnnie continued their sporadic conversation, as they waited, somewhat impatiently, for the time to pass until they could go up to their rooms. It wasn't as if they were eager to get into the possible violent action, it was just that it was emotionally exhausting hanging around, waiting for the night's events to begin. There was, though, one incident which occurred to lighten their mood for a short time. It occurred when one of the other customers, a slightly drunk 30-ish male, decided he would try and chat up Natalie. He approached her table and leant on it and said, in what he clearly thought was a sophisticated chat up line,
"Hi darlin', I hate to see a beautiful young woman sitting on her own so I thought I would give you the pleasure of my company. Would you like a drink?"
Natalie turned a languid stare on the presumptive Casanova, slowly looked him up and down and with disdain dripping from her voice, replied,
"No thanks."
Being fairly drunk, inept and definitely overconfident, he did not immediately recognize the finality of his rejection, he continued his awkward approach,
"Sure you do, I think you and me would be great together, we could be like strangers who pass in the night."
He had heard a line like that in a film somewhere and being easily impressed, he had always wanted to be able to use it

199

sometime. Fully expecting her to melt in response to his charm, he was just about to sit down next to Natalie.

David took a moment to look around the bar, noting that several members of staff were staring apprehensively at the unfolding situation. It was clear that they were clearly expecting an explosion. David returned his gaze to Natalie, wondering how she would deal with his persistence. A moment later he found out and it clearly was not what the man was expecting either.

"I already said no and have no intention of changing my mind, we are certainly strangers and, after listening to your pathetic chat up line, that's what I definitely intend to remain."

The man stopped, halfway between standing and sitting, as her words hit him. She gave him a hard, level stare and, finally recognizing his utter dismissal, and in complete confusion, as well as embarrassment, he sidled away from the table, avoiding looking at anyone else as he left the bar and then the Hotel. Natalie, on the other hand, appeared totally unruffled and casually signaled to the barman for another glass of wine.

"Abrupt, isn't she," commented David admiringly.

"Oh, yes, she doesn't suffer fools well," Johnnie replied.

"I can tell."

A short time later, Johnnie finished his drink and stood up to go.

"Well, I'm off, got to be up early tomorrow to get to a job. It's been great seeing you again, Davy. We must do it again soon."

"Yeah, it's been good to catch up. Give me a call soon."

"Will do. See you."

"Yeah, see you."

With that Johnnie left the bar and appearing to go to the toilet, it gave him a good view of the reception desk. Seeing that no-one was there at that moment, he veered to the stairs and quickly went up to Natalie's room. Once inside, he made himself comfortable for the wait ahead, making himself a cup of coffee, before settling down to see what the night would bring.

Back in the bar, both Natalie and David continued to drink sparingly whilst they waited to go up to their rooms. About fifteen minutes after Johnnie had left, Natalie made a show of lifting her glass and draining the last of the wine from it. She rose languidly from her seat at the table and took the glass back to the bar.

"Thank you," she said to the barman, "that was an excellent red."

"I'm glad you liked it, "the barman replied with a smile.

"Indeed I did. Goodnight."

"Goodnight," the barman responded, picking up her empty glass, but as he turned away from Natalie, his hand accidently caught the pint glass of another guest who was standing at the bar. Almost in slow motion, the nearly full glass toppled over, and the drink flew, like a tidal wave, over the shirt and trousers of the man. For a second the man and the barman stood, frozen in place, but then the man looked down at his sodden clothes and turned back to the barman with a look of drunken fury in his eyes. He took a deep breath and then launched into a verbal assault on the poor barman.

Chapter 15.

Then There Were Two.

"Bloody hell, this can't be happening, not tonight," thought David, his eyes taking in the sodden clothes and his ears, the angry tirade.

Recognising the potentially disastrous situation, Natalie looked across at David who, almost imperceptibly jerked his head to tell her to go up to her room. After Natalie had left, David hung around long enough for Tony to get to the bar to try and placate the obviously angry guest. Whilst he was there, David looked around the bar to see if anyone, staff of customer, was taking a great interest in the proceedings, but as everyone was looking intently, this didn't really help. When it was clear that the man would not be easily appeased, David moved to be in Tony's eye line and when he looked his way he, once again, jerked his head upwards a fraction, to let him know to come upstairs when he had finished with the man. To his credit, Tony nodded his head equally fractionally to show he understood, whilst he continued trying to pacify the guest.

When the altercation seemed to have died down, at least in terms of volume, David left the bar and quickly went upstairs to discuss the incident with Natalie and Johnnie. He made sure the corridor outside Natalie's room was empty before he knocked on her door and when she opened it, he slid inside quickly. Once fully inside, David explained what had happened after Natalie had left.
"The prat just wouldn't shut up, he just kept shouting at the barman. I let Tony know to come up when he was finished with him."

"This could well bugger's things up a bit, couldn't it?" Johnnie exclaimed.

"Just a bit." David acknowledged.

"What are we going to do, then, to cover both potential situations?" Natalie asked.

"We need to come up with a contingency plan," he replied, "but we first need to get his room details from Tony when he gets here so we can work out how to protect him if the killer decides to go for him."

"You really think he might be in danger then?" asked Johnnie.

"Based on what's happened before, I don't think we can risk ignoring the possibility, we can't take the chance of leaving him unprotected." David explained.

"Whatever his room is, it's going to stretch our resources a bit," said Natalie.

"We'll just have to sort it," said David, "we'll just have to come up with a plan to protect both rooms."

"How about if me and Johnnie stay here as planned, but you protect tonight's loud-mouthed guest," suggested Natalie.

"Oh thanks, you are so kind," David responded before giving her a brief bow.

"Don't mention it." Natalie replied, smiling sweetly at him.

Johnnie looked at the two of them critically, before saying,

"You're not supposed to be enjoying this, you know."

"A person should always enjoy their work; otherwise, what's the point in doing it?" Natalie responded, a sentiment which David heartily agreed with. However, he wasn't entirely sure that Natalie's suggestion was the best solution, but he kept that to himself for the time being, instead he merely said,

"Let's wait 'til Tony gets here. Until he gives us the details, we can't be sure what the best approach should be."

Johnnie and Natalie nodded in agreement as they settled down to wait for Tony.

A few minutes later there was a knock on the door. All three of them readied themselves for action in case it was the attackers.

203

David signaled to Natalie to open the door and she opened it carefully, ready to respond if it turned out to be the killer, however, she relaxed when she saw Tony stood there. She opened the door fully and Tony followed her into the room. Once there David asked him,

"Ok, what happened after I left?"

"What exactly do you want to know?" he asked.

"Basically, did he quiet down, did he apologise, and what's his room number," David demanded.

"Yes, no, 8,"

Natalie laughed at Tony's very succinct response and David said apologetically.

"Sorry, I didn't mean to snap. Thanks. Ok, where exactly is room 8?"

"It's the one almost directly below this one, but on the other side of the corridor, which mirrors this one."

"Do you know if there are any free rooms near room 8?"

"Actually, only rooms 1 and 4 are taken, so 5 or 6 are possibly the best one's free."

"I'm glad you can remember all these details," David said.

"Why don't you go and stay in room 5 or 6?" Natalie suggested to David.

"I was thinking along those lines, however, I can't just go in any room I feel like in case a late guest is given that room. Tony, go down to reception and tell the night porter that you are going to stay in room 6 overnight? It won't be suspicious as you often stay here."

"Ok,"

Whilst Tony left to get the key, David continued discussing the new plan with Johnnie and Natalie, before saying,

"First hypothesis, and please highlight potential problems so we can alter the plan. Natalie, you stay in this room, Johnnie, you go to my room and watch the camera so you can give Natalie a head's up if someone approaches her room, then you can follow on from behind to trap whoever, it is. There's one possible good

204

thing about this situation, if there are two killers they may well split up, so one goes for each guest. At least that will make them easier to deal with."

"Unless they both go for each guest; killing one and then going after the other."

"Yes, they could do that. That will be ok for you two; you should be able to deal with them easily enough. The real problem would be if they both came for the guy in room 8. I would have to take on both of them."

"Don't you think you could take them?" Johnnie asked.

"That depends on whether they are trained operatives or not."

"Also, you need to get to them before they enter the guy's room, this is all meant to be secret, after all." Natalie reminded them. "It might be a bit difficult to disable and capture two people in silence."

"Yes, that means it's too risky for me to be there on my own," David decided.

Just then there was a knock on the door. Natalie went over and repeated her previous performance but, again, it was only Tony. He followed her into the room and handed the key to room 6 to David, who absently took it as he was still working his way through the logistics of protecting two rooms.

"It's a pity we haven't got another radio," he said, "otherwise, I could call one of you down if there were two of them downstairs."

"What about the radios they use in the hotel, couldn't we use them?" Natalie said.

"Good idea," David said, as he continued working on a plan.

Whilst the others waited David continued to put the pieces in place in his head. When he was ok with his plan he turned to the others.

"Ok, here's the new plan. Johnnie and I will go downstairs. We will have one of the department's radios and Natalie will have the other, so we can keep directly in touch with each other.

Natalie will be here, also with one of the hotel's radios, and Tony will be in my room, watching the surveillance camera in case there are two killers, and they try to carry out the murders at the same time or come here first. Tony can use the hotel's radio to warn Natalie if something happens up here. If that happens, Natalie can contact us, and we can decide how to respond. Can anyone see any problems?"

"Can Tony operate the security camera?" queried Natalie.

"Yes, I showed him how to use the other night when we set it up. I thought it better to be prepared, just in case."

Natalie nodded and said,

"Good thinking."

Apart from a general feeling of being out of his depth, faced with the professionalism of the other three, Tony was impressed with the speed that David had come up with a new plan. This was a whole new side of David, who had always seemed so laid back, but his performance highlighted how incisive he could be. He was, though, unsure of his role, so asked,

"What do I do if I have to warn Natalie? Do I go and join her?"

"Oh, my knight in shining armour," Natalie said, bowing to Tony, who smiled in response. His pleasure was soon ended by David,

"No, you stay in my room, out of the way. You aren't trained for this."

Tony was both relieved and a little upset at David's response. On the one hand he knew he would be out of his depth if it came to a fight, but he had to admit, part of him actually wanted to be fully involved. He was thinking that he hadn't had this much excitement since, he was trying to think when, but then realised it was 'ever'.

"Ok, it's starting to get late so let's get organized. Tony can you go and get two radio head sets for us to use. We will get everything ready here." David told them all.

"Yes, boss," smirked Natalie.

Tony set off down to the kitchen area where the radios were kept. Luckily this meant he didn't have to disturb the night porter, who would be asleep in the office behind the reception by now. He reached the kitchen and opened the cupboard which housed the radios. He took two out but noticed that one of the others was missing. This was becoming a habit, quite a few times now someone had forgotten to return it to the cupboard. In Manager mode, he made a mental note to remind staff they should not take the radios home. Smiling at the incongruity of his worrying about that when so much might happen that night, he shrugged as he closed the cupboard and made to return to the others. At that moment his legs seemed to go rigid as the the full import of what was about to happen hit him and he found himself riveted to the spot. All these preparations were to deal with potential killers. The appalling clarity of it hit him; someone might die tonight. Fear threatened to overwhelmed him and he grabbed the cupboard to steady himself. Up until that point, it had almost seemed like a game, or a tv programme, but now, it suddenly felt very real. He noticed that he was sweating. Taking a tissue from his pocket he wiped his forehead and took a few very deep breaths, before forcing himself to go back and rejoin the others.

Knocking quietly, Tony waited to be re-admitted and again it was Natalie who carefully opened the door, checked it was him before admitting him. Once inside, he gave Natalie one of the radios and showed her how to use it. Natalie then put the radio on the bed next to the department radio, where she could easily reach both of them. With his new sense of self-awareness, Tony looked at the others in the room, noticing that all of them, including David, were very self-possessed and assured in the way they held themselves, with no obvious signs of fear as they prepared for what was ahead. He realised he had been sort of aware of it before, but now it struck him that all of the other three, had probably killed before tonight. Tony looked down at his hands, which he noticed were trembling. A feeling of shame washed over him, and he hurriedly thrust them in the pockets of his trousers, hoping the others hadn't seen them shaking.

A couple of minutes later, after he had checked all the equipment, David said,
"Right, is everyone sure what their jobs are."
Every one of them, including Tony, nodded and David said,
"Ok, let's go."

Chapter 16.

Well, That Was A Surprise.

David, Johnnie and Tony left Natalie alone in room 15 as they went out into the corridor and headed down to room 12. David opened the door to the room and gave the key to Tony, who went in. David held a hand up to Johnnie, saying quietly,

"I just need to drop some stuff off; I won't be a minute."

Johnnie looked briefly towards Tony, nodded and waited outside as David followed Tony into the room, patting his pockets and pretending to check for any sharp objects which might stick into him at the wrong moment. As he was doing this, he said quietly to Tony, who was placing his two-way radio on the bed.

"How are you doing? I take it you suddenly realized how serious this whole thing is."

His throat constricting, all Tony could do was nod; unable to speak. David put a companionable hand on his shoulder and said, with a touch of sympathy,

"It happens to all of us at some time. It's not as glamourous as people think, is it?"

Tony managed to find his voice.

"How did you know?"

"I could see it in your eyes; they seemed to be looking inward, more reflective than before. Will you be ok?"

Attempting to hide fear in humour, Tony said,

"I think I can just about manage being out of the way in this room."

"Can you remember how to operate the monitor?"

Tony nodded and David took out the monitor and keyed in the security code, before symbolically handing it to Tony, who put it on the table.

"Good. Later, when it's all over, we can get drunk."

"Oh, definitely."

David left the room and rejoined Johnnie, who cocked his head towards Tony's room as they began walking to the stairs.

"Is he ok?"

"You noticed as well, did you?"

"It was obvious to the trained eye, the sudden decline in enthusiasm and the opaque look in the eye."

"I'm sure he'll be fine. A few minutes thinking it through in there and he'll have rationalized it to himself, like we all did; one possible life to save others."

"Oh well, at least he is relatively safe in there, nothing should happen to him."

By this time, they had arrived outside room 6. Quickly and quietly, they let themselves in. They did not switch the lights on and left the door to the main outer corridor slightly open. Johnnie pulled up a chair and sat down to watch the corridor. David went to the room table and put the equipment bag on it, before taking the radio back and placing it on the floor, next to Johnnie. David looked at his phone and saw it was 12-47am, so they had probably still got about an hour to wait. He went back to the main part of the room and by the light from his phone, he made them both some coffee. Because the sound of voices travels clearly at night, they did not talk but just sat quietly. As they were both professionals, they were able to wait easily, not really thinking, almost trancelike, but still fully focused on observing and listening, totally ready to spring into action.

In room 15, Natalie was going through the same routine, waiting in that same state of trancelike readiness. She had taken the chair from next to the table and had placed it so she could comfortably watch the door to her room. Although she thought Tony was competent, he was not a trained operative and could possibly miss seeing someone approaching her room. She did not want to be caught unawares if someone entered her room unexpectedly.

That same sense of calm waiting was clearly not in evidence in room 12, however. Tony had settled into the chair at the table and picked up the monitor. He began to operate it as he remembered seeing David work it and very soon was fully competent in its use. He placed it on the table, fetched the equipment bag and put it on the table behind the monitor. He then arranged the monitor against it so it stood up and he could see it without having to hold it. For some reason he felt better having his hands free. Having satisfied himself that he was ready, he sat back and began to wait. As soon as he did, he realized he needed the toilet, but at least he could take the monitor with him so that he could keep watching. For some reason he felt embarrassed going to the toilet whilst holding the monitor but, despite the performance anxiety, he managed to complete the task and keep watching the monitor. Having washed his hands, he returned to his seat at the table to continue monitoring the surveillance camera, constantly afraid that he would miss seeing someone stop outside Natalie's room.

After about half an hour of just sitting, watching the screen, he began to suffer from nervous boredom. A deep lethargy began to invade his mind. His concentration started to drift, and his eyes started to close. With a sudden jerk, his head dropped. Startled, he woke up, momentarily wondering where he was.
'This is useless,' he said to himself, 'I need to do something'.
He got up from his chair, picked up the monitor and went to the bathroom; he grabbed the towel and placed it over his shoulder, before switching the tap on. He waited until the water was warm and then he quickly splashed his face whilst still trying to watch the monitor. He dried his face, still attempting to watch the screen continuously. Feeling fresher and more alert, he went back to the main room, his eyes still fixed on the monitor and made himself a cup of coffee. Sitting back down to continue his watching, he recalled what David had said and agreed,
'No, this definitely isn't glamourous.'

As he sat there, nerves taut, a touch of panic washed through him as he realised that he had forgotten to set up the two-way radio. Swearing at himself, he surged out of his seat, to get the radio off the bed. Just as quickly, he stopped, as he remembered he had to keep his eyes on the monitor. Confused, he looked from the monitor, to the bed, then back to the monitor, temporarily unable to do anything. After a few moments of complete indecision, he forced himself to breathe deeply to calm himself. Thinking logically once more, he looked back to the bed quickly, locating exactly where the radio was. Still keeping his eyes fixed on the monitor, he backed slowly towards the bed. When his leg hit the bed, he groped behind him to get the radio. It took a couple of attempts to locate it and then, without turning, he grabbed it. With a quick sigh, he pulled the radio to him and held it tightly, making his way back to his seat. As he sat down, he felt his heart beating far too quickly and thought,

'I am definitely not cut out for this. If it's not over soon, I could well have a heart attack'.

Even worse, he realised that he could have avoided all the paranoia if he had just picked up the monitor and carried it with him whilst he fetched the radio.

'Idiot,' he thought, 'get a grip on yourself.'

Sometime later, David and Johnnie, their coffees now long finished, were still in waiting mode, when Johnnie raised his hand to signal to David, pointing to the outside door. David crept closer to the door and saw someone walking down the corridor. Recognising the figure, he gave a sharp intake of breath before he turned quickly and mouthed,

"It's Vicky."

A range of thoughts tumbled through his mind.

Shock at seeing Vicky.

Was she there on hotel business?

Was she also staying overnight in one of the spare rooms?

Then David noticed the strange way she was walking and knew instinctively that something wasn't right. He made the decision to grab her just in case. After all, he could always apologise later if he was wrong. He signaled to Johnnie for both of them to grab her from behind and drag her back into room 6.

Johnnie nodded to show he understood and then David signaled that he would go high and grab Vicky at shoulder height and signed for Johnnie to go low. Again, Johnnie nodded to show he understood. All this took barely a couple of seconds and Vicky had not moved too far down the corridor.

They both crept out of their room and moved stealthily, but surprisingly quickly, up behind Vicky. As they got closer, they were both ready for Vicky to notice their approach and spin round to face them. Even if she didn't hear them, instinct should warn her of their approach. However, they were able to get to her without her giving any sign she knew they were there, so concentrated was she on the door to room 8. Still walking in that strangely wooden fashion, she was just about to reach the door to room 8, when two pairs of arms grabbed her simultaneously low and high. Before she had a chance to do anything, or even make a noise, David had covered her mouth and they were carrying her back to their room. Seemingly not understanding what had happened, she lay supine in their arms for a few moments, then, completely without warning, she began thrashing her body violently in a bid to escape. Her legs almost broke free from Johnnie's grip, but he just managed to hold on as they carried her into the room, thankfully still in virtual silence.

They pinned her to the floor as she continued to thrash, both of them struggling to restrain her. There was no logical way that, physically, Vicky should be able to cause the two of them so much trouble, but she did. David began talking quietly to her hoping to calm her down. He could tell something was wrong

213

with her, of course, but did not know what. Vicky did not acknowledge him at all, or even make a sound, she just stared at him intently. Shockingly, he realized he could see no trace of recognition in her eyes.

As he stared at her, trying to understand what was going on, Vicky's struggles began to ease as if she were tiring and so Johnnie, who had been struggling to keep hold of both of her legs, eased his grip and tried to get a better grip. As he did so, Vicky made a sudden lunge to one side, freeing one of her legs in the process. Before Johnnie had a chance to react, she kicked him in the stomach with her free leg. Breath hissed from his mouth as he fell back against the wall, losing his grip on Vicky altogether. Vicky kicked at him again, but was hampered by her position on the floor, so only caught Johnnie a glancing blow to his leg. Johnnie threw one hand out and managed to grab her leg and hold on to it, gasping as he tried to suck in some oxygen. David had also been thrown partly off balance when she had got free from Johnnie, falling back against the wall, allowing Vicky to get one arm free and swing a blow at David, who blocked the blow and instinctively made to hit Vicky with his other arm. Remembering it was Vicky, he held back on the hit, not wanting to use full force. At that same moment, Johnnie grabbed Vicky's other leg, pulling her slightly away from David. David's blow glanced off her head, hitting the radio head set and knocked it off her head to fall loosely at her side.

Vicky slumped on the ground, unmoving. David grabbed her again, holding her tightly. Vicky lay still for a few moments, breathing deeply, before her eyes slowly opened. Seeing David she said, very groggily,
"What the hell is going on? What are you doing to me?"
David looked into her eyes quickly and saw that they now recognised him again, though a mixture of fear and confusion circulated across her face. David eased his grip on Vicky as he realized that, somehow, she was back with them. When Johnnie

also recognised that Vicky no longer appeared to be dangerous, he let go of her leg, wheezing still, as he sucked oxygen into his lungs. Deciding that everything was under control, David stood up and helped Vicky, who was still staring around the room with a look of complete bewilderment on her face, to also stand. Frowning, she asked,

"What am I doing here?"

"Can you remember anything at all?" he asked.

"No," she replied slowly, a plaintive note in her voice. "The last thing I remember is finishing my shift and heading back to the kitchen to replace my radio. After that, nothing 'til I found myself in here being attacked by you two."

Her eyes watered and tears began to trickle down her face. With a mute appeal on her face, she pleaded,

"David, what's happening to me?"

Moved by the pathos in her voice David impulsively gave her a quick hug, before gently saying,

"Come and sit down whilst we try and sort this out."

Putting the room lights on as they walked back into the main part of the room, David said to Johnnie,

"You'd better radio Natalie and tell her what's happened here and to be ready, in case there is another attacker. We'll just have a quick talk with Vicky down here, whilst she recovers a bit and then we'll go back up. Hopefully this is it, but we can't be sure yet."

"Ok," replied Johnnie, moving to the table to pick up the radio.

Chapter 17.

And So Was That.

Still sat at the table in room 12, Tony was arranging the headset in the most comfortable position so he could speak and hear easily, whilst still watching the monitor. Switching it on, he sat back down on the chair, blowing his cheeks out and exhaling his breath quite explosively. Now feeling ready for anything, he settled back down to watch the scene from the corridor, wondering, as he did so, what was happening downstairs with David and Johnnie.

Down the corridor, in room 15, Natalie was also sitting, calmly waiting for events to unfold, when the department radio burst into life and she heard Johnnie say,
"Natalie, are you there?"
She quickly picked up the radio, pressed the send button and responded,
Hi Johnnie, what's up?"
"We have just caught Vicky trying to enter room 8; she put up a hell of a fight. There was something odd about her that we haven't worked out yet. She didn't seem to be aware of anything. It was almost as if she was possessed in some way."
"Is everyone ok?"
"Everyone is fine. We are just going to give her a few minutes to recover. Just be on guard in case there is someone else. Let us know if Tony calls you, otherwise we'll be back up shortly."
"Ok."

Natalie put the radio back on the bed, but continued looking at it without actually seeing it. Scratching her cheek, she thought about what Johnnie had said about Vicky, unable to grasp what that actually meant. Whilst she was standing there, she heard a key in the door. Fully focused now, she spun round and went cautiously towards the door. It opened slowly and Natalie saw Tony entering the room, sighing in relief she turned back into the room, still thinking about Vicky as she said,

"You've heard about Vicky then. It's weird, isn't it?"

Tony made no reply as he walked into the room. Natalie, her mind still focused on Vicky, was simply standing still, staring into space. Suddenly, some instinct made her throw herself sideways onto the floor, before, in one flowing movement, surging back to her feet. Once on her feet, she saw Tony's arm thud into the wall near where her head had just been. For a brief second, she stared in confusion at Tony, before noting his ungainly movement and unfocused stare. Tony continued moving towards her, and Natalie let her training take over. Keeping her eyes on him, she moved quickly backwards into the room, to give herself room to manoeuvre, holding herself ready for any attack. Tony continued moving towards her but, again, Natalie noted that his movements were sluggish and somehow wooden. Hoping to use that to her advantage she launched a sudden attack, moving in low and sweeping his legs from under him. Her attack caught him completely by surprise and he fell to the floor. Natalie aimed a strike at his throat, a blow that could be deadly, but she held back on her strike. 'This wasn't really Tony', she told herself. 'This must be what happened to Vicky'.

These thoughts passed in a fleeting moment, as Natalie adjusted how she was going to fight him. Deciding to try to disable him if she could, she also knew she would seriously hurt, even kill him, if she was forced into it. She threw a series of blows at Tony, aiming for different parts of his body, each of them hitting its target. They must have hurt him, but, apart from a few grunts, he seemed oblivious to them. She launched another flurry of blows, but her foot caught in a dangling bed cover, causing her to stagger and lose balance. Tony grabbed her and pushed her backwards, apparently trying to crush her against the wall. Natalie managed to free one of her arms, hitting Tony around the back of his head. Tony spun her round and threw her onto the bed. She bounced on the mattress, her head thudding against the headboard. Gasping in pain, she momentarily lost focus. Tony reached the bed, sat on her legs and wrapped his fingers around Natalie's throat, squeezing tightly.

With her arms still free she repeatedly battered Tony, but he seemed impervious to her blows. His face was close to hers but there was no glimmer of recognition, or even humanity, in his eyes as he stared at her.

Now struggling for breath, Natalie knew she was fighting for her life. Pulling the last remnants of her strength together, she lurched to one side, managing to free one leg and then kneed Tony in the groin. Tony grunted, but other than that, hardly reacted at all. Natalie was beginning to get desperate; her strength was leeching away. Realising she had reached the point where she would have to kill Tony, or she would not survive. Part of her felt sorry for the real Tony, but he was not really there, and she was running out of time. She held herself still for a few seconds, ignoring her mind which was screaming at her to attack. She inhaled as much air as she could. Hoping to take Tony by surprise, she violently arched her back. Unbalanced, Tony lost his grip on her throat. Using that split second, she kicked at him, catching him full in the stomach. He fell off the bed and Natalie, moving with a speed fuelled by self preservation and adrenaline, grabbed the duvet and threw it over Tony's body and then jumped on top of him, pinning him down. As Tony struggled to move, Natalie took several deep breaths, steadying herself and replenishing her oxygen levels. "Stop fighting please, Tony," she begged.

Looking him in the eyes, she tried to convey her sadness at what she was about to do, but Tony showed no sign of understanding and continued struggling in a confused sort of way, trying to get

218

loose. Natalie raised her hand, focused her eyes on a place just behind Tony head and prepared to hit him with a palm strike.

"I'm so sorry Tony," she said as her hand began its fatal strike.

Chapter 18.

No Time To Explain.

Vicky blinked several times, trying to force her brain to concentrate on the present. Amazement mixed with fear spread across her face, as David explained what had happened that evening, as she desperately tried to process the fact that she had been on her way to kill a guest.

"But I don't remember any of it," a plaintive note torturing her voice. "All I remember is you holding me down on the floor in this room. Why did I suddenly recognise you then?"

"That's a very good question," David said, looking up to Johnnie, who nodded his agreement.

"Can you remember what happened just before she recognised you?" Johnnie asked, "It might be important."

David thought back, going over the sequence of events that occurred just before Vicky came back to herself and spoke to him. The problem was, he had been fighting hard to hold on to her, so he wasn't totally sure what had happened.

"I was just about to hit her really hard when I remembered in was Vicky, so eased up on the attack so as not to seriously hurt her…"

Vicky gasped as the import of his words sank in.

"….and her head lurched to one side, so my blow hit the radio head piece instead, knocking it off her head."

A moment later he inhaled sharply, abruptly stood up and started moving quickly to the door.

"What are y…?" Johnnie exclaimed.

"Stay here with Vicky, I need to go upstairs," David hissed as he moved to the door.

Fighting the impulse to run, he walked quickly, but without obvious haste, upstairs. Even now, he didn't want to give anything away if he should meet an innocent member of staff or a guest. He went straight towards Natalie's room, noticing, as he got closer, that the door, which should be closed, was slightly ajar. Muffled sounds were coming from inside. Heart beating fast, he ran towards the door, all pretence of normality now gone.

Inside the room, he saw Natalie, hand raised, as she paused for a second, taking a steadying breath before she launched her blow at Tony. David threw himself at her, his body deflecting her blow, which thudded harmlessly into the carpet, inches from Tony's head. Momentarily caught off guard and fearing an accomplice, Natalie spun round, ready to attack. Seeing David, she blurted, "What the hell?"
 David ignored her and, instead, grabbed hold of a still struggling Tony, he pulled the radio headset off his head. Confusion flooded through Natalie. Why was he messing about with the headset, rather than subduing Tony? After a second or so, she saw David release Tony. She was about to warn David that Tony had been trying to kill her, but before she could say anything, a very dazed and confused Tony said the very same thing that she was thinking,
"What the hell is going on?"

Unexpectedly, David laughed, before he replied,
"You were a crazed killer, but we'll let you off, you weren't yourself."
"What?" was all that both Tony and Natalie could manage to say, staring open mouthed, at David.

David moved away from Tony so that he could get up, but then bent down again when it was clear that he needed help. Sweat covered Tony's forehead and pain was clear in every movement he made.

"God, what happened to me?" he said through groans.

"I did," Natalie replied. "I hit you, a lot."

Painfully, Tony raised a quizzical eyebrow as she continued, only a little defensively,

"Well, you were trying to kill me."

'Oh," was Tony's baffled response.

By this time David had helped Tony into a standing position and then supported him to the chair, where he collapsed, still groaning. With a fairly satisfied look, David assessed the overall condition of both Natalie and Tony, before saying, a pleased tone seeping into his voice,

"Well, that's that. We stopped both murders and found that no members of the staff were really to blame. Not only that, we also managed to keep the whole situation quiet. A good result, I think."

An exasperated Natalie threw up her arms and quietly yelled,

"I don't understand. What happened?"

A bruised and battered Tony, groaning as he only half raised one painful arm, added,

"Me either."

David, seeing their bewildered faces, laughed, relief etched on his face, before saying, as he reached for the radio,

"Let me just get Johnnie and Vicky up here, then I'll explain."

He pressed the send button and talked into the radio.

A few minutes later, Johnnie and Vicky came through the door. Vicky looked a little the worse for wear; shock, bewilderment, pain, all flitted across her face as she looked at the other people in the room, but it had to be said, she looked a lot better than Tony did. Vicky went to sit on the arm of the chair that Tony was sat in; feeling the need to be near an old friend who was a reminder of stability in a world suddenly gone mad. David turned to Vicky asking,

"Has Johnnie explained what the situation here is and who he and Natalie are?"

Vicky nodded, adding,

"It's all unbelievable. Here. In Belper?"

She turned to Tony, gently hitting him on the arm, "And you knew all about it and didn't tell me."

Tony grimaced in pain, but had the decency to look sheepish.

"David told me not to tell you," he said defensively.

Vicky turned to David,

"And you are part of them," waving her arm to incorporate Natalie and Johnnie. "I can't believe it."

"I used to be. I am still basically the same person you thought I was."

"You can do the apologies later," Natalie interrupted him, "I'm knackered and I want to know what happened before I fall asleep."

"Yeah, so am I, I think we could all do with some sleep. I'll make it brief."

"Good," agreed the others, virtually in unison.

David collected his thoughts, then said,

"Well, once I got close to Vicky, it was obvious that she was being controlled in some way, but I had no idea how. It was only when I was recreating the end of the fight that I remembered exactly when Vicky came back to herself. It was when the headset was knocked off her head. I've got no idea how it worked, but I suddenly remembered that Natalie and Tony were using the same headsets, so I rushed upstairs in case they were being controlled as well. I heard a struggle going on in here and I burst in, saw Natalie was about to hit Tony and so I threw myself at them before she really hurt him, or worse."

"Thanks," said Tony and Natalie, again virtually in unison, but for very different reasons.

"How did you know Tony was the potential killer and not me?" Natalie asked.

"I saw you weren't wearing the headset."

"Oh."

223

"Anyway, I pulled the headset off Tony's head and, luckily, it was the right move. Tony came back to himself, and the danger was over, for both of them."

Tony and Natalie stared at each other; both realizing what might have happened if David hadn't got there in time and intervened. Tony was definitely the more grateful; especially when he thought of the damage Natalie had done to his body anyway, before she had decided that her situation was desperate. He shuddered as he realised how close he had come to death.

After a few moments, Johnnie asked the question they were all thinking,

"So, how were they being controlled by the headset?"

"No idea," David admitted. "That's something for the experts to sort out. What we do need to do is confiscate the other radios before anyone else uses them later today. After all, we've got no idea who it is that's using the radios to control people. Vicky, can you do that, Tony can hardly walk. When that's done, we can get some sleep."

"I think I can manage that," Vicky said, struggling up from the chair arm and heading for the door.

David nodded to Johnnie, tipping his head in the direction of Vicky and Johnnie rose, saying,

"I'll come with you, just in case there are still any problems."

Vicky gave him a grateful look and the two of them went off to get the remaining radios.

Whilst they waited for Vicky and Johnnie to return, David asked Tony if he could remember anything at all about what happened, when he was wearing the radio headset.

"I remember putting the headset on and switching it on, then I sat back down and kept watching the monitor for a while, then nothing more until I found myself on the floor here with you above me, feeling like I'd got in the way of a steamroller."

"Ooh, can I have that as my nickname, 'The Steamroller'," Natalie joked.

"Suits you," a laughing David replied.

"When people have had some sleep, we'll need to take statements," Natalie reminded David, "The boss and the experts will need all the info we can provide."

David nodded in agreement, before adding,

"I don't know how much use we will be though; we haven't learnt a great deal that could be of use."

"Well, they still might get some new info from it all, though, particularly if they have the radios to study," Natalie said, picking up a radio and giving it a cursory examination.

"I hope so; I have a feeling this is going to become something big. Someone, with a lot of resources, has put in a lot of effort into this."

"The more I think about it, the more I think the only people with that sort of reach, and that amount of resources has to be a government organisation."

"That's what I was thinking too. But who?"

"I don't think it was one of ours, as we would have been warned off officially."

"Yes, so my guess would be one of our enemies."

"Or the US," Natalie added.

"As I said, one of our enemies," was David's ironic response.

At that, the two of them lapsed into an exhausted silence. A few minutes later David stirred, his brain still working, despite the tiredness he was feeling and turned to Tony, who was virtually oblivious to everything already,

"Tony, can you text Chris and tell him the situation has been successfully dealt with?"

It took a moment for David's words to filter through to Tony's exhausted brain. When it did register, he barely managed to say,

"I'm too tired, can't we tell him later?"

"No, we are going to be asleep when he gets here, plus he needs to know about the radios, so he can come up with an explanation for the staff to explain their absence."

Tony just stared absently at David and It was clear that he was unable to think coherently or really understand what David was saying, so David shook his shoulder and said,

"Just get your phone out and get me to the right page and I'll do the rest."

"Ok," mumbled Tony, fumbling in his pocket for his phone. Once he had got the right page up on the screen, he handed the phone to David, sighed and sank back into his chair. David wrote the text to Chris, sent it and put the phone down on the table.

A few moments later Johnnie and Vicky returned, carrying the remaining radios with them and put everything together in a heap on the table. Once that was done, David decided that enough was enough and they all needed some sleep. Johnnie, though, decided that he would prefer to drive back to headquarters straight away.

"I'm still feeling fine, so," he said, looking at Natalie, "if it's ok, I'll drive back and let Mark know what happened. I'll sleep later."

Natalie nodded.

"Are you sure, we can find you a room if you want?" David offered, looking at Vicky, who nodded.

"No thanks, I unwind best when I'm driving. Are you coming Natalie?"

"God no. I am going to tuck myself into this bed and sleep."

"Ok, see you back at the department when you get back."

David turned to Johnnie and said,

"I think the department's scientists will want to study these radios as soon as possible, so do you want to take them with you?"

"Good idea. I'd better take the department's radios with me as well; I brought them, so I'd better take them back."

As David packed everything in the equipment bag, he made sure that every radio from the hotel was completely switched off. He then told Johnnie,

"I'll sort the other equipment out later, I'm sure Sir will want to see me in the coming days, so I'll return it all then."

He gave the equipment bag to Johnnie, who hung it on his shoulder and, as he prepared to leave, David held out his hand,

"Thanks for everything Johnnie; it's been a pleasure working with you. Drive carefully,"

Johnnie shook his hand and smiled, before walking to the door. Vicky decided to go with him.

"I'll see him off the premises, then I'm going to sleep and hopefully, when I wake up, this will have all been a bad dream. I'll be in room 6," she said, picking up the room key off the table. With that, the two of them left.

David turned to Tony, to see what state he was in, only to find that he had fallen asleep whilst sitting in the chair. David gave a gentle laugh and said,

"Poor sod, he will really hurt when he wakes up. I'll put a blanket on him and he can sleep there."

"But I was going to sleep in the bed," Natalie wailed.

"Here, take the key for room 12, I'll sleep in here."

Natalie picked up the key for room 12 and, with a weary sigh, said,

"Thanks. Thank God that's over; I will see you later before I go."

When she got to room 12, Natalie picked up the 'Do Not Disturb' notice and hung it on the handle of her room. Turning back inside, she firmly closed the door, before collapsing onto the bed with a contented sigh.

Back in room 15, David also put the 'Do Not Disturb' notice on the door. He then checked on Tony, who was dead to the world on the chair, making sure he was covered up, before he too, collapsed on the bed with a contented sigh

Chapter 19.

It All Went Up In Smoke.

About 3 hours after leaving the hotel, a now exhausted Johnnie parked his van in the underground car park and trudged slowly up the steps that led to the department. He verified his identity and went straight to the night room to get some sleep before he made his report to Mark. A few hours later he woke up feeling refreshed and went to get himself some breakfast, after that, he found Mark and gave a quick verbal report on the main events of the previous night. When he had finished, Mark said,

"Good, that sounds like a job well done. Did Natalie come back with you?"

"No, she was pretty bruised after her fight with Tony and was going to get some sleep. She said she would report in later."

"Ok," Mark replied. "What about David, how did he cope?"

"Oh, very good; on the ball all the time and easy to work with."

"I'm sure the boss will be pleased to hear that."

"It was very quick thinking to recognise it was the hotel radios that were the problem, and that Tony was wearing one. If he hadn't got to Natalie's room in time, I think she may well have had to kill him."

"I'm glad it didn't come to that."

"Yes. I've brought the radios back with me so they can be analysed by the tech guys. I'm sure they will find something interesting there. They are in the van in the car park."

"Good, I'll get them to work on them right away. Good job. You can write up your full report tomorrow."

"No problem."

After Johnnie had left, Mark sat and thought for a few moments, committing the main points of Johnnie's report to memory for when the boss arrived. A short time later he made his way to Sir Peter's office, knocked on the door and entered.

"I see Johnnie got back, how did the mission go?" Sir Peter asked.

"A complete success, they stopped the murders and found out some very interesting information about the whole situation. It seems that the staff were being controlled somehow by the radio system they were using. Johnnie brought them back so we can analyse them and find out how they work."

"Good, is everyone ok?"

"Yes, tired and bruised in some way, but ok."

"Good and how did David perform?"

"Apparently very well. Johnnie said he was very good to work with."

"Excellent, we really will have to try and get him to come back to us."

"With luck he might not need too much persuading; his life hasn't been that great lately."

"Now, what have you discovered about our potential leak."

"I haven't been able to discover who it is yet. Whoever accessed the information used the department password and so is untraceable. I think we need to change the system so that everyone has their own password."

"Yes, do that straight away. I know it will be obvious that we suspect something but that can't be helped, it might even scare the person into making a mistake."

"There is also no trace of where the information went, so I assume it was sent manually."

"Damn, so we have no idea who we are dealing with."

"Not yet."

"Well, keep investigating and put the new password protocol into place. Oh, and take the necessary steps to make sure nothing about this becomes public."

"Yes Sir,"

With that, Mark left the office and Sir Peter was left thinking what other steps he might have to take to make his department secure. More important though, was finding the identity of the people using the information about David and discovering how they were able to remotely control people's actions. Like David and Natalie, Sir Peter knew it had to be a government sponsored agency, but which government?

As it was, his counterpart was himself on the phone, receiving a report from his deputy.

"So, what is the current situation?" he asked.

"The operation has been fully compromised. Sir Peter's operatives were able to stop the staff members from killing their targets. They also must have realised that the radios were being used to control them as they confiscated all of them. The tracking devices show that the radios are now at their headquarters."

"Did they discover our identity?"

"Not as far as we can tell."

"I see, still I think we need to close the operation down entirely at the hotel. I think we have enough information to enable us to evaluate how much progress we have made in controlling people's actions but, more importantly, what the limitations are."

"Yes Sir, but what are we going to do about the radios? We could do with getting our operative there to get them back; there are a few secrets as to their origins that would be best remaining secret."

"I don't think there is any way we will be able to get them back. I don't want to make it obvious that we have someone in their department, as we will need them to get us a copy of their report of the operation. It will be useful to know how they were able to negate our operation so we can assess whether the project has any further potential. Get the technicians to set off the self destruct mechanisms in the radios."

"Yes Sir. Is there anything else?"

"Yes, I think there are too many loose ends with the operation. See to it."

"Yes Sir, how far can we go?"

"As far as necessary to stop any information getting out, but make sure there is no trail back to us."

An hour after he had spoken to Sir Peter, Mark received a phone call from one of the technicians he had told to start investigating the radios that Johnnie had brought back.

"You need to come down to the car park; we have a problem with the radios." He said.

"What is it?"

"Well, they've melted."

"What the…. I'm on my way."

With that Mark hurried out of his office and down to the underground car park. As soon as he entered, he was hit by the stench of burning plastic and metal. He saw the technicians near to the van that Johnnie had used and quickly walked over to them. Once there, one of the technicians opened the rear door and stood back. Mark brushed past him and looked inside. Apart from the increased acrid smell, he saw a pile of twisted metal covered in foam, obviously from the fire extinguisher he had seen one of the technicians holding.

"Bloody hell, the Boss is going to love this. Who found it?"

"I did, well I opened the van door," said one of the technicians. "We were all here. It was obvious as soon as we entered the car park that something was wrong. We could obviously smell the burning and it got worse as we approached the van. I opened the door and saw smoke and Carl grabbed the fire extinguisher and sprayed the inside."

"Ok, clear the mess up and see if there is anything we can still use. Give me a report as soon as you can."

"Ok", said the technician.

With that, Mark strode off to report to Sir Peter.

Chapter 20.

Well, I'm Glad That's Over!

Much later that same day, a good few hours sleep away from the violent events of the night and after they'd explained everything that had happened to Chris, for the fourth or fifth time, David and Tony retreated to the bar.

"Well, that appears to be that, I think we've finally dotted all the I's and crossed all the T's," David said, weariness still clear in his voice, as he collapsed onto the leather sofa in the bar.

"God, I hope so," Tony said, slowly and painfully carrying a couple of drinks from the bar.

He placed the drinks on the table, before he too collapsed onto the sofa with a heartfelt sigh, supplemented by several groans. After a moment's silence, staring at nothing, they both lifted their drinks, clinked glasses and said 'cheers', before taking a long drink from their pints. Wiping some errant froth from his mouth, Tony exclaimed,

"I don't know about you, but I feel like getting absolutely pissed, the past few days have been bloody hard."

"I'm with you on that."

They both raised their glasses again, "Absent friends," said Tony, as they clinked glasses again.

At the same time Tony and David were beginning to get drunk, about a mile and a half away, Vicky was, once more, going over what she could remember of the events at the hotel and her part in them. She had spent most of the day resting her aching body and thinking. Understanding and acceptance of what she had done, though, were slow in coming. The main problem was that despite what she had been told by David and the others, she simply had no memory of anything that she might have done whilst she was being controlled. The idea that her mind and body had been controlled by some unknown person terrified her. By late evening she was feeling completely overwhelmed and a little paranoid. She decided to go back to the hotel. Hopefully, Tony and David would be there and she could talk to them about how she was feeling, but if they weren't, at least she would have some company, rather than sitting home alone. Putting on her coat, she picked up her car keys and left her house, closing the door behind her. In her car, she put the key in the ignition but didn't immediately turn the key; instead, she simply sat, staring out the windscreen, overwhelmed once more by dark thoughts. A few minutes later, she came back to herself with a start. Shaking her head in bewilderment, she decided that driving might not be a good idea, so she took the key out of the ignition, got out of the car and decided to walk to the hotel.

Still sitting in the hotel bar, Tony looked around the room, thinking back to when they had first sat down to drink. There had still been a few members of staff and customers drinking in the bar then, for whom it was just a normal night, but he remembered how he had felt very disjointed and separate from them.

"They've got no idea, have they?" he had asked David.

"Not the slightest, but that's why we did it."

"How did you deal with that side of the job? Doing things that you couldn't talk about. I want to shout at them about what happened."

"It was second nature, just a part of the job, now 'shut up' and get drinking."

Recognising that David didn't want to talk about it, at least, at that precise moment, Tony did 'shut up' and, when everyone else had gone their own separate ways and they were the last people in the bar, the two of them turned their attention to the very serious job of getting very drunk. At least now, Tony didn't have to pretend to everyone that he was suffering from a bad back, an excuse he had stolen from David. After two or three pints of Peroni David changed to 7 yr old Havana Rum, his favourite spirit, as he found there was too much volume in drinking pints. There was also far too much wasted effort in repeatedly staggering to the toilet, which seemed to get further and further from the bar as the night wore on. Tony stayed with lager, which he could consume at virtually the same rate as David's consumption of shorts.

Preoccupied with her thoughts as she set off for the hotel, Vicky failed to notice the darkly clad figure that slipped out of the passenger seat of an old van parked in the shadows near her house and then took up station about fifty yards behind her. After a while, the shadowy figure radioed his companion in the van.

"It looks like she's heading for the hotel," he said quietly.

"Ok, I'll get there ahead of her."

About half an hour later, Vicky was nearing the back of the hotel and headed towards the rear entrance. As she crossed through the staff car park she was assailed by a feeling of vague unease. Uncertain and scared, she stopped walking. She looked quickly around the car park but saw nothing unusual. She was about to resume walking when a strange, acrid smell, like disinfectant, assaulted her nostrils. Shrugging her shoulders, she gave a quick nervous laugh and, telling herself she was being stupid, started walking again. Passing near to a parked van, she again felt uneasy. Once more she stopped walking but before she could look round, she was roughly grabbed from behind. Two strong arms held her and before she had time to react, or even scream, another hand clamped a soft, pungent cloth across her mouth and nose. Panicked, she tried to struggle, but the arms were far too strong for her. As she was carried into the shadow of the van, she grew dizzy and her ability to focus began to slip. Her struggles grew even weaker as she quickly slipped into unconsciousness, her thoughts dark and scared.

When certain she was unconscious, her attackers laid her on her back inside the van and in a few short moments she was tied, hand and feet, with strong ties. Tape was then fixed over her mouth.

"Ok," said one of the men, "that was easy, let's hope the others are. Go check who's in the hotel."

The other man just grunted in response as he set off for the hotel, slipping quietly into the hotel through the back door, He came back a few minutes later to report that Tony and David were in the bar,

"It looks like they may be there drinking for a while yet."

"Ok, you go back in and keep tabs on them. I will keep watch out here."

"Ok," replied the second assailant, heading back for the hotel, whilst the other got into the van and settled down to wait.

"Don't like mixing my drinks," Tony mumbled sometime later, when David asked why he didn't change to spirits, his question triggered by the repeated groans Tony made every time he got up from the sofa to go to the toilet. David, who was a very placid drunk, squinted at Tony's face, thought about Tony's explanation for a minute, or possibly longer; time had lost its precision under the onslaught of the alcohol, before nodding sagely.

"Gotcha," he muttered.

They both sat in silence for some time, before, eventually, Tony stirred from his reverie.

"It'll be good to get back to normality," he exclaimed.

"Yeah," David replied with a distinct lack of enthusiasm, "back to pulling up weeds and coming home to an empty house. Can't wait."

They must have sat in silence for longer than they realised because both of them seemed to have sobered up a lot during their reverie.

"Well, it's time you got back out there and found somebody new," Tony said.

"You can talk, how long is it since you had a girlfriend?"

"A couple of years...... or so."

"Well then, why don't you find someone new?"

"Aagh, I spend almost all my time here at work, the hours don't suit having a serious relationship, and the staff here are mostly just passing through on the way to something better, so a long-term relationship with any of them doesn't work, but that's not the case for you, you have regular hours."

"Excuses, excuses. As for me, I'm not sure if I can be bothered anymore, I'm not sure the pain is worth it."

"What pain?"

"Tell me Tony, you always seem so cavalier about relationships, but wouldn't you like to be in love, to give yourself up to someone else; for that person to be the centre of your universe?"

"Honestly?"

"Yes, honestly."

"Yes, I probably would. I've never felt like that about anyone, but it sounds good."

"Yes, well, I have, or at least I thought I had, before I realised that all of it was just a mirage."

David looked up at the ceiling, then closed his eyes and started talking, but it was clear he was almost oblivious to Tony's presence.

"Working for the department, you can't really have those kinds of relationships. Then I left and for while I was on my own, literally, spending most of my time alone, just thinking about my life, before I met my ex. I gave myself to her, body and soul. We were like soul mates; I had never seemed so happy, or indeed laughed so much. Like others before me, I thought it would last

236

forever but reality decided to intervene. Whatever the cause of the split, I have had several years of being alone, no real friends, only acquaintances, though some of them could become friends over time, and only a few people to talk to. It was hard to deal with that sudden absence of a companion, although I have to admit that I made good friends with quite a few bottles of Havana rum and a few more bottles of wine. I really don't know if I can go through that kind of intense relationship again, getting to know someone, getting to trust them, getting to love them, only for them to leave."

"You can't stay alone for the rest of your life."

"Maybe not, but I'm seriously thinking I may go back to the department. Everything is so absolute there; you know where you stand with everyone. You don't get too close to your colleagues as there is always the chance that they could just disappear, for one reason or another. Not going through the pain of losing the one you care about makes killing the occasional malefactor seem like the less painful option just now."

After he finished, David sat quietly for a few minutes, eyes closed, whilst Tony sat, thinking about what he had heard. Then, with an apparent sense of purpose, David rose from the sofa, picked up his glass of rum, raised it in salute to Tony, before draining it and placing it, with a sense of finality, back on the table. After a moment, he began to walk carefully towards the door; halfway there, he stopped and turned to look back at Tony, "Look after yourself," he said, a solemn look on his face, and then he turned back to the door and walked out of the hotel.

Tony continued looking at the closed door for a few moments more, feeling a mixture of sadness and concern.

"See you," he said to the now closed door, raising his glass and draining it dry, wondering how long it would be before he saw David again. He had a feeling it wouldn't be for a long time.

In the shadows, a figure stirred, preparing himself for Tony's departure from the bar.

The following day, a still exhausted David was taking an afternoon nap to catch up on his sleep, when he was jolted awake. Disorientated, he lay in the semi dark, wondering what had woken him. From the last moments of his sleep, he vaguely recalled some sort of loud pounding but had no idea where it came from. A sudden renewal of the pounding made him realise that he had been woken by someone knocking very loudly on his door. Suddenly wide awake, he slipped out of bed and cautiously moved his curtains a little to peer out of his window. Anxiety hit him as he saw several police cars blocking the road outside his house and police officers at his door. Pulse racing, he quickly closed the curtain. Instinct told him he should try to escape but, almost immediately, he decided against it. If the police were after him they would probably have surrounded the house. It would look very suspicious if he tried to run and was caught. Just then there was another burst of pounding on the door and a voice shouted,
"Police. Open up."
David decided that the only realistic option was to see what they wanted, so he went back to the window, opened it and shouted down to them,
"Ok, ok, I'll be down in a minute."
"Be quick," one of the officers replied.
Frowning, David closed the window, quickly got dressed and went downstairs. He unlocked his front door but as soon as he went to open it, the door was barged open and three police officers, now holding guns, forced their way in. Knocked backwards against the table, David's initial instinct was to fight, but he held himself in check. There were too many police officers for him to deal with, apart from the three pointing guns at him. He was not in a good tactical position and he knew it. He put his hands up and stood very still.

One of the officers asked,

"Are you David Miller?"

"Yes, what the hell is this about?"

"You are under arrest on suspicion of murder. You do not have to say anything. But, it may harm your defense if you do not mention when questioned something which you later rely on in court. Anything you do say may be given in evidence."

Other works by the author.

The Albatross and the Plastic Human.
(*The Poetic Musings of an Aging Hippy*). 2018

My Life: Hidden In Words.
(*More Musings of an Aging Hippy*). 2019.

My Life: Spent in Shadow and Light.
(*The Aging Hippy Continues His Muse). 2021.*

Printed in Great Britain
by Amazon

20484886R00139